# Dangerous Knowledge

# Bryan Lawson

A crime mystery in which time, place, and the characters all play a part.

"Creativity takes courage." - Henri Matisse
"Art is dangerous." - Duke Ellington

- Imogen's favourite quotations.

About DANGEROUS KNOWLEDGE   Bryan Lawson

The badly mutilated body of a woman floats down the River Dee in Chester and disturbs evening drinkers at a popular pub on the riverbank. Detective Chief Inspector Drake and his sergeant, Grace Hepple, investigate. Their first problem is that it proves almost impossible to identify the victim, and nobody has reported a missing person.

She is identified as a highly successful painter. Her paintings sell well in Chester and the Far East. It is not long before Drake follows in her dangerous footsteps. Drake and Hepple are soon working on a confusing mystery. They discover a world in which they have no experience. It seems art has a dark side. It is run by ruthless crime syndicates working across at least three continents.

Gradually, the victim's tortured personal life begins to emerge. Drake and Hepple also discover a curious quasi-religious sect. It has had a disastrous effect on the victim's life. But has it also had a hand in her death?

DANGEROUS KNOWLEDGE is the fifth of Bryan Lawson's Drake and Hepple mysteries series.

Other books by Bryan Lawson
A DEGREE of DEATH, 2017
WITHOUT TRACE, 2019
FATAL PRACTICE, 2019
THE FLAUTIST, 2021

## About BRYAN LAWSON

Bryan Lawson is an architect and psychologist. He studies the relationship between people and place. He has published over 300 books and articles and practiced, taught and researched architecture for many years. He was Head of School and Dean of the Faculty of Architectural Studies at Sheffield University. He has travelled extensively and regrets that, so far, he has not worked in Antarctica.

He has now turned to crime. This is his fifth crime mystery.

Details of all books by Bryan Lawson, together with news of forthcoming publications and a blog may be found at: - www.bryanlawson.org

My thanks to Rosie for her invaluable support and help.

Wherever possible, this book uses real locations. To see images of many of these, go to the website www.bryanlawson.org

Select" "novels"
Scroll down to "Dangerous Knowledge"
Select "see locations"

You can see the locations for each chapter. Try not to look at those for chapters not yet read, as this may confuse the plot.

# 1

The water shimmered delicately in the evening sunlight. The River Dee was exhibiting its usual resolve to reach the Irish Sea. Drake thought it meandered a little as it passed through Chester. Perhaps it was to give the swans and gulls a smoother ride, or maybe it just enjoyed the surroundings of this historic city. Detective Chief Inspector Carlton Drake sat taking in the scene. He had grown fond of the Boathouse Pub. It was conveniently located just a few steps upstream from the house he had rented on The Groves, so it had become an easy habit to call in on an evening. Drake liked the alternatives of a cosy traditional interior or, his choice this evening, of sitting on the flat-decked barge moored against the river embankment. As usual, he chose a seat facing upstream. He found that this view would often help him to sift through the facts of his current case. The slowly fading light picked out swans and gulls against the darker water. This offered Drake just the calming influence he needed. It had been a busy and frustrating day full of bureaucratic obstacles. During his career, policing had become more a matter of paperwork than pounding the pavements. As a young copper, he had not particularly enjoyed patrolling the old-fashioned beat. Now, even that seemed preferable to all the paperwork that had become the defining feature of modern police life. Of course, he fully understood the need for documentation and accountability. He felt it had all gone too far, and even some happy medium seemed an impossible dream.

But it was all a lot better here. He was glad he had taken the chance to relocate to Chester from The Met. The promotion and departure of his protégé, Detective Inspector Martin Henshaw, had created the opportunity. Martin was off to the Far East for two years, acting in an advisory capacity to the Hong Kong Police Force.

This place allowed Drake an indulgence he valued more than he could say. He would occasionally find himself thinking of his wife. Many things triggered a memory of Cynthia. It might be what somebody said. It might be a mother with a child. Often, it would be a building or even just a place. He had always envied her architectural career without ever fully understanding it. Now, he was trying to put that right, but these unbeckoned memories would so often interrupt a present that he needed to concentrate on. She lived on in his mind. There was no escaping it.

Here on the banks of the Dee, he could allow his mind to wander where it would, bringing its choice of memories to the fore. A glass of wine sat invitingly on the table in front of him. Drake twiddled the stem between his first three fingers and thumb, and the red liquid swayed gently, tempting him to take one more sip. Inevitably, he wondered what he would be doing now if Cynthia had lived longer. Would they still be in London? Would they both still be absorbed in their careers? Would they have found a way of spending more time together? He idly watched the small girl at the front of the barge trying to tempt a swan with the bread her mother supplied from a plastic bag. She reminded him of his daughter, Lucy, when she was that age.

'Mummy, there's a lady in the water!' the little girl shouted suddenly.

'Is she swimming, dear?' asked the mother, her head buried in a glossy magazine. 'I bet that water is cold now.'

'Maybe that's why she's got all her clothes on.'

'That's silly,' grunted the mother without looking up.

'I think she's asleep,' said the little girl, tugging her mother's sleeve.

The mother's scream scattered the little group of gulls floating nearby. Most of the drinkers looked up from their mugs. Several stood up. One, a rather burly man, immediately took off his jacket, pulled up a shirtsleeve and lay down precariously on the edge of the barge. He fished fruitlessly. Another young lad grabbed one of the barge poles intended more for decoration than serious use. It proved just too long and cumbersome to manipulate accurately. A couple of teenage girls dressed for a later disco started to scream. A crowd soon assembled as people pushed forward to see what the fuss was about.

Drake arrived at the front of the barge and instinctively took over the increasingly chaotic situation. He spoke in that reassuring voice he had.

'I'm a police officer,' he said. 'Please move back.'


Two uniformed constables had arrived quickly in their patrol car. They soon got everyone back behind the blue and white plastic ribbon that was now across the entrance to the barge. The crowd of chattering onlookers stood on the riverbank, watching as an incident tent was assembled. The pub staff were trying to persuade people to move to the indoor bar. Drake watched as the woman's lifeless body was laid on the barge deck, out of sight, behind a temporary screen. That she was dead had been immediately apparent to Drake. He had seen many dead bodies in his time. They had met their end in a variety of unpleasant ways. Some had been drowned, a particularly nasty way to go, Drake thought. This one floated face down with her legs, arms, and head hanging down into the water in a way that he knew suggested she had been dead for some time. She was wearing black denim jeans and what looked as if it had been a black long-sleeve blouse. Drake's brain interrupted proceedings. Was the wearing of all black on a warm summer's day odd? The approaching ambulance siren made the watchers clutch their hands to their ears. The two paramedics were soon in discussion with Drake, who persuaded them to turn off their siren. The blue light flashed silently, insistently confirming that some tragic and alarming event had broken the peace of Chester's Groves.

'I think we have to assume this could be an incident needing investigation,' said Drake. 'I've called the pathologist, and he is on his way. My preference would be to leave the body undisturbed until he arrives.'

Professor Cooper, the local pathologist, was busy with his grisly work. He and Drake had worked together now on several cases, and they had learned to accommodate each other. Professor Cooper had slightly relaxed his meticulous manner and would give Drake his interim findings as early as possible. Drake stressed the importance of speed in the early hours of so many investigations. Cooper was more inclined to take his time but gave Drake a running commentary. It was always couched in appropriately cautious language. For his part, Drake agreed to abandon his habit of sitting in as a spectator at the postmortem. Professor Cooper appeared from the blue incident tent far earlier than Drake anticipated.

'That's quick, Prof,' said Drake.

'The body is a complete mess,' snapped the pathologist. 'Everything is entangled with reeds and water grasses. I need to do a lot of cleaning before I can even begin on the mortuary table.' Drake grunted a groan that the pathologist ignored. 'You are, of course, right about the time of death. Enough time has elapsed since death for the build-up of gases in the torso to float the body. People tend to assume dead bodies automatically float. They don't. The human body is slightly heavier than water, so it usually sinks. The decomposition gases take some time to develop enough to float the body. This is usually face down as the limbs can easily hang forward but not backward. It was exactly as you observed. The timing of all this is rather imprecise. I estimate she has been dead in the water for at least one or two days. Much longer, and we should see other changes to the corpse at the autopsy. That is the best I can do for now.'

'Thanks, Prof,' said Drake. 'I don't think I can do anything further here. I live just down the road, so I will head home and do my flute practice.'

'You play the flute?' snapped Professor Cooper.

'I'm learning,' replied Drake. 'It's a slow process. Thanks, Prof. I'll leave you to finish your work. One final question. I assume she drowned?'

'It looks like it, but I will need further investigation to confirm that. In the meantime, I think you ought to come and look at the body while it's still here. It will have been cleaned of all the reeds and other detritus once I have performed the postmortem. I will, of course, photograph it, but the actual reality is always more informative.' With that, Professor Cooper pulled aside a flap of the incident tent, and Drake followed him in. The body was now lying on its back, staring into the evening air. It was covered in weeds and plastic bags, all collected in the water. Drake was well used to confronting dead bodies. However, his sharp intake of breath admitted to Professor Cooper that even he was seeing something unusual.

'It is the head,' said Drake. 'The face is so covered in scratches and abrasions that its features are no longer apparent.'


Drake turned the key and opened the door of his rented house on The Groves. He instantly felt that weird, undefinable sensation mysteriously announcing the presence of another person.

'Hello,' he called.

'Hello, Dad,' returned the unseen voice from the living room.

'Tom? Is that you?' said Drake. Drake's son appeared in the doorway. The two men hugged and slapped each other on the back. There was a lot of uncontrolled laughter.

'Happy birthday, Dad,' said Tom.

'Surely you haven't flown from Singapore to wish me happy birthday?'

'I've got a present as well,' laughed Tom, pulling a small white box out from behind his back. Drake took the box and examined it.

'How the hell did you get in?' he demanded.

'I have a key,' replied Tom. 'Lucy had one, and she got it copied for me. Sadly, she can't be here. She is performing this evening.'

'Yes,' said Drake. 'She is doing so well. She's got one of the leading roles in Sleeping Beauty. Her mother would have been so proud of her.' Tom detected a sudden moisture in his father's eyes. He hugged him again.

'So, this is a present from both of us.'

'You really shouldn't spend your hard-earned money on me. Besides, I'm getting to the sort of age when you want to forget how old you are.' Tom shook his head.

'How kind,' said Drake, opening the box to reveal what he could see was a smartphone.

'It's the latest and best configured iPhone,' said Tom. 'I got it entirely tax-free on a flying visit to Hong Kong. It will replace that clunky old phone you still use.'

'Well, that is wonderful,' said Drake. 'Surely, you could have posted it?'

'I could, but I was coming over anyway. I'm beginning to feel that Singapore has given me all it can. I'm thinking of trying to find a job in London. These days, it's one of the most important financial centres, and Brexit has given it a new purpose.'

'Oh, that's marvellous news,' said Drake, dabbing his eyes with his handkerchief. 'I shall see more of you. This is a wonderfully generous gift, but do you think I can learn how to use it?'

'Lucy tells me you are learning to play the flute. By comparison, learning to use the iPhone must be a real doddle. Look, you only have to touch this camera icon, and you can take high-quality pictures. You can even take movies. You could record the room you are investigating. Then, at your leisure, you can look at it again. Now that you have mastered email, you can do it from your phone without waiting to find a computer. It needs some final setting up, and I've contacted your technician, Dave. He is ready to do that first thing tomorrow morning.'

'I see,' said Drake, warming to the idea. 'I could have done with it ten minutes ago. We've got a badly injured body to investigate. I kept trying to imagine it as I walked back here. There are so many things I should have made a note of. I'm getting old and forgetful.'

# 2

Detective Sergeant Grace Hepple held the rear door of the Range Rover open for Drake to climb in.

'Thank you, Grace,' said Drake as he slid across the seat. 'I thought PC Steve Redvers was driving me to see Professor Cooper this morning.'

'Yes, Sir,' said Grace, 'but I wanted a quiet word. It's only a brief matter, but I can't speak about it in the case room.'

'No problem,' said Drake. 'It will be good for you to see the postmortem process anyway. I don't wish to be cruel, but you need to get hardened to these things a little more, and you will be able to do that as much as you feel comfortable with today.'

'Thank you,' said Grace. 'I am grateful not to be thrown in at the deep end. The matter I need to raise with you is about a new team member.'

'Oh good,' said Drake. 'I thought they hadn't listened to me. I've been telling them for some time that we need at least one more pair of hands.'

'It's a chap called Dan Ford. He has been a PC in the uniform branch but got nastily knocked over and trampled on in a riot at a football match. He suffered badly for a while and lost his partner as a result. Understandably, he now struggles with crowd control duties and the like and has expressed an enthusiasm to come and work with you. I've interviewed him, and he seems fine to me. I thought it would be a good solution, but I just wanted you to know about his problem before you meet him.'

'Not an issue,' said Drake. 'I'm sure we can give him some equally terrible experiences and help him a little in the process.'

'I expected you would see it that way,' said Grace, smiling. 'He starts tomorrow.'

Drake sat in the rear seat of the Range Rover as Grace drove to the mortuary. He was particularly anxious to discover the findings of the postmortem. After its dramatic beginnings, this case had come to a grinding halt. Drake was heard to complain of boredom. There had been no reports of missing people in the last couple of days. No one had rung the police despite a short article in the local paper encouraging anyone with any information to do so. Drake had even done a short interview for the local TV news, but he had been unable to begin any serious work. Was this an unfortunate accident, or was some foul play involved? The phone call from Professor Cooper had been somewhat enigmatic. Secretly, of course, Drake liked that. He preferred his mysteries to be mysterious. Only then would they suitably occupy his mind and help to prevent it from wandering negatively around his situation.

'Ah, Drake and Grace too,' said Professor Cooper. 'I'm sorry to drag you both over here, but there are some features of this case that we could discuss before waiting for me to write my formal report.' Drake nodded and grunted. 'First things first,' continued the pathologist. 'We have an apparently healthy woman of slightly above average height. I would estimate her age to be the late thirties or early forties. The first important thing I must tell you is that this woman did not drown.' He paused, waiting for Drake to react.

'I see,' said Drake slowly. 'That is indeed interesting. Do tell me how you know, and are you certain?' Professor Cooper looked at him over his gold-framed half-glasses and raised his eyebrows.

'Of course,' he snapped. 'She was no longer breathing or trying to breathe when she entered the water. An examination of her lungs makes this nearly certain.'

'So how did she die?' asked Drake. 'Is it possible she could have fallen into the water, accidentally, banged her head and died from the injury?'

'I can't eliminate that for certain, but, as you will see, it is unlikely,' replied Professor Cooper. 'She certainly wasn't shot or stabbed or anything representing a murderous assault. There is no evidence of any fatal poison in her system.'

'So, what does that leave us with?' demanded Drake.

'Good question. That brings us to the next unusual feature of this case. The body is seriously damaged. There is a clear sign of a significant blow to the rear of the head. The skull is fractured. This could have been a fatal injury, though looking at it, I doubt this. However, I cannot say either way for certain. There is also what looks to be a blow to the front of the right shoulder and forearm. There are many injuries to the body. Most of these could have been sustained during her time in the water. I have contacted the river authority. They have a good understanding of where an item floating at The Groves could have entered the water. She probably passed over some sharp rocks upstream, and these could have been the source of many injuries. However, the blow to the rear of the head seems different and could have been made intentionally with the famous blunt instrument.' Drake forced a smile at this attempt at humour. He had heard something like it before.

'However, there are some other injuries that might be important. The face has been seriously mutilated, as we both observed at the river. This is to the extent that it might prove impossible to identify her facially. I could have sent you photographs, but somehow these don't capture the reality of the situation.' Cooper put a swatch of small snapshots on the table. 'Would like you to look at the body itself.' Drake nodded, and Professor Cooper pulled back the sheet to reveal the head of the unknown victim. Grace gritted her teeth and bent over alongside Drake.

'Goodness!' exclaimed Drake. 'It seems even more astonishing now, lying here in such a clinical environment. I've seen many injuries, some so graphic that one hesitates to imagine the pain that must have been suffered, but never have I seen a face that looks so unlike a face. There are so many injuries and cuts that the actual face is no longer apparent.'

'Exactly,' said Professor Cooper with an air of satisfaction. 'At first sight, I could only see the totality of lesions. Now, this is where I begin to introduce doubt into your considerations. The body had been in the water for perhaps two or three days. Not a long time, but long enough for the current of the Dee to carry it over all sorts of obstacles. At first, this would probably have been dragging along the bottom. Later, as the body began to float, it could have encountered other objects.'

'So, you think all this injury was inflicted on the already dead body?' queried Drake.

'Some, probably quite a lot. The section of the Dee just upstream from where she was found is shallow near the banks in many places.' Professor Cooper pointed to a map of the Dee on the wall to the side of the mortuary table. It showed a myriad of spot heights denoting the depth of the water. 'My investigation suggests there may be three almost distinct sets of injuries. Cuts made to a living body will bleed in a particular way. Cuts made to a recently deceased body can usually be distinguished from them. In this case, we have a third set of lesions. These have most likely been caused while in the water. What we have here are injuries before and possibly causing the death. Then there are other injuries postmortem, but before the body was in the water. Finally, we have the damage caused to the body in the water. It is a complex situation.'

'I wonder if this complexity was intended,' said Drake. 'Was the body dead for long before immersion?'

'That I cannot tell for sure. From various pieces of data, I would hazard a guess that it was most likely, one or two days. One injury is to the left rear of the head. You can see it if you come around the table here. This may be the cause of death, but on balance, I am inclined to think this unlikely. There was no evidence of significant injury to the brain. Sometimes, a major blow to the head can cause a brain aneurysm. If it bursts, this can lead quite quickly to death. There is no evidence of this. However, much of the data I need to be sure of has been eradicated by the period in the water. The right forearm is broken. There are signs of a blow to it. The front of the right shoulder is similarly damaged. Again, you can see these injuries here.' Professor Cooper drew the covering sheet further back and pointed to the shoulder and arm. He continued once Drake and Grace had both inspected these sites.

'I cannot be certain, but I am doubtful that the river runs fast enough to have caused these injuries. Serious lesions like these appear differently when the heart pumps blood around the body. Such injuries after death do not bleed in the same way. However, a body in rough water for some days will have these differences considerably disguised.'

There was a long silence while Drake thought all this through. Eventually, he spoke.

'So, our best guess is that this young lady was hit on the back of the head with a heavy but blunt object, but this did not cause her death. The actual cause of death remains uncertain.'

Professor Cooper responded immediately. 'There is a raised level of carbon dioxide in the blood, which can indicate suffocation. It is possible that she fell into such a position that she could not breathe when the blow was delivered to her head.'

Drake continued thinking aloud. 'She was then transported from the scene of the murder, possibly inflicting other damage upon the body, most particularly the face, or was that a deliberate act on the dead victim? In any event, it was taken to a location, presumably rather a quiet place, along the banks of the Dee upstream from The Groves and dumped in the water. To begin with, she sank but later floated as you have explained, all the while being dragged along by the considerable current of the Dee until it was entangled in reeds and other rubbish.'

'Yes.' Professor Cooper nodded. 'That sums it up well, though none of this is certain, and you omit one important finding. She was almost certainly dead before entering the water.' Professor Cooper drew Drake forward.

'Now, please look carefully at the face, or what is left of it, and tell me what you see.' Drake bent over the body and began looking in detail, trying to imagine how the face might have looked. It was hard to appreciate that there was a human face in his field of vision.

'I see many cuts, some deep and wide, others little more than scratches. There are so many that you are right; we could not use this for identification.'

'You will see across on the next table is the black blouse she was wearing,' said Prof Cooper. 'That seems featureless too. You will see it is covered in marks and rips, with one of the buttons missing. The button could have been lost earlier, but the damage to the fabric suggests it was ripped out. The overall pattern of marks and damage to the blouse is far more extensive on the front than on the back. This is consistent with damage to the body and suggests most of this was caused when the body was face down at the bottom of the river.'

'So,' said Drake, 'there is the usual question of whether we have an accident, suicide, or murder. I guess from what you have said, you might have an opinion on that?'

'We have already seen that an accident is unlikely. Suicide would also be highly unlikely,' said the pathologist. 'People just don't commit suicide by drowning themselves. All the natural human instincts come into play when in water. If you can swim, then you are unlikely to be able to commit suicide by drowning. It just doesn't happen. Of course, it could be someone jumping from a high bridge and being knocked out by hitting the water, but I don't think we have any suitable bridges upstream from The Groves.'

'So, I have to consider this may be murder,' said Drake.

'Yes,' said Professor Cooper. 'The body was deceased before it entered the water. Of course, it is possible that somehow, she fell and managed to inflict a fatal wound on herself, but then some other party would have had to take the body to the river.'

'That seems implausible on the face of it,' grunted Drake. 'So, we do not know how she died. There was a blow to the head, but this is probably not the cause of death. Somehow, she died, and her body was taken and dumped upstream of Chester in the River Dee.' The pathologist did not attempt to reply. Professor Cooper considered it was his duty to present the facts, not to arrive at conclusions, a position that he sometimes found difficult to maintain. He turned to Drake and looked straight into his eyes.

'I know this doesn't help you a lot, but it is generally estimated that we pathologists cannot determine the cause of death in about a tenth of our cases. It looks as if this is one of them.'

'Our other problem,' muttered Drake. 'Is that we have no identification. No one has come forward to report a missing person. I presume you have no other way of helping with that?'

'Well, that is also interesting,' said the pathologist. 'The pockets of her jeans were empty. She had no rings on her fingers.'

'That sounds suspicious to me,' grunted Drake. 'Who goes without a phone or credit cards these days? Was she perhaps killed for theft of some kind?' The pathologist shrugged his shoulders, unwilling to join in such speculation.

'I do have one object, however,' said the pathologist as he held the door to his office open for Drake. 'Under her blouse, she was wearing a necklace. I have it in here. It is a fine and long chain with a piece of what I take to be ceramic. It is quite small and would hang well down the torso.' Drake looked as Professor Cooper pulled out a small evidence bag. The two men peered at a simple link gold chain with an oval piece of ceramic about three centimetres long by half that wide. It had a swirling pattern of bright colours, mainly yellows and reds.

'At least this looks unusual,' said Drake, brightening up a little. 'Hopefully, it might mean something to somebody. I might try putting an image of this out in the papers and on local television.'

'One warning,' said the pathologist. 'It would not be visible under the black blouse she was wearing. Only a low and revealing neckline would enable others to see it.'

'So, it might only be very close friends who might know of its existence,' groaned Drake.

'On that theme,' said a smiling pathologist pulling the sheet further down, 'I have one more item for you to see. She has a tattoo and a rather unusual one at that. It is, however, also on the front of the body below a normal neckline. It is roughly where most people put their hands to indicate the heart. This is, of course, inaccurate. The heart is far more central than is commonly believed.' Drake had always admired how Professor Cooper would naturally try to teach his audience, so he smiled and nodded. Professor Cooper turned the sheet covering the body further down. 'You will see here on the left chest on the side of the breast, we have this little tattoo.'

Drake bent over to examine it more carefully and began talking to himself as if trying to commit what he could see to memory. 'It's quite small. I would estimate less than two centimetres across. It is mostly a collection of straight lines in the traditional tattoo blue. There are three quite thick vertical lines spaced apart. The outer two are connected by a horizontal bar much nearer the top than the bottom of the uprights. Then we have a central third line dropping from the middle of the bar to below the level of the bottom of the two outer lines.'

'Agreed,' said Professor Cooper, 'and then you have this red horizontal rectangle filling the space over the bar between the outer lines.'

'So at least I can put out a press release calling for anyone who knows a middle-aged woman with such a tattoo. Grace, perhaps you could do a press conference and show a picture of the tattoo.' Grace nodded and made a note of her duty.

'Of course,' said Professor Cooper. 'Many people who know this woman may not have seen the tattoo; such is its location.' Drake grunted while making a note and photographing the tattoo on his phone.

'Identification may remain a difficulty here,' he said. 'There may only be a few people who can identify her.'

'Yes, and one further problem,' said Professor Cooper. 'I would say that it is probable that the tattoo was done not too long ago. There are signs that the tattoo may not have fully healed. You can see a little blurring if you look carefully. This might suggest that it was submerged before it was fully healed. Remember that a tattoo is a wound to the skin. I have looked up some research on this issue, as it is not something I have seen before. As I understand it, the ink can leach slightly in water until it has healed. However, given that it is only slightly blurred, I would guess it must have been about four weeks before the submersion. I cannot be sure about any of these times. Again, I shall have to say that provisionally rather than certainly. Events don't seem to be on your side in this case.'

'It certainly has the makings of teasing mystery,' said Drake. 'We need to start digging.'

# 3

Detective Sergeant Grace Hepple was sifting through reports of people missing from around the country. This was a tedious and, so far, unrewarding exercise. She was anxious to reach a result. Drake had been irritable, to say the least, since the unknown woman's body had been found in the Dee. Try as he might, Drake couldn't get going. So far, there seemed no way to get a handle on the case. The case was stalled until they found out who the poor woman was. Drake was stamping around the case room like a chained bear. At one minute, he would stumble around as fast as his ageing body would permit. The next minute, he would sit down in his chair, irritably turning the sheets of the latest copy of his beloved Times newspaper. Then, he would put that down and read the Pathologist's report. Grace had lost count of how many times this had happened that morning.

Suddenly, Drake stood up and called Grace over. 'Stand in front of me,' he demanded. A puzzled Grace duly obliged. Drake raised his right hand over his head and moved towards Grace, bringing his hand down towards her head. She instinctively raised her right arm to defend her face and ducked down. Drake checked his movement.

'As I thought,' he said triumphantly. 'That is surely how an assailant carrying some heavy weight might have attacked the victim and injured her forearm and shoulder. What would you do next?' Grace gulped for breath, having been perturbed by Drake's imitation attack.

'I guess I would turn and run away', she said. Drake grunted with satisfaction.

'And that is how the victim would have received the more serious blow to the back of her head from an aggressively pursuing attacker.' Grace nodded, relieved that the curtain had come down on Drake's little piece of theatre.

'So then,' she said, entering into the spirit of the performance. 'She might have fallen to the floor, perhaps injuring her face on something.'

'Maybe, maybe,' said Drake, in that way of his that usually meant he was not convinced. It seemed that he did not want Grace to jump to conclusions.

Grace returned to her work, and Drake sat back in his usual chair with his copy of The Times open at the crossword. His copy of the pathologist's report was on the coffee table beside him. Occasionally, he would pick up the Times crossword and enter a clue with a grunt of satisfaction. He would stare at another clue while scribbling odd letters on a notepad. This action would cause the chair to creak. It was a welcoming sort of chair. Drake made extensive use of its rotating and reclining capabilities. The resultant creaks and squeaks generated a mounting irritation for Grace Hepple, who was trying to concentrate on her task. Occasionally, Drake would pull out the pathologist's report from under the crossword and flip through the pages seemingly idly, though Grace was sure it was a purposeful enquiry. Although Drake often appeared to, she was sure he never did things idly. Everything about him was calculated, especially doing his beloved crosswords. Then, a phone rang in competition with Drake's creaking chair. Grace answered it to discover Sergeant Denson calling from the front desk.

'I've got a young lady down 'ere,' he said gruffly. 'She says she may 'ave something to say about the River Dee case. Do you want me to bring 'er up?'

'Absolutely,' said Grace. She was relieved she could put her missing person reports to one side. A few minutes later, Sergeant Denson escorted a smart-looking woman of average height and dressed extravagantly in brilliant primary colours.

'This is Miss Philippa Crehan,' said Denson, puffing from climbing the stairs. He bowed out and left the guest standing by the door. Grace showed her to a chair by the freestanding table in the centre of the room. Drake rose from his chair in instalments and stumbled across the room.

'I believe you may be able to help us with the case of the unknown lady found deceased in the River Dee,' he said.

'Well, I don't know,' said Philippa. 'I hope I'm not wasting your time. No, that's wrong. I hope I am wasting your time because I don't want Imogen to die.'

'Imogen?' said Drake quizzically.

'Yes, Imogen Glass,' said Philippa. 'I have been away for a couple of weeks myself, and when I came back, I went to look for Imogen, and she was not there. Imogen often goes away. She works a lot in the Far East. I seem to remember her saying she was going out there soon. I hope it's not her, but I've become increasingly concerned that it might be.'

'Perhaps you'd better start from the beginning,' said Drake, smiling reassuringly.

'Yes, of course. We live in the same house. It's my house, but I let out the annexe. Imogen has been there for about three years now. She has a bedsit that she mostly uses when she is in Chester. I think she also occasionally stays a night with her younger sister. It was the other room that attracted her. It is huge and has roof lights. She has turned it into her studio.'

'Studio,' repeated Drake quizzically.

'Yes, she's an artist. A good one, I think, and in recent years, has become rather well known. Her work is in demand and fetching quite extraordinary prices. Her success is remarkable. She seems to have created a niche for herself. Most of her work is influenced by Chinese culture. She was brought up in Hong Kong, which gave her a unique insight into traditional art from that part of the world. Apparently, as a young child, she would spend hours creating paintings that local people would think were Chinese. I am sure her fame will spread, both here and over there. Her work is unique and beautiful.'

'Ah, yes,' said Drake. 'I thought the name was familiar. I read an article about her in The Times recently. 'Tell us what you think has happened to her.'

'When I didn't see her for a couple of days, I assumed she'd gone away. When you requested help, I got the spare key for the annexe. There was no sign of anything out of order. Her white van kept in the carport at the back is missing. She doesn't have a car, and she hates driving the van. Normally, she only uses it to take work to an exhibition or an auction. Usually, that would be a day trip or perhaps an overnight one, at best. However, when she travels overseas, which she does a lot, the van is left behind, but her usual travelling bags are still there. So, I began to think she had gone out somewhere and had an accident or something.'

'You said she travels overseas a great deal,' said Drake. 'Can you tell us where she goes?'

'Yes, mostly, it is to the Far East, sometimes Singapore, but more often to Hong Kong. I've lost track of how often she's been to Hong Kong in recent months. She's almost been living there. In recent times, she has also been going occasionally to the States. She is trying without much luck to get her work known over there. Oh dear, I hope she is away. I hope it's not her who has died.'

'Well, normally, in such situations, we'd ask you to try to identify the body,' said Drake. 'But sadly, in this case, that's not sensible. I doubt you could identify the face. It is distorted by injury. Could you describe Imogen to us?'

'Oh, dear. I'm not very good at that sort of thing. She is a little taller than me. I'm five foot six, so she might be around five foot nine or ten. She has straight, long, dark hair. That's not very helpful. That could be millions of women. She almost always wears black jeans and a black blouse. It's a sort of uniform. She says it saves time in the morning when deciding what to wear.'

'What a good idea,' growled Drake, interrupting.

'I think it's more of a design statement. Sorry, I'm rambling. I'm in a bit of a state with all the worrying. Is any of that any help?'

'It might be,' replied Drake, looking at Grace, who nodded knowingly. 'Is there perhaps anything unusual about her? Never mind the clothes. It would be more helpful to know any distinguishing features.'

'Well, she has quite classical features. It is her fortune in life to look perfect.' There was a strange tone in Philippa's voice that Drake thought was rather grudging. He made a mental note. Perhaps the relationship between his guest and the dead woman, if it was her, might not have been entirely amicable. Philippa looked upwards, obviously trying to think of other things she could say. 'Oh yes, there is one thing about her that is odd. It is far from perfection. The fourth finger on her right hand is unusually long. It's almost as long as the third finger. It's only on her right hand. She plays the bassoon. She always says that has caused this finger to get longer trying to reach the keys on her instrument. I've no idea whether that is true, but that's what she claims.'

'Do you know if she has any piercings or tattoos?'

'She had once told me she disliked tattoos on women. I remember that because I wondered about having one done and abandoned the idea,' replied Philippa. 'Strangely, a few weeks ago, she showed me a small tattoo on her chest. I thought it ugly, but she said it made her feel safe. She often had romantic notions of that kind. Although she is a deep thinker, she also has some silly ideas.'

'Can you describe the tattoo?' asked Drake.

'No, sorry, I only took a cursory look at it. It just seemed like a bit of scribble.'

Drake pulled out his phone, scrolled to his picture of Imogen's tattoo and showed it to Philippa.

'Could this be the tattoo?' he asked.

'It could be,' replied Philippa, 'but I really couldn't be sure.'

'As for her extra-long finger,' said Drake. 'I've heard similar claims from flute players about their third finger.' He went over to his chair and picked up the pathologist's report. He started to flick through to the final pages. Eventually, he found what he was looking for and grunted with satisfaction.

'I can tell you that the pathologist has commented in an appendix about this finger. I'm afraid it may be your friend who was found in the Dee. Certainly, she was wearing clothes like those you describe, and her hair and height match your description.

The match for the finger and the tattoo suggests it might be her. I'm sorry.'

Philippa Crehan began to sob uncontrollably. 'I knew it. I knew it,' she cried.

'Do you happen to know who Imogen's dentist was?' asked Drake quietly as Grace went over and put an arm around Philippa's shaking shoulder.

'Yes, of course. We used the same dentist. It's a practice called Richards.'

Grace made a note and fetched Philippa a cup of tea. She took sips while staring blankly at the floor in front of her.

'Can I just check with you, Philippa?' asked Drake quietly. 'You said that originally Imogen didn't have a tattoo and didn't like them. Then, apparently, out of the blue, she showed you one. Have you any idea why she changed her mind?'

'I've thought about that,' said Philippa. 'Not long ago, she was commissioned by a local tattoo artist to design some tattoos in her style. He thought there was a market for them from enthusiasts of her work. Perhaps he persuaded her to have one, but I don't know that for certain.'

'I see,' said Drake slowly while scratching his head. 'Do you know the name of this tattoo artist?'

'No, sorry. I've changed my mind completely and agree with Imogen's original dislike of tattoos, so it didn't interest me.'

'Do you have any sense that there may be someone who would wish to do Imogen harm?' asked Drake.

'Not really. There is nothing that I can say for sure. She did say a few things about people handling her work in Hong Kong. I don't think she liked some of them much. It seemed she had recently lost her trust in them. I don't know why. I seem to remember she said she hoped to get some help soon.'

# 4

The following morning, Drake came out of the rear door of the police station and clambered stiffly into the back of the Range Rover. He did not speak and immediately opened his notebook. The Range Rover set off in almost complete silence as if respecting the situation. Grace was driving. She understood that Drake preferred comfort to speed. They were followed by a small scene-of-crime team, which Drake had demanded as a precaution. Drake took out his crossword, which had been going slowly that day. Grace was concentrating on a busy section of the route. It was several minutes before she spoke to Drake.

'Good morning, Sir. You might notice we have someone else with us.'

'Yes,' replied Drake. 'I can see the back of a head. Unless I'm much mistaken, it's a tall person.'

'We have Constable Daniel Ford sitting in the front,' she said. 'He has just joined us from the uniformed branch.' The head turned to reveal its face, hesitantly peering around the front seat headrest.

'My apologies,' said Dan Ford. 'I am taller than average, but I can't compete with you, and this seat back is rather high.'

Drake laughed. 'Welcome to our little team.'

'Constable Ford is going to take notes,' said Grace. 'He can then compare them with mine to see how we do things.'

'Excellent,' said Drake. 'You couldn't have a better mentor than Detective Sergeant Hepple. I suggest you shadow her throughout this case or at least until further notice.' With that, he returned to 7 across, which was particularly obstinate.

Grace drove around the new bus station with its plant-covered roof and set off along Hoole Road. Gradually, the houses began to get larger and more set back from the busy road. Grace was looking for the property where Philippa Crehan had said she and Imogen Glass lived. Some of the houses had been converted into small hotels. Drake was about to write in a clue when the Range Rover jolted over the pavement, knocking the pencil from his hand. They turned through a generous gateway and crunched across a gravel driveway. Straight ahead was the house. It was an elegant, though far from extravagant, affair. Drake thought it would be worth a significant sum. Somehow, Philippa had seen them and soon appeared through the front door. She stood on the porch, waiting for the little cavalcade of vehicles to arrive, and then stepped out to meet them. Grace was holding the rear car door open for Drake, who was struggling to get his large ageing frame out. Philippa stepped forward to help.

'Thank you, how kind,' said Drake. 'I'm afraid I don't move as easily as I did, especially early in the morning. This looks like a splendid house in a pleasant yet handy location.'

'Yes, I inherited it,' said Philippa. 'I can't afford to run it, but I have such lovely memories of my childhood here that I couldn't imagine selling it. There is a charming annexe to the side and rear. To help with the costs of the house, I let the annexe out. I was lucky to find Imogen, who has turned it into a flat with a studio for her work. Please come, and I will open it for you.' She turned her key in the lock and stood back to allow the police officers through.

Drake briefly stuck his head into the living room with its offshoot kitchen to the left. It seemed a bare room. Its current residents appeared not to take much interest in it. He looked around the bathroom and the bedroom. They were generally tidy but uninteresting spaces. He was most interested in the studio across to the right of the little hallway. He stood in the doorway, inhaled the air, and looked around. This was not quite what Drake had been expecting. He had seen many productions of Puccini's opera, La Boheme. They all presented a typically messy and chaotic artist's studio. The one such space he had seen for real in Sheffield confirmed this pattern. Imogen Glass, however, had an exemplary tidy version.

Drake's first impression was of the scent in the place. It changed as he moved around. Near the doorway was a distinct aroma of oriental incense sticks. On the far side of the room was a distinct whiff of oil paint. There were two paintings and a selection of blank canvasses stacked vertically against the far wall. Above them was shelving that held materials all stored logically. The brushes of all sizes and kinds were on the lowest shelf. Above were paints of various mediums arranged by colour. There was the unmistakable odour of oil paints and solvents. Large rolls of paper and piles of sheets were on a counter against the right-hand wall. It had two doors on the front, which Drake tried. They were both locked. He chose deliberately to sniff the sheets of paper. They had their own rather delicate aroma. Drake thought it was rather like the smell of a newly opened book. That smell had lured the young Drake into a life-long passion for reading. The room was an adventure of attractive and distinctive aromas.

He was warming to the place. In parts, it looked and smelt like an artist's studio. Elsewhere, it took on a domestic feel. The centre of the room was occupied by no fewer than three easels, two with work in progress. The third was empty. To one side was a double bed covered in pillows and an upright chair. Beyond the easels was a carefully stacked pile of heavy-looking wooden poles, each about a metre long. Their diameter was such that an average person could comfortably get a hand around them. Lying next to them were several coils of rope. Drake assumed they were intended to be part of some three-dimensional work of art. Perhaps Imogen had been interested in sculpture. He pulled on a pair of blue rubber gloves and lifted a pole. They were even heavier than they looked. Drake guessed they must be hewn from a dense timber.

The left-hand wall had a huge window that flooded the whole room with daylight. Drake checked his map. Sure enough, the window faced north to reveal a sun-free sky. Drake knew that artists preferred that for their studio. In the opposite corner was a music stand next to a bookcase full of musical scores and recordings. Next to this was a bassoon proudly upright on a dedicated stand. The bare wooden floor was the only indication that this was a place for creative work. It was covered in dabs, spills and pools of paint and ink.

Drake began examining the stacked paintings and a few others hanging on the wall in which was the doorway. The stack of frames was generally uninteresting. Most were empty, awaiting some work yet to be imagined. A few had paintings that were either abstract or landscapes. A certain amount of purely graphical work suggested Imogen might have been commissioned for more commercial purposes. Some of the graphics were elaborately decorated. It looked as if they might be based on Chinese characters. A couple of the landscapes hanging on the wall in portrait format resembled those Chinese paintings of towering scenes showing huge waterfalls and treed hillsides. Seeing Drake looking at these paintings, Philippa Crehan stepped forward to explain.

'Imogen creates what she calls "fusion art." She named it after the fashion of fusion cuisine that combines Western and Chinese cooking. It is quite common in countries such as Singapore and Hong Kong. This sells well over there, and there is a growing body of avid collectors of her work.'

'It's all very charming,' said Drake. 'The world has lost a real talent.' He walked over to the right-hand side, where he discovered a small kiln. Sitting on a stool next to it were several pieces like the one Imogen Glass had been found wearing under her blouse.

'This is new experimental work, I think,' said Philippa. 'I don't know anything about it, I'm afraid.'

'Did Imogen sell her work here in the UK?' asked Drake, toying with one of the ceramic pieces.

'Oh yes,' replied Philippa. 'Especially here in Chester at a shop on St Werburgh Street called The Orient. She had become good friends with the owner, Angela Marchment.' Philippa looked around and idly flipped through the empty frames. 'Usually, I think she has more work on view. Perhaps she has a current exhibition or has been selling unusually well recently.'

Drake ran his fingers across the wall. His hand flicked against several nails where more paintings had once hung. He sat on one of the two simple upright chairs on either side of a small round table. Grace picked up the A3 portfolio that was sitting on the table. The cover announced Imogen Glass as its author. Grace flipped through it. Inside were countless prints of paintings. The final page was a numbered list, which Grace assumed was an index. Finally, there were several sheets of transparent plastic wallets containing business cards. Grace thought they might be from the purchasers of the paintings.

'Ah yes,' said Philippa. 'This is her collection of the work that she is satisfied with. She would show it to prospective galleries, possible commissioners or buyers. She has a version on her laptop that she could take with her. That's her laptop over on the table.' Grace and Drake could see the enormous range of her work in the portfolio. Imogen had been prolific. This did not look like the work of a tortured artist but rather someone confident and capable of working at speed.

'This looks like some sort of catalogue of all Imogen's work,' said Grace, still flipping through the portfolio.

'OK,' said Drake, 'bag it and let's take it so you can study it. Philippa, you mentioned a missing white van normally kept at the rear. Can you show me where it is normally parked, please?'

'Yes, of course,' said Philippa. 'Come this way.' She took Drake and Grace Hepple back into the small hallway and pointed to a door between the bathroom and the living room. 'Through that door is a short corridor that takes you to a door out into the carport. Follow me, and I will open it for you.'

Drake's brain was sifting through all this new information and suddenly started shouting alarm signals at him. 'Stop, Philippa, please,' he said so suddenly and loudly that Philippa jumped slightly. 'Sorry to be so abrupt,' said Drake. 'It is possible that Imogen was attacked here. We must provisionally assume that this may be a crime scene, and there may be important evidence around here that we must not contaminate. Please allow my team here to proceed.' One of the scene-of-crime team came forward to put what looked remarkably like blue plastic bags over Drake's shoes as he held each foot in the air.

Philippa stood back. Drake and one of the suitably clad SOCO members donned gloves. Drake slowly turned the door handle. The door opened into a corridor, perhaps five metres long, with a solid door at the far end. Drake and his colleague walked carefully towards the door. Drake turned the internal latch on the lock, pulled down the handle and opened the door. They were in the open air. It was a concrete-floored space with a corrugated plastic roof above. It was open to the air on the other three sides. To the left was a driveway giving access to a side road. Two sides of the carport were overgrown with dense shrubs and grass rising almost to waist height. Drake closed the door through which he and his colleague had come. Drake stood and proudly took photos with his iPhone around these spaces and grunted to himself in a satisfied sort of manner.

'Get our locksmith to examine the lock, please. Can your boys look carefully at the corridor and then in the studio? The other spaces in the apartment can wait until later. I need a report on all this as soon as possible, please. The investigation may be held up until we get this.' The SOCO officer nodded and returned to collect his colleagues. Drake walked back inside to join Grace and Philippa in the studio. As he arrived, he spoke again to Philippa Crehan.

'I'm afraid we must take this whole area into our investigation. I would be most grateful if you could make yourself available. Please leave the whole annexe to my officers. We shall also need your fingerprints to conduct our investigation.' Philippa nodded and gulped. It suddenly seemed to hit her that they were in the middle of what was probably a murder investigation. Drake continued. 'Do you know the registration of Imogen's white van?' Philippa shook her head silently, still gasping for air.

'What about close family?' asked Drake. 'Did she have any relatives who may be able to assist the investigation?'

'She has a younger sister who lives here in Chester. They see each other quite a bit, I think. Mostly, they seem to discuss the situation created by their parents.'

'What situation?' demanded Drake.

'They are old now and quite mad. They are religious fanatics and think Imogen and Felicity lead sinful lives. They keep threatening them with fire and brimstone!'

'Ok,' said Grace. 'I'll get onto the DVLA about the van and track down the family.'

Drake stood centrally in Imogen's studio, asked Grace and Philippa to sit down, and panned his iPhone, taking a video of the whole space. The iPhone chirruped cheerfully as Drake put it back in his pocket and tapped it through his jacket.

'Right,' said Drake. 'We need to leave the SOCO boys to it. Let's get back to the station.'


Drake remained silent in the rear of the Range Rover while Grace drove. Drake's silence persisted as they returned to the station and into the newly assigned case room. Drake went straight to the coffee machine, pressed a button, and it obligingly leapt into action, pouring out two cups. He took them over to the table in the middle of the room and sat down, beckoning Grace to join him.

'There's a pattern suddenly developing here,' he said. Grace wished she could see it. Right now, there seemed to be a plethora of evidence that she had yet to get together in her mind. She felt this was unfair as she had been driving through the Chester traffic. Drake took a sip of hot coffee and pushed the cup away to cool down. He began talking, apparently to Grace, but she thought he was probably thinking aloud.

'We find the body of Imogen Glass, a relatively young and successful artist, disfigured in the River Dee. Her van is missing. There are two possibilities here. Either she drove the van, or someone else did. Where did the van go, and why? We need to find it, Grace.' She nodded, having already put in a request for information to DVLA. Drake continued talking to thin air, but clearly for her benefit. 'Perhaps, quite innocently, Imogen drove the van somewhere, maybe with some paintings. Her studio suggests a rather well-organized young woman. I think you collected her laptop. I guess that she might keep a diary on it. Get Dave to boot it up and look for it if he can. Whatever appointment she may have had, it eventually proved fatal. Are these two things connected?' Drake took a sip of his cooling coffee. It seemed to his taste, and he held the cup in both hands up to his lips and froze before beginning to speak again slowly and deliberately.

'Another possibility is that Imogen was taken from her studio by persons, so far unknown. Perhaps they drove her in her van to meet her fate. Why? We need to find the van. Philippa said there are fewer paintings in her studio than normal. Why? Have some been stolen? Was it a theft that went wrong, and she got caught up in it and had to be disposed of?' Drake finished his coffee. 'I have a sneaky feeling the little corridor to the outside world via the carport may hold some secrets we need to uncover. We need the scene-of-crime boys to do their thing for us. Until then, we need to keep our minds open.' Drake fell silent, and Grace went to take the laptop to Dave, the technician.

When she returned, Drake was sat in his favourite chair doing the Times crossword. He looked up over the paper.

'Yesterday, you might have noticed that Philippa Crehan was aware of the tattoo,' he said.

'Yes, I remember,' replied Grace, laughing. 'It suggested their relationship might have been more than landlady and tenant,'.

'Yes indeed. I take your point. They must have at least been good friends. However, she could not confirm that it was the same as the tattoo found on our victim's body. This makes the dental record even more critical,' grunted Drake.

'I've arranged for some constables to go from house to house up and down the road,' said Grace. 'They may turn something up.' Drake grunted his approval.

# 5

The case room was unusually crowded. Most people were sitting around the large table in the centre of the room. A few lesser figures and assistants had to sit behind. Over to the side, Drake's famous case boards had been erected. They stood exuding authority and purpose, even if still mostly blank. They were nearly two metres tall and were arranged in a large U shape. There had been worryingly little to post on them. There were Drake's phone pictures of the site where Imogen's body was found floating in the river. His photographs of the studio where Imogen worked were next in line. Notes from the interview with Philippa Crehan were posted next to the pictures that Drake had taken of the studio. The most eye-catching items were the gory images of the victim's face taken by the pathologist on his table. No one in the room seemed interested in these pictures of poor Imogen Glass. While a few people sat silent, most were chattering and laughing in a manner that a casual observer might have thought inappropriate, given the tragic nature of the case. But these people dealt with death almost daily and needed at least some relief to maintain their sanity.

There was an empty chair next to Detective Sergeant Grace Hepple, who was quietly thumbing through her notes. She wore the characteristic black suit that contributed to her air of calm competence. There was a loud scratching noise that interrupted the general hum of conversation. Grace knew instantly what caused it. She looked at her watch; he was right on time.

'Sorry,' said Drake as Grace opened the door for him. 'I seem to have lost my keys again.' Several faces of people in the know smiled and winked at their neighbours. Drake struggled into the empty chair, groaned, and muttered something about chairs without arms. Everyone gradually stopped chattering as Drake sat looking around the table. He leaned forward so he could see all the faces around him.

'I intended to start by hearing comments from our pathologist, Professor Cooper,' said Drake, 'but he does not seem to be here.' An excitable young-looking man at the far end of the table tentatively waved his arm in the air like some enthusiastic schoolboy who knew the answer to a difficult question. 'Yes,' said Drake. 'I'm afraid I don't know who you are.'

'I'm Professor Cooper's trainee assistant,' came the rather bombastic reply. 'I thought it might be helpful to hear me first. Professor Cooper is sorry he cannot be here and hopes you don't mind. He has received the deceased's dental records from her dentist. Professor Cooper can now formally confirm that they match those of the body exactly. He is happy to accept this as identification. It is indeed a female name of Imogen Glass.'

'Good. I can claim at least some progress to the powers that be,' said Drake. 'Please thank Professor Cooper. Now, we can get on without further uncertainty. We are investigating the death of Imogen Glass. She has probably been murdered. She might have been killed somewhere along the riverbank. It is also possible that this happened in her studio. There is a short corridor connecting the studio with the carport. An image of that corridor keeps creeping into my mind. I have a sneaky feeling it is important. It is possible that there was some illegal entrance this way. I'm anxious to hear about any evidence that might support this hypothesis. Perhaps someone can tell us about the door lock first,' he said, turning to the locksmith.

'Yes, James Bull, locksmith,' came the reply. 'First, I can report that we managed to unlock the two cupboard doors under the large counter. The cupboard was empty except for four large cardboard tubes.'

'What was in the tubes?' asked Drake.

'Nothing, they were all empty.'

'Perhaps they were used to store or package up paintings for posting. Why keep them locked up if they were empty?' grunted Drake. 'Sorry to interrupt you, please carry on.'

James Bull continued. 'As for the door into the carport down the short corridor from the studio, that's a more complicated story.' Drake sat back in his chair and listened intently. The locksmith continued. 'There are some scratches in the mechanism visible under the microscope. These are characteristics of a clumsy attempt at picking the lock. It rather suggests the would-be burglar was ham-fisted. To pick a lock, you must insert special blades into the lock to cause each tumbler to operate. These are sharp and, in the hands of the inexperienced, they can leave microscopic scratches. There is also some damage to the cylinders that suggests the lock has been bumped open.' The locksmith paused and looked around the table. Drake asked the obvious question that was in many minds.

'Can you explain bumped open to the uninitiated?' he demanded.

'It's an alternative way of opening a lock to the well-known but difficult and skilled process of picking. When picking a lock, you manipulate all the pins in turn. It needs a delicate touch and careful feeling and listening. It is not easy without considerable experience. When bumping a lock, you insert a blank key-like tool into the lock and hammer it. Hopefully, the pins can be encouraged to drop. It is more hit-and-miss and doesn't always work, but it doesn't need as much experience. I guess the intruder tried to pick the lock, failed, and turned to bumping.'

'When was this done?' asked Drake.

'I can't tell,' replied the locksmith, 'but some of the scratches are quite shiny, so I think it is fairly recent.'

'Are we talking days, weeks or months?' demanded Drake. The locksmith shrugged his shoulders and looked frustrated that his efforts were not more warmly applauded. The sergeant in charge of the scene-of-crime team waved his hand for attention.

'If it's any help,' he said, we found this. It was in the undergrowth right next to the door.' He pulled out a transparent evidence bag and dropped it on the table, pushing it towards the locksmith, who grinned broadly.

'There you go,' said the locksmith, picking up the bag. Those sitting nearby could see a large ring with seven almost identical objects. They looked like keys but with much thinner bodies. Some curled into elaborate shapes, and others were nearly straight. 'That's a set of professional lock-picking tools,' he said proudly. 'You must select the right tools for the situation and each pin. It is not easy.'

'It's a wonder anyone ever learns to do it,' grunted Drake. 'So those have been discarded by the intruder?' asked Drake.

'More likely dropped,' replied the sergeant. Everyone looked at Drake, who paused as if to take everything in. He spoke slowly and carefully.

'So, we think an intruder tried to use these to pick the lock, failed and turned to another more substantial but cruder tool,' said Drake deliberately. 'As he did so, he dropped the picks, which fell into the undergrowth. If this was at night, he couldn't find them, or perhaps he didn't know he had dropped them.' There was much nodding of heads around the table. Eventually, the sergeant in charge of the scene-of-crime team broke the silence.

'We have found shoe or boot prints on the floor in the corridor between the outside door and the studio,' he said. Drake looked up as he continued. 'There are at least three sets of prints of what appear to be men's footwear. It might have been wet outside, but the concrete there doesn't allow us to find reliable prints. We must assume these are recent. If this is a well-used corridor, they could have been easily scrubbed out, so we assume there has not been much traffic since the footprints were made. Nobody would go down the corridor from the studio unless they wanted to go outside through the door.'

'You didn't find a woman's shoe print?' asked Drake.

'Not definitively, but some marks might be of the boots worn by the victim as shown in photographs in a publicity folder we found in a filing cabinet.'

'Ah,' said Drake enthusiastically. 'Can I see the photograph?' He looked closely at the image passed to him and pointed it out to Grace.

'Yes, these look like the clothes worn by the body recovered from the River Dee. Her landlady said it was almost a kind of uniform.' Drake immediately went to his case boards to post this image next to the ones of her lifeless body. It was a stark reminder of the job ahead. Grace reported that the house-to-house enquiries had not yielded any lines of investigation. The house next door was locked and showed signs of the residents being away. Further visits will be made in due course.

'What do you think then, Grace?' demanded Drake after the meeting had closed and everyone had left. 'At least we now have a dental identification rather than relying on a slightly long bassoon-playing finger. Then there is her peculiar tattoo, which her landlady reported. Of course, the location of the tattoo was always a possible obstacle, but even so. It is also intriguing that Imogen showed it to Philippa. I wonder what that tells us. Did she perhaps see more of Imogen's body than most? I wonder! The more important matter now is how and why she died.'

'Well, there is one idea that keeps churning around in my mind,' interjected Grace thoughtfully. Drake raised one eyebrow and looked at her across the room. 'It's that maybe three people have broken into the studio. Was it their intention to steal rather than murder?'

'Yes,' said Drake. 'But it would seem odd that three people went to a well-planned burglary but were collectively so inept at opening a lock. Taken together with something we heard from the landlady Philippa, what was her name?'

'Philippa Crehan,' said Grace.

'Ah yes, Philippa Crehan. She told us that there were normally more paintings there.'

'Exactly,' said Grace. 'It makes me wonder. Is it possible that this was a planned break-in to steal paintings? Perhaps Imogen caught them at it and, in a struggle, received a serious blow on the head.' Grace paused to wait for Drake's reaction.

'Taken at face value,' he said slowly, 'that seems quite feasible. Perhaps this group panicked and attempted a rather crude way of disguising the body as a drowning victim. If so, they didn't fool our friendly local pathologist.' Drake paused and grunted. 'It's probable from what we know now that Imogen Glass is sufficiently well known for this to be a speculative robbery. Or could it be something done on demand? Is there some reason we don't yet understand for her work to be targeted?' Grace shrugged her shoulders.

'I've studied the portfolio we found in the studio,' said Grace. 'Nearly all the paintings are recorded as sold, and there is usually a name of the owner. There are a few paintings in the studio that don't look finished. They are not yet catalogued. However, there seem to be some twenty-four paintings given names and numbers but no owners. Perhaps these have been stolen and perhaps taken away in the missing van. Given the prices shown elsewhere, this would be quite a haul. It could be worth quite a few million pounds. It feels that it could be a professional job, perhaps done to order in a planned way. Do we have any informers who might be able to help?' she asked. Drake grunted.

'There might be some people at The Met who could help with that,' he said. 'We need to do some digging around. Perhaps it's time to issue a press release. It might trigger something. It is about time we announced the name of our victim. Try to get my photo of her tattoo included. It needs to be a colour reproduction. You never know if that might get a reaction of some kind. Let's get something in the local evening papers, and maybe local television news might run an item for us this evening. I have a hunch that there are a couple of places that might be worth some exploration.'


That evening, Drake walked down to the Boathouse Pub for a glass or two of red wine with his son, Tom. Drake bagged a table on the barge while Tom went in and ordered. Drake regretted that he was no longer incognito at the pub. He was now greeted by other drinkers who wanted to know how the investigation was going. He was not used to being such a celebrity and had begun to appreciate how irritating fame could be. He wondered about the latest possibility of a planned theft, perhaps interrupted by Imogen, who had then been killed. Tom arrived with the first two glasses of wine. He sat down, and father and son sipped their drinks and enjoyed the scenery. Tom knew his father's moods better than most and maintained the silence for several minutes. Eventually, he spoke first.

'I suppose the trouble is that this river is no longer just a lovely spot to you,' he said, taking another sip of wine. 'It is the place where an awful crime was committed.'

'Not a problem,' said Drake. 'I have long been able to separate crime scenes from their surroundings. We had to solve that Singapore case when a body was found on that lovely bridge.' He pointed downstream over his shoulder to where the beautiful iron suspension bridge soared over the river. 'I still walk to the centre of it and admire the view. If anything, I can associate it not with the crime but our success in solving it.'

'I'm going to London for a few days,' said Tom. 'I've lined up a couple of interviews for interesting-looking jobs. May I return and stay for a few more days before I go to Singapore?'

'Of course,' said Drake. 'You never know. We might have solved this one when you return. Somehow, I doubt it. There are so many loose ends.'

# 6

The following day, Grace pulled the Range Rover off The Groves onto the short driveway at the front of Drake's house. Drake sat in the front passenger seat, completing a clue in the day's Times crossword. As Grace pulled open the door, he pushed his propelling pencil back into his shirt pocket and swivelled around to dangle his legs out of the car. With a brief shuffle forward, his feet conveniently reached the ground, and he could push himself up to a standing position.

'You would think that they measured me up before making these cars,' he said with a grin. Grace nodded and laughed. It was common knowledge in the force that Drake was always to be transported in the Range Rover. Even though age was causing a slight stoop, his six-and-a-half-foot frame was impressive and caught the eye of a couple walking along the riverbank road. Drake looked up at his little cottage and back across the River Dee. He had been so lucky to find this place. It now felt like home. He stood wondering what Cynthia would have made of it. He was pretty sure she would have approved. There was nothing pretentious or fake about this spot. The house, the road, the trees and the river all fell into place, and the view upstream was beautifully composed by a gentle bend with rising land behind. A little further downstream, the white suspension bridge elegantly asserted its claim to be the focal point. But his target today was just a few paces along the river in the opposite direction. Luckily, the table that the little girl who discovered Imogen's body occupied with her mother was free. Drake motioned to Grace to join him at the table.

'Grace, see if you can find the landlord or manager or whatever he is and ask him to spare us a few minutes. Oh, and bring a couple of pints of that rather nice local bitter they have on tap here.'

Grace returned accompanied by a man almost as tall as Drake carrying a tray with two pints of beer and a glass of red wine. 'They tell me that your preferred tipple is this nice red and that you always order it after a beer,' he said as he put it down in front of Drake. 'So, I've saved you the trouble.'

'Good gracious,' exclaimed Drake. 'I didn't know I was being watched.'

Drake's host smiled and nodded his head.

'I'm afraid that after the events of a week or so ago, you are quite a celebrity. The locals tell stories about the cases you have solved. The local paper's editor dug them out of his back numbers.'

'And I thought I was having a quiet incognito drink or two,' laughed Drake. 'I must admit I have noticed the odd stare recently. But tell me, what do your customers say about the current case that began here the other evening? No, wait. First, thank you for helping so brilliantly that evening with the crowds. It was a real bonus that you kept everyone in good spirits. You kept them all back from the work my officers had to do in a way that was dignified and respectful to the dead.'

'You're most welcome, and by the way, my name is James Staniforth.'

'Drake is the name I am most usually known by.'

'Yes, we know. A couple of your constables often drink here, and they have told us about your stellar career.' Grace was sniggering behind her beer mug, and Drake looked nonplussed. 'There are all sorts of rumours, to be fair,' said James Staniforth. 'Some people thought they knew who she was. One chap said he thought he had seen the body previously upriver, though he wasn't sure enough to report it. Another was sure he had seen it here the previous evening but didn't appreciate it was a body.'

'And what do you think?' demanded Drake.

'Oh, a pub like this is where people tell stories. I doubt any of them have any real substance. I always do a circuit as we lock up, and I think I would have spotted her if she had been here the previous evening. The most credible story was from a stranger. I hadn't seen him before. He claimed to have seen a man and a woman arguing on the riverbank further upstream near the ferry. He thought it was a couple of days previous.'

'Really!' said Drake. 'Grace put out a press release on this, asking anyone who saw anything to contact us. First, drive me to Imogen's Studio. I have unfinished business there.' A slightly surprised and puzzled Grace decided not to ask Drake what his business was. If he wanted her to know, he would have told her.

Drake stood as near as he could to the centre of Imogen's studio and slowly looked around. His gaze halted at what Grace thought was the double bed over to his left. Then he walked over to the right and poked about with his crossword pencil amongst the components of what Grace assumed was a work in progress for some sculpture. Drake walked back to the centre of the room and finally spoke to Grace.

'I'm still trying to put the words of Professor Cooper into perspective. His final and formal version of the post-mortem report arrived this morning in the post.'

'Does it contain anything new or surprising?' asked Grace.

'Not really, but it has reminded me of some unresolved issues,' replied Drake as the door opened. In came a rather flustered pathologist.

'You wanted an urgent meeting. Is there something wrong with my report, Drake?' he demanded.

'Not in the least,' replied Drake. 'It has done its job admirably. However, it reminded me of two issues that might dominate our investigation. I wondered if you could help us with them.'

'I'll try,' snapped Professor Cooper slightly irritably.

'Please look over there,' said Drake, pointing to the bed. 'Does anything surprise you?'

'No, I'm afraid not.'

'Well, look again at the double bed. Isn't it surprising to find one in an artist's studio? I have built a mental image of this sort of space. It is somewhere intrinsically hard and probably rather mucky. It's a workplace.'

'Well, isn't it something a naked model might drape herself over?'

'Possibly, possibly,' grunted Drake. 'Except we have no evidence of Imogen Glass painting that. Look at all the pillows on it. They are set out for comfort, not posing. Notice one pillow has tumbled onto the floor.' Drake looked at the pathologist in total silence. Eventually, Professor Cooper spoke again.

'Does the fallen pillow have something to do with it?' he asked.

'Could Imogen Glass have been smothered with a cushion?' snapped Drake. Professor Cooper scratched his chin and grunted.

'Well, yes. It is possible, but there are some problems with that hypothesis. Firstly, smothering takes a considerable amount of time, at least three minutes and maybe as many as five.'

'Why is that a problem?'

'Because the victim would have to be restrained,' said Professor Cooper with a slight air of exasperation at such a question. 'Even a momentary lapse in the hold and the victim will gasp a lot of air surprisingly quickly. Although the body was heavily damaged by being carried along in the river, there were no signs of restraint that I could detect. To hold a body still would require restraints that would leave clear marks on the skin.'

'Point taken,' replied Drake. 'But could the wound to the rear of her head have caused her to remain unconscious long enough?'

'That is certainly possible. A second problem needs investigation. It has to do with how airtight the pillow is. Sometimes, people talk about someone being smothered by a pillow. The contents of most pillows and some cushions are far from airtight. They are just a collection of material stuffed into the case.'

'What about these pillows?' asked Drake.

'I could test one if I take it to the lab. The pillows may not all be the same, of course. If you are happy that I am not damaging material from a crime scene, I can look now.' Drake beckoned the pathologist over and gave him the cushion from the floor. The pathologist opened the pillowcase and pulled out the contents. He pulled and pushed at the material inside and grunted.

'OK, this feels like it may be filled with down. This consists of many separate items and is not airtight. Some pillows are made from closed-cell foam rubber. Some foams, such as those you might use for washing up or cleaning the car, have open cells. This means you can press them, exhaust most of the air, immerse them in water, and they will expand, taking water in and filling the cells. This enables us to use them, gradually letting the water out to clean. Closed-cell foams have isolated cells. This is why they spring back after being compressed. This makes them comfortable for mattresses, pillows and cushions. Some foams can be a little in between. I will test this pillow to see if it is airtight in the lab.'

'OK,' said Drake with a grunt of satisfaction, 'Now, please come over to the other side of the studio and look at this collection of stuff. We think it was intended to be constructed into a sculpture. There are a couple of crude sketches leading us to this conclusion. Now, could any of these wooden poles have been the instrument used to hit Imogen Glass on the head?'

'I would say that her wound is compatible with her receiving a blow with one of these. May I pick one up?'

'Yes, they've all been fingerprinted,' said Grace. Professor Cooper picked up one of the poles and wafted it about as if testing a blow to Imogen's head.

'What do the fingerprints show?' demanded Drake. Grace consulted her notebook.

'All of the poles had at least two sets of fingerprints. One set belongs to Imogen Glass. The other we have not yet traced. Two poles have one additional set of prints. They are both different and unknown to us so far.'

'So,' said Drake. 'Perhaps the second set of fingerprints belongs to the craftsman who made them. They would have had to touch them all, and it seems logical that Imogen stacked them into this neat pile. However, is it possible that the murderer may have just picked up one pole? Perhaps the fingerprints suggest there were two people involved. It is possible that Imogen Glass was hit on the head with one of these poles, causing her to lose consciousness for long enough to smother her to death using one of these pillows.'

'Yes, I cannot say that is what happened, but the evidence is compatible with that. On the other hand, the murderer might have used one of the lengths of rope used in the sculpture. There are several lengths on the floor. If so, she would have marks on her neck, but I might have missed these because of all the other injuries.'

'So,' Drake continued. 'If we develop this scenario, it all suggests that she was murdered in this room and then later taken to a site along the river upstream from the pub where it is possible to drive right to the riverside. The mystery begins to clear just a little. Of course, we still don't know who murdered her and why. We have most of the investigation before us. Thank you, Prof. You have been a huge help. I am still puzzled by the facts. We have at least three people forcing the lock on the rear door and tramping through the rear entrance. Some twenty-odd paintings go missing. It is hard not to see these two things as connected. We also know that Imogen's white van, which is normally kept outside this entrance, was missing. If, as the footprints suggest, three or more people were involved in a break-in and theft, did Imogen disturb them and was then attacked and beaten on the head with one of her wooden sculpture components? Do we know any more about these poles?'

'Yes,' replied Grace. 'The scene-of-crime team found a business card under the poles. We checked with the supplier. They were delivered only two weeks before Imogen's body was found.' Drake grunted an acknowledgement.

'Does the scene-of-crime team have any more information for us about the footprints in the corridor?'

'Yes. There are three sets of shoes or boots, each leaving their distinctive pattern of prints. As you know, Sir, it is impossible to accurately translate a footprint into a shoe size because of the variation in shoe soles. However, the estimate is that all three fall into a range of perhaps nine, nine and a half or ten. This is average for UK men, so there is no unique clue.'

Professor Cooper stood holding a pillow and a pole, listening to the conversation.

'So,' continued Drake. 'There were at least three to carry out twenty or so paintings. This would not have taken long. Why then go to the trouble of smothering Imogen?'

'Perhaps at least one of the attackers was known to Imogen, and she would have been able to identify him or her,' Grace interjected.

'Yes, good thinking, Grace,' said Drake, 'but why not just leave the body? Why go to all the trouble of dumping it in the River Dee?'

'Perhaps they were hoping her body would not be found,' said Grace slowly.

'Possibly, possibly,' replied Drake, 'but if so, why dump it upstream of Chester city centre? It would have made more sense to use a downstream location.'

Three people stood in the centre of the studio with puzzled expressions on their faces. Grace shrugged her shoulders.

'It remains a mystery,' she said.

'We're missing something,' said Drake. 'The facts are not yet neatly falling into place in our hypothesis. Perhaps we are on entirely the wrong track. Perhaps the robbery and the murder are separate but coincidental events. If so, the murderer could have had a different motive, which we don't yet understand.'

# 7

Drake left Grace to drive back to the station. He had another place to visit and said he was "going digging in an exploratory sort of way." He made his way up into the centre of the town, arriving on Foregate Street, where he turned left to pass under the great Eastgate. The gilded initials of Queen Victoria on the clock were glinting in the summer sunlight. He took a picture of the clock tower. He wondered if any other clock had been photographed as much. Maybe Big Ben, he thought. As he passed under the arch, he looked up to check his watch against the ornate clock. Of course, it was correct. Drake's watch was always right, but this had become a habit that he had no intention of breaking.

A short distance further on, he was turning right onto St Werburgh Street. He headed to the point where the street turned sharply to the left. It then wrapped itself around the cathedral precinct. Sure enough, to his left was a shop proudly announcing itself as The Orient. It was set back from the street under overhanging upper-floor half-timbered gables. This was where Philippa Crehan had said Imogen Glass used to sell her paintings. Drake had unconsciously imagined a more touristy affair, but it was elegant and restrained. He thought it would be more accurate to describe it as a gallery. The extensive premises were on the opposite side of the street to the cathedral, largely obscured by trees. From the way the windows were arranged, Drake thought it had earlier been a series of small shops. He could see paintings, sculptures, pottery, and even furniture. To his uneducated eye, it all looked Chinese.

Drake reached the entrance. The door had caught the spirit of the place. As it opened, it wafted a great puff of oriental-scented air in Drake's direction. He was instantly charmed as he began to explore the interior that was divided into a series of bays. He imagined Cynthia's voice confirming his suspicion that this had been a row of shops in an earlier life. This worked well as each bay seemed to represent different kinds of art. Everything was displayed with space around it. There was nothing cluttered about this place. The owner or owners certainly knew how to curate such an exhibition, for that was what he was exploring. Inside, it was even more like a gallery. He passed through rooms with paintings on the walls and a few large brass and ceramic items in central cases.

He eventually arrived at a space that contained only one item. It looked like a huge four-poster bed. It had a polished dark wood floor rather than a mattress. It was the size of a small room. It was littered with brightly coloured cushions, all delicately decorated. The frame was also made from rather dark wood, which was in immaculate condition. Drake leant forward to read the notice on a stainless-steel plaque held by an elegant stand. He soon learned that he was looking at something called a daybed. It was believed to have been owned by some illustrious figure of the upper reaches of the Chinese community. It had six posts, not the four Drake initially noticed. There was an ornamental railing wrapped around it. The extra posts were at the front, making an opening. It was carved into a series of interlocking squares and circles, all fashioned from the same wood that looked to Drake something like mahogany. The notice claimed that this was from the Ming Dynasty and explained this for Western viewers as running from 1368 to 1644. Drake did not doubt that it was old and from a sophisticated early culture. It was in good condition. Amazingly good for its age. Drake assumed it was for sale, but there was no price tag. Drake smiled as he remembered that famous saying, "If you have to ask the price, you cannot afford it," but made a mental note to ask anyway.

Drake wandered into the next room, where smaller pieces of furniture from the Chinese past were displayed. The price tags for these items suggested that you would need to sell a rather large and luxurious car to raise the money to buy the daybed. It would carry a price tag of at least six figures. Drake looked back at the windows in the frontage of the gallery. They were heavily glazed, each with an alarm to detect any breakage. This was where substantial sums of money were exchanged between wealthy people. He tracked back, looking again at the prices and descriptions of more items. He found some silver items labelled as from the Tang Dynasty. He checked a table on the wall listing all the dynasties and discovered that the Tang ran from 618 to 906. Drake made a mental note that he should learn the dates of the Chinese dynasties. These rooms contained highly precious items of a kind that you might expect to find in a museum. He worked his way back to the first few rooms that concentrated mainly on paintings.

He scanned around and eventually found a sign showing three paintings by Imogen Glass. Drake thought they had a dreamy quality. They reminded him a little of Turner's great landscape scenes. But these were different. All three were in portrait format. They had towering vertical landscapes, not the more usual horizontal ones. There were vertiginous waterfalls with mountainous backgrounds. Even Drake could tell they were influenced by traditional Chinese art. Discreet labels indicated that these paintings were expected to fetch sums of tens of thousands of pounds. His victim was indeed a valued artist. Drake took photos with his iPhone of the three paintings. He would look at them in more detail later.

'Can I help you at all, sir?' The gentle, enquiring voice came from behind. Soft as it was, it startled Drake, who was deep in the study of Imogen Glass's work. He stumbled around.

'Perhaps you can help,' replied Drake. 'I would like to see the manager, please.'

'I am the joint owner, together with my husband, Wang. I am Angela Marchment. We have noticed you walked down our gallery and back again, so you are interested in all things oriental. What sort of item are you looking for?' Before Drake could decide how to answer this question, she spoke again. 'I see you are looking at the work of our wonderful artist, Imogen Glass. We were the first gallery to feature her work, and we are still lucky enough to get many of her fascinating paintings. These days, she is in great demand in the Far East, and most of her most recent work is sold there. Our prices can be considerably lower than you could pay in Hong Kong or Singapore. These three are perhaps a little small, but they represent excellent value. Some of her work has already sold for several million pounds in the Far East.'

'Good gracious,' said Drake. He had been pondering how to play this interview and, unusually for him, had not previously resolved the matter. For some reason, in an instant, he decided to use a direct approach.

'Good afternoon,' he began, pulling out his ID. 'I am Detective Chief Inspector Drake. I am investigating the death of Imogen Glass.'

'Death! What death. You mean Imogen has died?'

'I'm sorry,' said Drake. 'That was clumsy of me. I thought that you would have heard.'

Angela Marchment spun round on her heels and shouted down the gallery.

'Wang, Wang. Come quickly, please. I need you.'

Drake was taking in Angela Marchment. She was of average height, middle-aged and dressed in an understated but expensive way. Her dark hair was drawn into a tight bun on the back of her head. She stood in black stockings and shoes with mid-height heels. Her tight skirt ended just below the knee. Suddenly, from round behind one of the dividing walls appeared a Chinese-looking man. Drake thought he was unusually tall and large for someone of his race. A little on the chubby side, but Drake assessed large rather than fat. He wore perfectly round black framed spectacles perched on the end of his nose. He had a full head of black hair cut short in spikes. His shirt was collarless, in the Mandarin style. There were elaborately decorated toggles down the front. He arrived notably breathless and concerned by Angela's command.

'What this is?' he asked.

'I am told that Imogen Glass is dead. Did you know this?'

'No, of course not,' Wang looked bemused. Angela was almost in tears.

'But she was such a huge talent,' sobbed Angela. 'She had most of her creative life yet to live.'

'But this important to us. We sell lot of her work,' Wang almost spat out his words. The faster he spoke, the less accurate his English became. 'But sounds awful. Not mean it that way. She was friend of many years. Why I not know?' Wang shrugged, his arms partly outspread as if helpless to know how to respond.

'I am sorry,' said Drake. 'Clearly, I have introduced this clumsily. I also assumed you would know. I want nothing more or less than justice for Imogen. There is at least some suspicion that she may have been murdered. I'm in charge of the investigation. I hope you both will be able to help me.' Angela began to shake and sob silently. Wang came to hold and comfort her. She patted his arm around her shoulders.

'I need a cup of tea,' she said. 'Perhaps we should close the gallery and go into the office.'


Drake was ushered through a door and up some rickety stairs to a large workshop.

'This is where Wang does all his wonderful work,' explained Angela. 'He frames pictures for many local artists, especially Imogen Glass. He has an array of mouldings. We have an office here,' she said, opening a door. They all sat around a small circular table. Unsurprisingly, the tea was Chinese and served in tiny cups from an equally small teapot. This reminded Drake of the refreshments he had been given during his times in Singapore and Penang. Wang fussed around making the tea. Out of respect, Drake nodded deeply, almost into a bow, as Wang pushed the cup across the table. Drake noticed that he was naturally left-handed in everything he did. Drake recalled the work of a psychologist friend who had shown that left-handed people were more than averagely dyslexic. Perhaps this, as well as his background, gave rise to

Wang's struggle with English. Angela Marchment was more composed. She began to sip her tea appreciatively. Drake was enchanted by the ceremony surrounding tea in the Chinese world. The first cup was consumed in respectful silence. Wang poured out another round. Drake thought it was appropriate now to restart the conversation.

'How long have you had this wonderful gallery?' he began. He had learned early in his career that it would often be more productive to ask a witness a question about themselves rather than pitch directly into the case.

'I've lost track,' replied Angela. 'But it was the project that brought us together.' She smiled at Wang, who bowed his head. 'We met at a conference in Hong Kong about Chinese art. I spoke about how the West was getting more interested in Oriental art. Of course, Western and Oriental art use value systems quite differently, and I talked about that. Wang spoke so eloquently about the relationship between past and present in Chinese culture, which is one of the ways it differs from the cultures of the West.'

'That is interesting, Wang,' said Drake. 'Can you explain that to me simply?'

'Simple, not possible. Briefly yes,' said Wang smiling. 'We not differentiate between them as you do. We see history as continuous flow that is still present. So, we use more traditional symbolism in modern art and design.'

'Yes,' said Drake. 'I hadn't thought of that clearly, but I see what you mean. My wife, Cynthia, was an architect who worked a lot in the Far East. She had commented to me how Chinese architecture students would mix traditional ideas with more modern ideas in their work.' Wang bowed again. Angela nodded her head.

'Wang has a natural understanding of his culture,' said Angela.

'Ah, but you study, you so wise,' said Wang, 'but no idea how to run business.' He shook his frame with laughter.

'This is true,' said Angela. 'Wang looks after the contracts, the accounts and, of course, the money.'

'Angela live on higher plane,' said Wang, smiling and patting her arm. Drake saw that Angela was now smiling. She had revealed a truth about their partnership that amused them both. Wang shrugged his shoulders.

'Wang,' continued Angela, 'brings me down to earth occasionally. Perhaps a little too often.' They both smiled, and Angela took up the story.

'So, we moved to this deeply historical city, Chester, which charmed us both. Luckily, we stumbled on a little craft shop called The Orient, which was closing. It was a rather small shop. We bought it cheaply and kept the name. We were able progressively to buy more of the neighbouring premises. We need a larger gallery now. Perhaps we should be in London, but it is less expensive here, and we have both fallen in love with this city. As Wang expected, our Chinese friends love the city too because its past is so apparent.' Angela stopped abruptly, pulled out a handkerchief and dabbed her eyes. Wang patted her hands on the table.

'I'm sorry,' she said. 'It is so sudden. Imogen was a long-standing and good friend. She was so talented. The world has lost a wonderful artist.'

Wang nodded his head in agreement. 'More important,' he said in a stuttering voice, 'We will see no more new paintings from her.'

'What will happen to those you have hanging on the wall here?' asked Drake.

'In topsy-turvy art world, will probably command higher prices,' replied Wang.

'As a matter of interest,' Drake spoke slowly. 'How does the financial side of it all work?' Angela shook her head and pointed to her partner. Drake thought she was just a little reluctant to explain. 'This is what Wang does,' she said.

'No, you tell,' said Wang. Angela nodded and took a deep breath before starting.

'Sometimes Imogen would sell a painting to us. It would then be up to us to value it and exhibit it. On other occasions, Imogen would bring a painting and leave it with us. Perhaps she was not immediately in need of the money. We would exhibit it, make a sale and return the sum minus a small percentage to cover our costs. In the case of the paintings here, we own them and will probably keep them for a while out of respect. We might eventually auction them. She is very popular in Hong Kong. Wang found galleries for her in Hong Kong and did all the exporting of paintings over there.'

'When was the last time you saw Imogen Glass?' asked Drake.

'I can't remember,' said Angela.

'Must be many weeks,' said Wang.

'When did you get the paintings you have on display here?' asked Drake.

'Oh, a couple of months,' replied Angela. 'We usually keep them on the wall to raise interest before we either decide for ourselves on their value or we might hold an auction. We don't like to be without at least a few of her paintings on the wall.'

'She come see you when I in Hong Kong last month?' asked Wang, looking at his partner.

'No, she was also away in Hong Kong then,' replied Angela.

'Thank you for your time,' said Drake. 'I may come back again if some more questions arise. There is perhaps one more thing. Do you know of people who may have wished to do Imogen Glass harm?' The two proprietors of The Orient shook their heads silently and in unison.

Drake arrived at the station to find Grace anxious to speak to him. He poured himself a cup of coffee from the machine. She went for her notebook, which was next to the phone.

'We got a response to our request for information from anyone seeing anything along the riverbank. It turned out to be the man previously mentioned talking in the pub. He was walking along the riverbank with his dog when he passed a couple having a huge row. It stuck in his memory because they seemed oblivious to anything around them, including his dog, who tried to get their attention. He described the man as wearing dark trousers, although he wasn't sure. However, he was certain the man wore a bright red plain knitted jumper. He remembered thinking it was a warm day, and the chap was getting overheated in the argument and his jumper. He described the woman as dressed in lightweight clothes, all in black. Again, he remembered because she contrasted with her companion. Unfortunately, he can't remember just where he was at the time. He takes a long walk with his dog, and it could have been anywhere along the river, but he is sure it was upstream from the pub. Annoyingly, he also cannot remember what day it was as he takes this walk daily. He thought it was a couple of weeks before Imogen was found.'

'Well, well,' said Drake. 'It could indeed be Imogen. Philippa Crehan told us she always wore black, just as she was found, but if so, who was the man? Surely, the murder could not have been committed in such a public place. Yet again, we have more questions than answers.'

# 8

'I've had a curious phone call,' said Grace as Drake arrived in the case room, shaking the rain off his overcoat. 'It was Tom Denson who took it and transferred it to us. It was a woman who insisted on whispering. She said she wanted to talk to us about the death of Imogen Glass. She said it may not be quite what it appeared, but she thought she might be in danger and could only speak to us in a safe place.'

'Did she give her name?' asked Drake.

'No, but she seemed closely connected, so I asked her how she wanted to meet. She said she was too frightened to come here as she thought she might be followed. She wouldn't leave her number, which was unavailable on our phone. She said she would call again later to find out how we proposed to meet her. She said she was in Chester. She seemed in a dreadful hurry.'

'Well,' said Drake. 'For the time being, we must treat this seriously. I suggest we book a room in the Grosvenor Hotel in town. She could easily be in town and walk in. Our friend, the manager, will surely set it up for us. Get her to suggest a time, and then get on to the hotel.' Drake pulled The Times out of his coat pocket and settled down with his favourite pencil to attack the crossword. Grace busied herself with more internet searches about Imogen Glass. It was becoming increasingly apparent that her work had international significance. Grace was preparing a summary of it for Drake.

'By the way,' said Grace, 'Imogen's white van has been found in the Grosvenor Centre Car Park. Our lads are going there to recover it so a search and examination can begin.'

Late in the afternoon, the telephone rang. Grace picked it up. Drake looked across over the top of his glasses. 'It's Tom Denson,' said Grace, holding her hand over the phone mouthpiece. It's the same woman again.' Drake cocked an ear to listen to Grace.

'Yes, good afternoon. It's Detective Sergeant Grace Hepple here. It was me who spoke to you earlier…. No, I'm not the OIC, sorry, officer in charge of the case, that is Detective Chief Inspector Drake.' Drake picked up a second handset. 'Yes, of course, you can speak to him.' Grace nodded to Drake as she switched the call.

'Good afternoon. This is Drake. How can I help you?'

'I'm worried that they may be following me,' said the voice on the phone.

'Who are they?' asked Drake quietly.

'I'd rather not say. They may be tapping my phone. I've borrowed this one from a friend, but even so.'

'When would you like to meet?' asked Drake.

'As soon as possible.'

'OK, how about tomorrow morning at eleven? We will book a room at the Grosvenor Hotel in Eastgate. My colleague and I will get there before you. You go to reception and say you are Miss Simpson. We will get reception to bring you up. They will not mention any room number. I suggest you tell Grace now what you will be wearing. Come to the hotel by walking from the Cross. Grace will give you a phone number to call when you get there. We will have experienced detectives watching, and they can tell if you are followed. When you are walking, do not keep looking around. Just walk as you would normally. If we think you are in any danger, we will intervene. You will be perfectly safe.'

'Yes, OK, thank you.'

Drake put down his phone handset, and Grace continued to get details from the caller.

Drake, Grace and Constable Ford sat in a specially arranged room in the Grosvenor Hotel. Drake was working on The Times crossword. Grace was going through her notes. Constable Ford was walking up and down by the door. Occasionally, he stopped and looked fruitlessly through the spyglass.

'Oh, sit down, Dan,' said Drake. 'There is often some important waiting around to be done in the plain clothes branch. The moment you feel frustrated is exactly when the situation bites you, and you miss something.'

'Sorry, Sir,' replied Dan Ford. 'I just want to open the door as soon as she arrives.'

'Good thinking, Dan,' said Grace, 'but just cut out the pacing up and down.'

At that very moment, there was a tap on the door. Constable Ford was there instantly and opened it to reveal a woman looking anxiously along the corridor. A hotel receptionist nodded to her silently and scuttled off down the hallway.

'Come in, do,' said Drake, struggling to get out of his chair and dropping his paper and pencil on the floor. Dan Ford scurried across to pick them up. 'You must be Miss Simpson.' The woman nodded anxiously and was soon sitting in the chair opposite Drake. Grace and Dan Ford sat on either side with notebooks at the ready. Drake's phone chirruped cheerfully, and he checked the incoming message. 'My team reported that they are certain you were not followed,' he said. 'I doubt anyone could remain undetected by them, so let's relax just a little.' The woman nodded, smiled and loosened her jacket buttons.

'I hope you don't think I'm being silly over this?'

'Of course not,' replied Drake. 'Your safety is of the utmost importance to us.'

The visitor waved her phone and put it down on her lap.

'A good friend has lent me her phone while she uses her business one for a few days. I heard breathing noises on my phone. He has always been known as a noisy breather. I'm sure it's him listening in.'

'Who is him?' asked Grace softly.

'My father.'

'Perhaps we should go back to the beginning,' said Drake. 'Please tell us who you are. I've studied faces for most of my life, and yours gives me a clue.'

'My name is Felicity Glass. Imogen is my older sister. Most people have difficulty telling us apart. We were born only a year apart.'

'I thought perhaps so,' said Drake. 'I'm sorry about your sister. Please tell us how you think you might help our investigation.'

'Our parents have been waging some terrible quasi-religious war against us for some time,' said Felicity. 'They have been involved in a dreadful cult for several years. It all started with a life coaching group in Hong Kong.' She paused and pulled out a handkerchief to blow her nose.

'The family lived in Hong Kong?' asked Drake.

'Yes, Imogen and I were born in Hong Kong. Our father was a dealer in the stock market there. He made a substantial fortune. To begin with, we were lucky, I suppose. We had privileged childhoods. The only problem was that our parents started to control how we lived in line with their new religion, but as kids, we just played along. We grew up there, and that was when Imogen got interested in Chinese history and culture. I did as well, for a while, but Immy became obsessed with it. In those days, ex-pat families like ours never really mixed with the locals or tried to learn about them. It wasn't long before my father decided he and our mother would move to the States. It seemed to change them. They became more aggressive and dogmatic. Immy and I decided to stay in Hong Kong to go to university. Our parents became more extreme in their demands. Eventually, they agreed to pay our fees and living expenses. This was on condition that once we graduated, we would join them in America. They seemed to have lost sight of the fact that we were independent adults, but we accepted with no intention of ever going over there. This was also on condition that we took degrees in Religious Studies and Philosophy. I obeyed, but Immy registered for Fine Art. The course stimulated her interest in art in the West and the East. Father didn't know. I left the university after a few months. The course was probably excellent, but it wasn't for me.'

'Felicity,' said Drake. 'Your parents seem to have become important in this case. Can you tell us their names?'

'Of course. They are called William and Dorothy. However, Immy and I thought they might use different names in their sect.' Grace made a note. Drake beckoned Felicity to carry on with her story.

'I got a job in a fashion shop just to stay near Immy. We've always done things together. This was the first time in our lives that we were apart during a normal day. One of Immy's tutors was a jewellery designer, and she got me a job in a jewellery shop. After a while, I started learning the jeweller's craft and did some designs, which sold surprisingly well. Our parents didn't know we weren't getting religious studies degrees. When Immy graduated, they somehow found out and were furious. They demanded their money back, but neither Immy nor I could afford to pay it then. They never came back to Hong Kong. They said they were too involved in the headquarters of this cult they were in as it opened a new centre down in Texas. When Immy finished, they again demanded that we go and live with them, but of course, we were horrified at the idea.'

'Felicity,' interrupted Grace. 'You look tired. Could I get you a drink?'

'Oh yes, please,' said Felicity. Dan Ford put down his notebook, got up and made cups of coffee from the machine on the sideboard.

'So, what did you do?' asked Drake after Felicity had taken a few sips of her coffee. As usual, Drake put his aside to cool down to his preferred tepid temperature.

'Of course, we were devastated but had to accept that we had effectively lost our parents. They had become different people. We no longer had anything in common with them. We had kept in touch with our grandparents who lived here in the UK. Our parents had bought them a small house here in Chester where they lived. They were sympathetic to our cause and welcomed us. It was not long before our father started to threaten them. They were my mother's parents. They thought my father brainwashed us. Immy and I weren't so sure. Certainly, most of the aggression emanated from Father. It stressed them out, and by then, they were quite old. I'm pretty sure the stress killed them. Immy believed they had been poisoned, but their doctor said they died of normal old age. They were both in their eighties. They died within a few months of each other, my grandfather first. Immy accused Father of murder. After that, things went downhill.'

'Did your father ever come over here?' asked Drake.

'No, they told us that they lived in a closed community. It's a sect called Xi Dong. Members are not allowed to travel. Immy started researching their cult and found they had started in Hong Kong and China. They have a place somewhere in Texas that my parents went to the USA to open. They have just opened a place in the country just south of London. I think it's called Fairlawns. As far as we could tell, this UK centre is not yet a closed community, so Immy was sure Father got people from there to come and spy on us. Recently, Immy thought she was being stalked. That's why I came to tell you. I think they will be after me now.'

'If you get any evidence or even real suspicion that is happening, then you must let us know. We can do our best to take care of that,' said Drake. 'Grace will give you her direct line phone number. Do not hesitate to call.'

'Thank you. I cannot tell you how grateful I am. It is bad enough that I have lost Immy. She meant everything to me, as I did to her. To have all this going on as well is just too much for me.'

'We're sorry to bring you extra distress,' said Grace. Drake grunted his agreement. Grace looked at Drake, who nodded.

'We understand that Imogen often stayed with you,' said Grace.

'We jointly own the house,' said Felicity. 'Our grandparents left it to us when they died. Originally, Immy lived there with me even though it was rather small, but then she got this place with a studio, which she needed. But Immy is also often away. She goes back to Hong Kong a lot.'

'Yes,' said Drake. 'We have met her landlady, Philippa Crehan?'

'Landlady?' queried Felicity.

'We understand that Miss Crehan owns the house.'

'I don't think of her as a landlady.'

'So, what do you think about her?' asked Drake.

'Well, I'd rather not say,' said Felicity deliberately. 'For many years, Immy and I had an agreement. We never talked about things that we strongly disagreed about. That way, we stayed as close as sisters should. I don't talk about Miss Crehan.'

'Are you suggesting that the relationship between Imogen and Philippa was more than landlady and tenant?'

'You could put it that way,' said Felicity, laughing. 'But I never talked to Immy about it, so I can't say any more.' Drake and Grace exchanged sideways glances. Grace made a note.

'Did Imogen have any other enemies, do you know?' asked Drake.

'Not that I know about here,' said Felicity. 'I can't say anything about her life in Hong Kong. The world there is extremely competitive, but I do not know of any problems she might have had.'

After Felicity had left in a taxi, Drake and Grace compared notes with Constable Dan Ford listening in.

'I think we need to investigate this sect that the parents are part of,' said Drake.

'I'll chase it up on the Internet,' said Grace. 'If I can find their place, Fairlawns, it might be worth a visit.'

'Yes, but be careful and take someone with you,' said Drake. 'If Felicity is correct, there may be some jeopardy. A well-built constable like Dan here might be a good idea.'

# 9

Constable Dan Ford was reading through his notes for the Imogen Glass case. He was alarmed about how little he remembered correctly. Drake had told him how important it was to keep all the information alive in your head. He understood this was one of the objectives of the famous boards Drake had erected in the middle of the room. He had already seen Drake walking around them repeatedly. He checked his watch. It was OK. He was still slightly early for the meeting that Detective Sergeant Grace Hepple had called. As he turned back to his notes, the door opened, and Constable Steve Redvers walked in.

'Morning, Dan,' said Redvers. 'How are you getting on?'

'Just reading through my notes and getting worried that I am already forgetting things that were said or that we saw.'

'Yes, Drake is rather hot on that,' replied Redvers.

'We are so lucky to have Drake here in Cheshire,' said Dan.

'Ah, well, there's something of a story about that,' replied Redvers. 'Drake was seconded over here from a special unit at the Met when we had a rather tricky case concerning a distinguished foreign politician. So, Detective Inspector Martin Henshaw, then based in Chester, worked with him and Grace Hepple on the case. Much of the investigation took place here in Chester. Drake became rather enchanted by the place. His wife had just died, and he wanted to leave London, where they had both lived most of their careers. Then, this opportunity came up for him to go to Hong Kong to advise on handling diplomatically sensitive cases. Originally, the Hong Kong Police hoped Drake would go. His reputation has spread even that far, but it wasn't the right time for him, and he suggested Martin could go. Martin jumped at it, and Drake came here, bringing Grace Hepple.'

'Grace Hepple is quite something, isn't she?' said Ford, grinning.

'Ah,' replied Redvers. 'I've noticed you looking at her more than once.'

'Well, who wouldn't? Especially when she wears that black suit she has.'

'It might be a good idea to make it less obvious,' laughed Redvers. 'Make no mistake, she isn't going to go out with a mere constable like us. She has much more ambitious plans.'

At that moment, in came Detective Sergeant Grace Hepple, complete with her black suit. The two constables sent each other surreptitious grins.

'Right,' said Grace Hepple. 'Apparently, loads of Imogen's bank statements are on her computer. They are password protected, but if you try to access them on her computer, it automatically inserts the password. There are five accounts. I guess she moved money between them for some reason. Look for any regular transfers either in or out of her accounts and between them. Also, make a note of any large amounts. All that sort of thing.' The two constables nodded. Grace continued.

'We also have the complete record of all her calls and messages on her mobile phone. Unfortunately or not, whichever way you see it, we don't get the calls or messages themselves. Make notes of all the people she contacts and again look for any patterns that might throw up clues about what happened to her. If you can, please try to map out a diary for Imogen. There may be some clues from the calls. We haven't yet found a diary or address book or her phone. The only other things Dave has managed to find on her laptop are images of her work and of things that seemed to have interested her.'

At that moment, the door started to rattle irritably. Grace began to cross the room, but she was still only halfway across when the door opened and in stumbled Drake.

'I swear that lock has taken to dislike to my key,' he grumbled. He dropped his coat and copy of The Times on his favourite chair. He stamped across to the case boards that occupied a large part of the room. He unhooked the large map of Chester from the first board and carried it across to the nearby table.

'Does anyone know where Dave is?' he demanded.

'I think he's next door working on Imogen's laptop,' replied Grace.

'Fetch him, would you.'

Drake bent down over the map and began tracing a line along the River Dee when Grace returned with Dave, the computer technician.

'Right,' said Drake. 'We found Imogen Glass's body in the river at the Boathouse Pub. Someone must have dumped it into the water somewhere. It seems unlikely that they would do this right by the pub. Even at night, there are people around. So, we must assume that the location was upstream from the pub and where a vehicle could be drawn up close to the riverbank. So, can you local lads help us identify such places? After all, wherever it was is now a crime scene, so who knows what clues it might reveal.'

The two constables and technician Dave poured over the map while Drake groaned and stood up to straighten his ageing back.

'I would say that the first place where she could have been dumped would be down Sandy Lane,' said Dave.

'Yes,' added Steve Redvers. 'It's quite close. You drive through Broughton here and turn right. The lane takes you down to the riverside and turns left to run alongside the Dee.'

'Agreed,' said Dan Ford. 'Not far along, a car park is next to the river, and a bit further, there is a park, but I don't think you can get a vehicle down to it. Then, there is a large hard area where boats are stored. I doubt you would be able to get a vehicle through there. I think it might even get locked at night, and it is supervised during the day.'

'Are there houses on either side of the road up here?' asked Drake.

'Yes, both sides, more or less as far as the car park,' replied Dave.

'What about coming the other way?' asked Drake.

'A bit further, beyond the park, there would be houses on both sides again,' said Dave. The others nodded their heads in agreement.

'OK,' said Drake. 'So, we have found the first possible location. What happens if we look further along the river?'

'So,' said Dave. 'You can see that Sandy Lane curves away from the river after a while, and, as far as I can remember, there wouldn't be another point of vehicular access to the river for some miles.'

'Yes,' said Dan Ford. 'That's dead right. A huge water treatment plant and a great area of solar collectors occupy the riverbank. There's no way through there. I think you've got to go to the other side of the river. Look, here is Eccleston Ferry. After that, there is Eaton Hall, which is gated, and then it is open countryside with fields on either side of the river for miles.'

'So how would you approach Eccleston Ferry,' asked Drake.

'Well, there is no road bridge over the Dee at all. You'd have to go into town and cross the river there. Then, you would turn left and drive out into the country until you came to Eccleston village. You go through, look here, and then take a left down to the ferry. Straight on, I think there is a gate because it goes into Eaton Hall grounds.'

'Where would the nearest house be?' asked Drake.

'Eccleston village, I guess,' replied Dave.

'OK,' said Drake, 'so we have two likely locations, and after that, it would be a long way to another. Let's begin by investigating these two. Grace, I want you to take Dave out there and look for cameras positioned along those two approaches. Our best bet is security devices on house walls that point towards the road. See what else you can find. Dave, you need to seek permission to access the cameras that seem to be the best bet and download the video. I suggest that we start the day before Imogen's body was discovered. Then, search back about four days before that. We need to see what more we can learn from Imogen's white van. The most likely thing was that the murderer loaded the body into that. It would offer ideal transport. See what you can find.'

'By the way,' said Grace. 'I've just been told that the van has Imogen's fingerprints all over it, as we would expect, but there are at least two more sets. One is Philippa Crehan.'

'Can I make a suggestion?' asked Dave.

'Go ahead, Dave,' said Drake.

'Why don't I load Google Earth on your laptop, Sir? I can show you how to drive along those roads. I will have my laptop with me anyway. We can keep in touch by phone, and any suggestions that you make from what you see, we can take a closer look.'

'Great idea,' said Drake. 'If only I can get it to work. Why don't you demonstrate it to us all?' said Drake. 'Then, if I get muddled, these boys can help me.'

Dave loaded Google Earth on Drake's laptop and showed how to swap between aerial and road views.

'That's brilliant,' said Drake. 'I could play with that for hours.'

'One caution,' said Dave. 'It will inevitably be out of date. We don't know how long ago they took the videos used to build the model. Some things might have changed.'

'While we are talking computers,' said Drake. 'What have you found on Imogen's computer, Dave?'

'There are hundreds of images. Firstly, all her work. Everything in that folder you found is on there, and there are loads of images of all sorts of things that she has almost certainly downloaded from the Internet. There are also pictures that the system has transferred from a phone. However, she didn't use the computer at all for everyday matters. She hasn't used the in-built diary, which probably means it wasn't on her phone either.'

'That's odd, don't you think?' said Drake. 'This person is efficient but doesn't keep her diary on a computer or phone. Of course, we've still not found the phone, so that may be wrong. We have also not found a good old-fashioned diary. I can't believe she didn't have one. So why has it disappeared? Did someone want to hide the information it would hold?'

Drake turned back and walked around his case boards, grunting to himself. Grace and Dave set off. The two constables returned to their tasks, and Drake made a coffee and settled down with his crossword. Occasionally, he would get up and walk over to the map. Standing looking at it or the laptop, he grunted, sometimes with frustration and at others with satisfaction.

The following morning, Grace was briefing the team on her work with Dave.

'We found three useful cameras were working over the period we are interested in. Two were along Sandy Lane, and one was in Eccleston Village. Dave is now trying to find the right plugs and cables, to say nothing of the software to download all this video to our computers. He will scan it, first for the white van and then more slowly, looking for anything unusual or striking. He is starting work on the best-looking camera in Sandy Lane.'

'Excellent, Grace. Now, drive me over to Imogen's studio. I want to look around now that the scene-of-crime boys have gone. I wouldn't mind a word or two with Philippa Crehan while we're there.'

Grace drove the Range Rover over to Hoole Road and onto the more secluded parallel road where Philippa Crehan's house was. She pulled onto the drive that ran down the side of the house, which had the annexe at the end. Grace grabbed the ring of labelled keys related to the case and opened the door. No sooner were they inside when Philippa Crehan appeared.

'Hello,' she said. 'Is there any way I can be of assistance?'

'I just wanted to look around this annexe in more detail,' said Drake. 'But since you are here, I did want to ask you to tell us more about your relationship with Imogen Glass.'

'There's nothing to tell,' replied Philippa, frowning. 'I advertised in the local paper. She saw my advert, took over the annexe and converted it into her studio. It saved my bacon in terms of income and allowed me to keep the house. I guess you would say we became friends as time went on. I don't pretend to understand the finer points of her work, but I find most of it beautiful.'

'You said that you became friends,' said Drake. 'From what we have heard, I think that might be an understatement.'

'Well, I don't see how our personal affairs are relevant to your investigation.'

'The nature of your relationship may have a bearing on your motivations, and they are certainly relevant.'

'Are you suggesting that I might be a suspect in her murder?'

'Everyone is a suspect until I decide otherwise,' snapped Drake.

'Well, I'm sorry,' replied Philippa, 'but I'm not prepared to discuss our relationship.'

'Obstructing a police officer in the process of an investigation may be an offence,' said Drake slowly and firmly. 'I put it to you that you and Imogen became lovers.'

'No comment,' said Philippa. 'Why don't you concentrate on who she thought was stalking her?'

'She told you about this? Did she know who it was?'

'No, but I always assumed it was her boyfriend. Perhaps finding him might be a more fruitful line of enquiry.'

'Imogen had a boyfriend?'

'Of course.'

'Do you know his name?'

'No. I was never interested. Now, I must get back to work.' With that, she turned and left. Drake was slightly taken aback. Grace had never seen him looking so non-plussed. She waited for him to say something.

'We seem to have touched a nerve,' he said. 'Now I wonder just what all that is about. We need to call Miss Crehan to come and see us. We can't just have her dropping bombs and then disappearing. I need to get to the bottom of this. First, Imogen's younger sister will not discuss it, and now Philippa gets tight-lipped. There is more to this. I need to go digging. Perhaps another chat with the sister might be a good idea first.'

# 10

The following morning, the incident with Philippa Crehan at Imogen Glass's studio was still amusing Grace. It was not as she had assumed. Drake was not worried about or offended by Philippa's somewhat rude and dismissive manner. He was pleased to have triggered some emotion from a potential witness and was busy trying to understand what it meant. He was prowling around the case boards erected in the middle of the room.

In came Dave in a hurry, followed by Dan Ford. Dave immediately started to set up his laptop on the central table.

'We got a preliminary finding for you, Sir,' said Dan Ford. 'We'd like you to look at it.'

Drake broke off from his wandering and came over to the table.

'Dave's been working all night on it,' said Dan Ford dramatically.

'Not quite,' said Dave. 'Have a look at this if you would.' He pressed a key on his laptop, and up came a video taken from the upper floor of a house. Drake could see the River Dee.

'Is this Sandy Lane?' Drake asked as a white van appeared from the right and drove across the otherwise static picture. 'Replay that slowly, can you?'

'No problem,' replied Dave, pressing buttons on the screen with his mouse.

'It certainly is Sandy Lane,' said Dan. As you will see, the camera is pointing directly across the road, so we don't get a view of the registration plates. It was four days before the discovery of Imogen's body and late in the evening before dark.'

'Could be it,' muttered Drake. 'Well, it could be the van, but it could also be one of the thousands, if not millions, of similar white vans.'

'Oddly, there don't seem to be any others around at that time,' said Dan.

'Well, there's a problem,' said Dave. 'Look at this next clip.' He hit the keyboard again and up came the same view, empty of vehicles. Suddenly, the white van appeared from the left and drove across the picture.

'What's the problem?' asked Drake.

'That was only four minutes and twenty seconds later,' said Dave.

'I see,' said Drake. 'That doesn't leave much time for dumping a body.'

'I think it may have been a delivery van,' said Dave.

'Possibly, possibly,' muttered Drake. 'Maybe not even time for knocking on a door. Getting a response, handing over a parcel and getting a signature, although these white van guys work to a demanding schedule.'

'So, what should we do next?' asked Dan. Drake stroked his chin for a few seconds.

'I suggest you look on the same day at the other location,' he said.

'Can do, of course,' said Dave. 'But I don't see what that will achieve.'

'It is a long shot, but I might be right,' said Drake. 'Grace and I have another meeting with Imogen's younger sister in the Grosvenor Hotel. Dan, perhaps you had better join us to take notes.'

'Good morning, Miss Glass,' said Drake as the visitor entered the room. 'How was your walk this morning?'

'OK,' replied Felicity Glass, but I could swear I was being followed.'

'Sergeant Hepple has been on the tracking course much more recently than I have, so why don't you explain this feeling, Grace.'

'What clothing was your follower wearing?' asked Grace with a reassuring smile.

'I couldn't say, I didn't get a good look. You told me not to keep looking around.'

'Were the streets busy?'

'Yes, they always are in Chester.'

'Let's imagine you saw a hundred people. The chances of you seeing one who was looking at you are quite high. Perhaps someone walked the same route. Perhaps someone stopped and looked in a shop window when you did look around when perhaps you were crossing a road. We could go on. Add together all these chances, and you get quite a high probability. It is quite likely that one or more of them are present in your view. But then imagine all these people turned out to be wearing the same clothes, and you get a low chance of that happening unless, of course, they were the same person. So, it is normal to feel you are being followed when you aren't.'

'Yes, I see. I suppose you are right.'

'I'm sure Sergeant Hepple is right,' said Drake. 'My team outside reported they saw no one following you, and they are trained to see such people. Please rest assured you are here safely.' Drake waited while Grace poured out coffees for everyone on the tray that had arrived on the table in the middle of the room. 'Thank you for coming. We appreciate it. We need your help with a couple of things.' Felicity smiled nervously. Drake nodded to Grace.

'Did your sister have a boyfriend?' asked Grace softly.

'She had lots of boyfriends. She was a lovely person.'

'The most recent boyfriend, was he perhaps the most serious?' Felicity grimaced and looked up at the ceiling in silence.

'I suppose I'm going to have to tell you,' she said. Grace and Drake remained silent, and Felicity took a deep breath.

'It's rather a lovely story. Quite romantic, I suppose. We met Elliott Chan when we were teenagers back in Hong Kong. His parents and ours were close friends, so we got introduced that way. He soon became her boyfriend, but we did a lot together. Occasionally, he would mistake me for Immy, and sometimes we played jokes on him. When we left Hong Kong to come here, we lost contact. I think Immy would email him occasionally. Then, of course, she was a little older. We were finally independent, and we met other people. She would always have boyfriends. Sometimes, they lasted little more than a week. Sometimes several months.' Felicity paused and took a sip of her coffee. Dan broke off from making notes to top up her cup from the pot on the table.

'Then quite suddenly, one day, Elliott appeared. He had left Hong Kong in a hurry. He had been one of the activists arguing for a free Hong Kong. He got a message from a friend saying the authorities were looking for him. Things were beginning to get tough out there. It has got a lot worse since, of course. He didn't dare email us before leaving as he guessed his messages were being monitored. Of course, we gave him a room in the house while he settled in and decided what to do. However, the inevitable happened, and he and Immy fell for each other. He found a flat, and they were soon an item. I could tell this was different from all the other boyfriends. Immy was always travelling for her work, and often, it would be Hong Kong. Elliott couldn't go with her to Hong Kong, but they would go together when she went to other countries. It must have been going on for a couple of years when Immy got her studio. That was when it all started to go wrong. I sometimes think Phillippa had planned it all along. She seduced Immy. Immy easily fell in love, perhaps too easily, and she got confused. Elliott found out, and there was a row. They split up, and Immy became infatuated with Philippa. Elliott was devastated. He kept trying to contact Immy, but she never replied. Eventually, he came to see me and asked me to help. I had already had cross words with Immy, but we reminded ourselves of our sisters' agreement never to discuss things we disagreed about. Elliott kept coming to see me. Then suddenly, one day, we just made love. It seemed right, and so I guess Elliott stopped chasing after Immy.' Felicity paused, took a breath and dabbed her eyes with her handkerchief. She sat silently, staring at the floor.

'Thank you, Felicity,' said Grace. 'We know it must have been difficult for you to tell us all that.'

'The story isn't finished,' said Felicity between sobs. 'Quite recently, Immy came to see me. She told me that she now thought it had all been a mistake. She said she had split up with Philippa. She had tried to contact Elliott, but he wouldn't return her calls. She was in a real state and wanted me to contact Elliott. Of course, I had to tell her what had happened. She broke down and said she had messed up her life completely and couldn't paint anymore. It was a terrible mess. Of course, the person who had caused all the trouble was not Immy but Philippa Crehan.'

'So,' said Drake. 'I'm sorry we had to put you through recalling it all. Please give Grace the details of how we can contact Elliott Chan.'

'He is living with me here,' said Felicity as she pulled out a pen and wrote on a piece of paper Grace handed her.

'Normally, Immy was strong,' said Felicity. 'When things went wrong in Hong Kong or with our parents, I tended to collapse or panic. Immy kept everything together. But at one point, I worried that she had become suicidal. When I first heard she had been found drowned in the river, I honestly thought she might have committed suicide.'

'Was Immy able to swim?' asked Drake.

'Oh yes, she was a strong swimmer.'

'If it is any comfort to you,' said Drake. 'I think from what we know and have been told by our pathologist, it seems highly unlikely that this was suicide.' Felicity nodded and smiled weakly through her occasional sobs.

'I keep turning it all over in my head. I can't sleep. I couldn't decide whether Immy committed suicide or our parents got one of their agents to kill her. Or perhaps the awful Crehan woman did it. Immy said she was extraordinarily emotional. She could easily have got in a rage.'

Drake sat silently in the rear seat of the Range Rover on their way back to the station. Grace was driving and knew well enough never to interrupt his thoughts, but she could see Dan Ford itching to say something, so she gestured to him to keep quiet. As they arrived and walked together to the case room, Drake broke his silence.

'Grace, would you try to get Elliott Chan to come in and see us as soon as possible, please? Dan, I hope you've got good notes on all that. You can help me transfer everything to the boards in the middle of the room. It is going to take a bit of sorting out.' Dan shuffled his notes, anxiously hoping that he hadn't missed anything. Grace opened the door and passed him her notes. Drake walked in what, for him, counted as a rush towards his boards. He turned and addressed Dan.

'On these boards here, we need people, events, places and objects. We connect them as best we can. Over here on this board, we try to establish a timeline from the earliest event we know about to the discovery of the body and on through the post-mortem into the investigation. We put notes about things that we haven't been able to locate on the final board. That is, of course, just the start. We then gradually shuffle things around as new information appears. We are always trying to see new patterns.'

Dan was about to start when in rushed Dave and Steve Redvers. They were whooping and looking rather pleased with themselves.

'Have a look at this video, Sir,' said Dave. He pressed a button on his laptop. Up came a view of buildings on the other side of a street.

'This is Eccleston village,' he said as a white van appeared and swept across the screen. 'It has the same mark on the side we saw on the other van. We're sure it is Imogen's van.' Drake nodded his head, grunted and gestured for Dave to carry on.

'Now we need to see the next video. It is about half an hour later.' As everyone expected, the white van crossed back in the opposite direction. Everyone turned to look at Drake to see his reaction. He took a long breath and smiled.

'So, this is my hunch,' he said. 'Those responsible for disposing of Imogen's body in the Dee did more or less what we did. We looked at the map, identified some possible locations, and then went to find them. Sandy Lane was too dangerous, and Eccleston Ferry was more remote, so it was chosen. OK, Grace, get a scene-of-crime team and go down there, cordon off as usual and search. Something might be found in the water, so I want the team to look around for a reasonable area in the river.'

'What are we looking for?' asked Grace.

'Anything that might be interesting. We need to remember that so far, we have never found her phone or diary. Either might give us a real breakthrough.' With that, Drake retired to his favourite chair, and Grace went to set up a scene-of-crime team. All was quiet, except for the noise of Drake's chair complaining as he persistently rocked it. Suddenly, this pattern was broken by the sound of a phone ringing. Grace looked around for the offending instrument. Drake's mobile was sitting on the table next to his chair. This did nothing to stop him from fruitlessly patting a couple of jacket pockets before seeing where it was.

'Hello, Drake here.'

'Ah, Drake, this is Bristow.'

'Bristow?'

'Yes, I helped you on that case at the opera house.'

'Oh, yes. You are The Met's link to MI5.'

'Correct. That's why I'm calling. They've heard about this case you're on now. They have an interest in it. This might help you. I need to come and see you. Would tomorrow be OK?'

'Yes, sure. Let Detective Sergeant Grace Hepple know what time your train arrives. She will arrange for someone to come and collect you.'

# 11

'Ah, good morning, Drake,' said Bristow as Drake and Grace entered the interview room. 'I'm grateful that you got this private room for us. The less our conversation is overheard, the happier MI5 will be.'

'No problem,' said Drake, shaking Bristow's outstretched hand and beckoning him to sit down. Grace pulled up two chairs on the other side of the small table in the centre of the room. A knock on the door heralded three cups of coffee brought in by Sergeant Tom Denson.

'I am intrigued to know what is so secret about our investigation,' said Drake.

'It's not your investigation as such,' replied Bristow. 'The fact is that Imogen Glass was a person of interest to MI5. They were keeping tabs on her.'

'Exactly what does that mean?' asked Drake, stirring his coffee and pushing it to one side to cool.

'Imogen Glass has been attending meetings at 10 Downing Street about a sensitive matter. A foreign country is involved; we don't want them to know about our investigations. More recently, it was discovered that Imogen Glass was also frequently meeting someone who, if she discovered our work, would be quite likely to reveal this information to the government of this country. Naturally, we are anxious that your investigation does not complicate matters.'

'I see,' said Drake, 'or rather, I don't. It all sounds a bit cloak and dagger. If we are to avoid inadvertently creating a problem, then I think we need to know more.'

'We understand,' said Bristow, 'and it is for that reason that I am here today.' Bristow dunked one of the ginger nut biscuits on a tray into his coffee and inspected the result before taking a large bite. 'Before I go any further, can I ask if the name Irene Lee has come to your attention?'

'No,' said Drake. 'I've never heard of her. Have you, Grace?'

'It does ring a bell,' said Grace. 'Can I go and look at something in our evidence store? I won't be more than a few minutes.' Drake and Bristow swapped stories about past Met colleagues while Grace was out of the room.

'Maybe I was right,' said Grace, returning with the A3 portfolio of the Imogen Glass paintings. She turned to the back and pointed to a small business card in one of the plastic wallets. 'There is someone here called Irene Mei Lien Li.'

'That's her,' said Bristow. 'I hadn't expected you to have the full name. It can be a bit complicated to understand these Chinese names. Her name in China is Li Mei Lien. They use the family name first rather than last, as we do. The name "Li" is the most common in China, where it is spelt with the letter "i" as opposed to the double "ee" as we do here. It is an ideal name for someone in her business as it is also common here, so it doesn't attract any attention. Chinese people, particularly in Hong Kong, will often add an English first name, in this case, Irene, and put the family name last as we do. Hong Kong Christians often use an English name and put it first. MI5 have been watching Irene Lee for some time. She is what they call a person of concern.' Bristow paused and took a sip of his coffee.

'So, what does Irene Lee get up to that is causing concern?' asked Grace.

'It is likely that the Chinese Communist Party control her. There is evidence of her meeting people quite high up there, and she has an address in Beijing. She is one of a host of agents who mostly operate on the margins of our espionage laws. Her role is to infiltrate our government at as high a level as possible. She has been quite successful and knows several members of parliament well, including a couple of ex-ministers. So far, we believe she hasn't penetrated the current cabinet, but the membership has changed recently. She is unlikely to attempt any serious espionage but will seek out vulnerabilities where they exist and pass this on to the Chinese Communist Party, who may then set a full-blown spy to try and turn them. In any case, she sees and hears material that interests her handlers. She has at least three names. The one we are talking about here is the identity she has used most frequently. May I see your business card?' Grace passed it over, and Bristow studied it carefully.

'Yes,' he said. 'She calls herself an art agent here. She will have spent some time mugging up on that and be capable of seeming competent even to someone like Imogen Glass. She recently tried an extraordinary enterprise using Imogen.'

'Are we allowed to know what that was?' asked Drake.

'Yes, I can tell you a bit about it. I don't know all the details myself. Imogen Glass was approached some time ago to sit on a committee that meets at 10 Downing Street. It sometimes has one or more ministers involved. It investigates the world of fraud and fakery in China, especially Hong Kong. The Chinese run a major part of their economy through people who make fake copies of anything you can imagine. It can cause considerable problems for parts of our industry. Recently, Imogen was recruited when the committee began to look seriously at the art world.'

'You said that Irene Lee tried something recently,' said Drake.

'Yes, indeed,' said Bristow. 'The committee met recently in Downing Street. Imogen Glass told them she had a contact who might be helpful to their work. It was someone knowledgeable about the situation in China. She said this contact might be prepared to join the committee. Of course, the person in question was Irene Lee, who most likely had prompted her with the idea. The suggestion was certainly not followed up. This is despite her indirect offer to be a British agent. Someone prepared to be a double agent with China must have a highly secure setup and be extremely confident in her position. This might be attractive to MI6 but also fraught with many dangers. However, it raised further concerns about Glass and Li, so MI5 have been tracking them quite intensively.'

'So,' said Drake, 'to return to our investigation, do you think Irene Lee may have been somehow involved in Imogen's death?'

'We have no direct evidence of it, but this brings me to the main reason for coming today. MI5 routinely track Irene Lee. I can't tell you how this is done, and I understand they use several methods. She was observed to come to the centre of Chester a couple of weeks before you found the body of Imogen Glass. Irene Lee went out into the Cheshire countryside, where our tracking is less precise. Perhaps this was deliberate on her part, but I doubt it. She kept one of the phones we know she uses regularly turned on during this time and had some calls. We cannot be sure she met Imogen Glass, but it remains a distinct possibility. I can also tell you that MI5 track Imogen Glass, though nowhere nearly so intensively. She normally either leaves her phone behind or carries it turned off. Whether this is deliberate, we rather doubt, but that is also a possibility.' Bristow paused to make sure that Drake was absorbing this news.

'How long was Irene Lee here in Chester?' asked Drake.

'She returned to London the following day,' replied Bristow. 'Since then, and before you discovered Imogen Glass in the River Dee, Irene Lee flew to Hong Kong from Heathrow, and we have lost track of her. I cannot know whether this impacts your investigation, but I imagine it might. However, we need you to be extremely careful here. I know you are focused on the murder of Imogen Glass, but MI5 have bigger fish to fry here, and you must please tread extremely carefully.'

Drake was nodding his head in a self-consciously slow manner as he tried to absorb all this information. Bristow began again.

'These people can be ruthless. If one has their identity threatened, the situation can become fluid. Imogen Glass was either in on what Lee was doing, or Lee may have thought her identity was in danger of discovery. Irene Lee may still be in Hong Kong or have gone to mainland China. However, MI5 would prefer that you didn't investigate Irene Lee or at least go extremely carefully and keep me informed. I give this advice on behalf of MI5 and to protect your safety. If these people get wind of your interest in them, there is no question that your life could be in danger.'

'I see,' said Drake. 'This case is already proving frustrating, and this does nothing to simplify matters.'

'I do understand,' said Bristow. 'As you know, I am only the link between MI5 and police forces. I sympathise. There is one more piece of information that might be useful to you. Some time ago, Imogen Glass introduced her boyfriend to us. A chap called Elliott Chan. He had been well-connected in Hong Kong and could give us the names of people in important positions there. He was also able to identify people of interest from photographs. If there is anything I can do to help, I am only too glad to assist.'

'We have contact details for Elliott Chan,' said Grace. 'They were given to us by his current partner, Felicity Glass. He lives with her. However, we don't seem to have a mobile phone number or email address.' Bristow opened his phone and read out an email and mobile phone number.

'What on earth do you make of all that?' asked Drake when Grace returned from delivering Bristow to the train station. Dave, the technician, was with her.

'I was going to tell you about something that came from Dave's investigation of Imogen's laptop. I wonder if it is related to everything Bristow was on about. Dave, why don't you explain it? You understand it far better than I do.'

'Sure,' said Dave. 'There is a new thing on the block called crypto art. It is a bit like Bitcoin or other blockchain currencies. This uses digital art. Art created on a computer can only be produced practically when you have bought the rights digitally to reproduce the actual work of art. Usually, only a few people are allowed to buy the rights to this, so the value is protected. We know that international crime syndicates have immediately shown an interest in this since it must be subject to computer fraud. However, all this becomes extremely technical and complex. The UK is one of the main centres where activity is found. The other place seems to be Hong Kong.'

'My brain hurts,' said Drake. 'I just don't understand this. What is to stop someone simply photocopying this art?'

'Two things,' said Dave. 'Firstly, much digital art is now produced for virtual reality only. This means that you can only see it while using the right digital kit. It is exciting because it moves art from two to three dimensions. In a way, it becomes more like sculpture, except that situations that would be impossible in the real world can be created. If you own this art, you can be inside it, moving around and experiencing it in the round. Such a thing cannot be reproduced on a two-dimensional computer. It cannot be copied without giving away that it is a fraud. Every time it is reproduced, it can have unique features. Although, in theory, such a thing could be copied, it is more difficult in practice. Of course, anything digital becomes susceptible to fraud, and this is where organised crime has got interested.'

'I see,' said Drake, 'but I only have a vague grasp of what you describe. If this is the world Imogen Glass inhabited, we need real technical help on the case.'

'I'm not sure how much she was involved, but there is evidence on her computer that she has been playing around with the art end of the business.'

Drake groaned.

'Grace, can you see if we can get hold of the boyfriend? Elliott Chan was the name. Felicity Glass also told us about him. I'm a little surprised that he hasn't appeared before. We ought to hear what he has to say. The other idea that Bristow has introduced is that Irene Lee may have met Imogen Glass when we believe she was killed. However, we have no access to Irene Lee and have been strongly warned off trying to find and investigate her.'

'It's a bit tricky to be sure,' said Grace. 'I suppose the only way we can handle that is to imagine how she could have killed Imogen and disposed of her into the Dee all in no more than a day.'

'Agreed. You have a good point,' said Drake. 'It certainly suggests she must have planned it all rather carefully. Perhaps that means other people may have been involved. Perhaps we could try to reconstruct those days.'

'Good thinking,' said Drake. 'But I'm not sure how we might start on that. There is another question that remains unasked at this stage. So far, we have no idea what her motive might be. Maybe we could think about that a little. Maybe Elliott Chan could help us if he knows about Irene Lee. See if you can get him to come in and talk to us. I've got a sneaky feeling that MI5 are going to interfere. I hope I'm wrong!'

# 12

'Mr Chan, thank you for coming in to see us,' said Drake, entering the interview room where Elliott Chan was drinking tea. 'I hope our rather basic Chinese tea is to your liking.' Elliott Chan smiled weakly and politely nodded his head. Drake turned to Grace, who had agreed to lead the questioning.

'Mr Chan,' said Grace, 'may we call you Elliott?'

'Yes, of course.'

'We understand that your girlfriend was Imogen Glass. Is that correct?' Elliott Chan nodded his head again silently.

'We assume that you did not live with Imogen Glass. Is that correct?'

'Not recently.'

'You had done so some time ago then?' probed Grace.

'Yes.'

'So why not recently?'

'We had broken up some time ago.'

'I see,' said Grace. 'So, when was the last time you saw Imogen Glass?' Elliott sat silently, looking up at the ceiling as if his diary was projected up there. Then he spoke slowly.

'Probably about three months ago.'

'So why did you break up?'

'It is a long and complicated story. I do not enjoy thinking about it.'

'I'm sorry about that,' said Grace. 'Unfortunately, we must ask you these questions. We are investigating her death, which is seen as possibly suspicious. How long had you known Imogen?'

'Since we were children in Hong Kong many years ago. We went to the same English school. My parents wanted me to be educated in English.'

'So, have you known her continuously since then?'

'No,' said Elliott Chan rather wearily as if he had been asked these questions many times. 'I will explain. Our parents knew each other when we were children. Imogen's parents became rather odd. They began to believe in a weird sect. Even so, my parents stayed friends with them, but eventually, they left for America, where the sect is also based. Things have been getting more difficult in Hong Kong recently. The American centre is becoming the headquarters. Imogen and Felicity eventually came to England to live in a house their grandparents had left them.' Elliott paused and took a sip of his drink. Drake and Grace waited silently until he picked up his story.

'We lost touch. In recent years, I have been active in the freedom movement in Hong Kong. We didn't want independence; we wanted the one-country, two-systems policy to be properly observed by China. I know that Hong Kong is far from perfect as it is. There is much petty crime and some major crime syndicates, but we have freedom. Freedom is invaluable. Once you have that, you can choose your leaders and work for a democratic society. This gradually became a hopeless ambition, but by then, I and a few others had been identified as troublemakers. One night, two of my friends disappeared. I haven't seen them since. It was time for me to leave quickly. I had already got a British passport, so it was simple. I had to leave everything behind. Imogen and Felicity were kind. They had been left a house here in Chester by their grandparents, and they let me have a room. I got a job as a structural engineer in a large practice in Manchester. I suppose then it gradually happened that Imogen and I became close, and she rented some accommodation that we moved into. It was a mistake.' Elliott Chan stopped abruptly and looked at the palms of his hands as if telling his future.

'Why was it a mistake?' asked Grace.

'At first, I thought it was our separate professional lives. Imogen did a lot of travelling back to Hong Kong and China. Her work was inspired by a crossing of the two cultures of East and

West. Then, one day, she suddenly told me.' Elliott paused as if remembering painfully.

'She told you what?' asked Grace quietly.

'She said she was now in a relationship with a woman called Philippa, who was her landlady. I was astonished. She said she hadn't previously felt those sorts of feelings. She said we could continue our relationship, but I felt that was not viable. I left immediately and returned to my old room in what is now Felicity's house.' Elliott went silent again. Grace and Drake sat, respecting his introspection. Eventually, Grace started again.

'Well, thank you, Elliott,' she said. 'I understand the story is painful to you.'

'Ah, but it isn't finished,' said Elliott. 'One day, about a month ago, Imogen called me and said she had finished her relationship with Philippa. She knew now it had all been a mistake, and we could get back together if I wanted. I told her it was too late and explained the situation. She was furious and shouted dreadful things at me. Eventually, she shouted down the phone in a big huff and cut me off.'

'Forgive me, Elliott,' said Grace, 'but what was your explanation?'

'Felicity and I had fallen in love. We are now happy. It is a strange thing to love sisters. I can't explain it. She seems to have many of Imogen's traits and looks, but she has a gentler and more caring personality.'

'A complicated life,' grunted Drake.

'It was complicated, but now it feels simple,' replied Elliott. 'So, when I heard that Imogen had died and you thought it might be murder, I didn't want to get involved. I suppose I wondered if Imogen had committed suicide. If so, I wanted to have nothing to do with it. She was trying to make my life a misery. I wouldn't allow it.'

'We are fairly certain that Imogen did not commit suicide, and it is not an accident,' said Drake.

'Really?' said Elliott, looking astonished. 'I suppose I had just assumed that but why would someone want to kill her?'

'That is one of the things we are trying to discover,' grunted Drake. 'We have talked to Felicity, and she briefly mentioned you.'

'She is a much more private person than Imogen. She and Imogen were incredibly close for most of their lives, but when Imogen and I moved into her studio, they seemed to have much less to do with each other. In a way, that is rather sad, but I suppose it is irrelevant now.' Elliott Chan sat staring at the table for a while, and Grace waited for him to continue.

'I don't know what Felicity may have told you, but she is convinced that Imogen was killed by someone sent by their parents. I've tried to understand all that, but I still find it hard to believe. However, Felicity is now terrified they will be after her. I suggested we move to another city, and she changed her name. I've done all that once. I can do it again. I changed my name when I came here as there is plenty of evidence that the Chinese Communist Party can reach people well outside China. They have introduced the new Security Law in Hong Kong. Even people outside Hong Kong can be charged with undermining the state.

'Felicity has been to see us and has told us something of her fears,' said Drake. 'So far, we have no evidence to support her fear that she is being followed.'

'I'm also sure of that. I've been used to people following me in Hong Kong, and somehow, I don't understand how, but I get a feeling when it is happening. At least Felicity and I understand each other's fears and can support each other. We are happy together.'

'We have just one more question,' said Drake. 'Does the name Irene Lee mean anything to you?'

'I assume you mean Li Mei Lien,' replied Elliott. 'I believe over here she calls herself Irene Lee. Technically, in Hong Kong, we would call her Irene Mei Lien Li.'

'Yes,' said Grace, seeing Drake's confusion. 'That is who we mean.'

'OK,' said Elliott. 'I think it would be correct to say that I only know her a little, but I know a lot about her. She is a dangerous woman who works in dark corners. Why do you ask?'

'Well, MI5 know about her too and have been tracking her. Imogen Glass knew her and recommended her to be a member of a parliamentary committee on fraud in the Far East. We found a folder containing copies of Imogen's paintings. Irene Lee's business card was inside.'

'Silly girl,' said Elliott.

'Please explain,' asked Drake.

'I warned Imogen to stay clear of her, but it seems she didn't.'

'Maybe if you told us what you know of Irene Lee, that would be helpful,' said Drake.

'Well, she uses several aliases. I think here she claims to be an art expert. Of course, she is no such thing. She will do anything to worm her way into people, companies or governments that interest the CCP.'

'CCP?' asked Grace.

'Sorry, the Chinese Communist Party. They run the government of China and are gradually taking over Hong Kong. Imogen's work is much admired in Hong Kong, so typically, Lee would try to get to know her and influence her. She would also use her to spread disinformation about China. I think you call it Fake News.'

'Yes, of course,' said Grace.

'The least I owe to Imogen is to help find her killers,' said Elliott.

Drake nodded his head and grunted. Elliott spoke again.

'In Imogen's case, we discovered that Lee was trying to include her in a massive fraud scheme. This involves many expert Chinese painters who are excellent at creating fake paintings. Because of the value of Imogen's work, this would be a multi-million-pound business.'

'So, was Imogen playing along with this?'

'I don't know what she was doing, but anything to do with Lee is dangerous. She is likely to be untruthful to Imogen about what she is doing. You can be sure Lee will win and Imogen will not. I could probably find out more, but it would be risky and difficult to do while being certain Lee did not find out about it. Lee has friends who can act anywhere in the world. They regularly take people out who get in their way. I only recently learned about Imogen's involvement and warned her seriously to steer clear. Sadly, she did not heed my warnings.'

'Do you think Irene Lee may be responsible for Imogen's death?' asked Drake. Elliott Chan sat silently for a while before speaking slowly and carefully.

'It is possible, but I would say unlikely. The possibility is that Imogen knew more than Irene would like, and she got worried about her. However, I think it is more likely that it might be Philippa. Of course, I dislike the woman intensely, but I think she seduced Imogen into their relationship and was furious when Imogen told her it was over. Perhaps she didn't intend to kill her, but they argued violently. Perhaps it happened as part of that. I have no evidence, though.'

'When was the last time you saw Imogen?' asked Drake.

'She's been away in Hong Kong a lot,' said Elliott. 'She said she was going there to do research. I assumed this was for her paintings, but her relationship with Irene Lee makes me wonder. One thing I can say about Imogen is that she was a real terrier. If she got interested in something, she would want to know all there was to know about it.'

'What might that be, Mr Chan?' asked Drake.

'She has become more interested in politics recently. Politics in Hong Kong these days is a dangerous pastime. I suppose the last time I spoke to her was when she told me her relationship with Philippa was over, and we could pick up again.'

'What was your reaction to that?' asked Grace.

'I was furious. She was treating me with disrespect. She was also angry. It was not a good time.'

'Are you sure you haven't seen her more recently?' demanded Drake. 'Perhaps you met again, had another argument, and there was some sort of accident.'

'No, that's not true, and I certainly didn't kill her if that is what you are suggesting.'

'It's you that has suggested it, Mr Chan, not me,' growled Drake. 'OK, thank you for your time and help. May we call you again if we need you to help us some more?'

'Of course.'

'Thank you again, Mr Chan,' said Drake abruptly. 'We are grateful for your time. I hope you will agree to our technician Dave taking your fingerprints. We need to eliminate those that you will have left in Imogen's studio.'

'I'm not sure I want that,' said Elliott Chan. 'I have no control over where they go. This could do me harm.'

'I can assure you they will remain entirely confidential to this enquiry. They will never enter any database unless you are later convicted of a crime.' Drake smiled to indicate this was a weak joke. Elliott Chan reluctantly nodded his head in agreement and left with Dave, who had just arrived.

'Well,' said Drake, as Grace returned to the interview room after seeing Elliott Chan out. 'What do we make of all that?'

'He is a young man with a huge load on his shoulders,' said Grace. 'Although they can support each other, I would guess that he and Felicity can also reinforce their paranoia. No, perhaps that is the wrong word. I'm sure their fears are based on quite real suspicions. I feel sorry for them.'

'It makes me think of quite a new line of enquiry,' said Drake. 'Remember how alike Imogen and Felicity were. What if Imogen was killed in error by someone looking for Felicity.'

'Good gracious,' said Grace. 'I hadn't thought of that, but it is worth keeping in mind.'

'We now have several strands to our investigation,' said Drake. 'We have the family with all its complexity. We have the possibility of straightforward theft. We have some connection with fraud and even espionage with China. We must do a proper analysis of this. Only then can we decide where our efforts should go.'

'They may not be entirely separate possibilities,' said Grace. 'Imogen's paintings are now of such worth that professional theft by crime syndicates is possible. If this turns out to be the case, it may be driven internationally and bring us back to China.'

'Well done, Grace,' said Drake. 'You are right there.'

'One possibility we cannot yet eliminate is that Elliott Chan was so obsessed with Imogen rejecting him that he murdered her. Alternatively, he worried that Irene Lee and her henchmen might come for him if Imogen did something dangerous.'

'Yes,' said Drake. 'On the surface, that might seem far-fetched, but of course, it could have been the result of an argument that got out of hand, and Elliott hit Imogen with some hard object that he unintentionally killed her.'

'On a similar basis,' said Grace, 'perhaps the sisters argued over Elliott, and that got out of hand. Of course, he has introduced this possibility that Philippa Crehan killed her in a rage.'

'Rage in such matters can be a terrifyingly strong force,' said Drake. 'So, of course, can fear. Elliott Chan is worried because he only half knows something dangerous.'

'I've just got a report from forensics about the van,' said Grace. 'Of course, Imogen's DNA and prints are all over it. However, we found another set that is even on the driving wheel. Somebody else has driven it and opened the rear door. Perhaps they loaded something in or out of the back.'

'I see,' said Drake. 'That just could be the person we are looking for. We need to start eliminating all our current contacts on the case. We need to get prints and DNA from everyone we are investigating. Especially anyone who could have driven that van. Get forensics going on it.'

# 13

'They told me I would find you here.'

To begin with, Drake only half heard these words. His brain treated them as just part of the general hum of conversation and not needing attention. He was preoccupied partly with his analysis of the Imogen Glass case and partly with watching the antics of gulls out in the middle of the River Dee. If he had been honest with himself, it was the anniversary of his wife, Cynthia's death, and, during the morning, the emotion of it all proved too much for him. The Boathouse pub provided some remedy where he could temporarily get relief from the hustle and bustle of the case room.

'This place where Imogen Glass was found?'

Drake turned as he heard the rather curious language. It was Wang from The Orient Gallery standing just beside him. Drake could admire the substantial figure. From his chair, Drake had to look up to talk to him.

'Sorry,' grunted Drake. 'I was miles away. Yes. I fear it was not a pleasant way to end an evening for most of the customers in the pub.'

'Suppose not,' said Wang.'

'Do please sit down,' said Drake, pointing to the empty chair on the other side of his table.

'How the investigation is going? It important to us she finds justice,' said Wang as he pulled the chair out from under the table and sat staring straight into Drake's face. Drake thought his understanding of personal space perhaps lacked some sophistication. Or was it just Drake's inability to understand Chinese culture and norms? Wang was a jolly fellow, and Drake did not mind chatting with him.

'Like all investigations,' he replied, 'it is gradually getting more complex. Hopefully, eventually, it will simplify as we pin things down.'

'You not have a prime suspect yet?' asked Wang.

'We have many suspects,' said Drake. 'Actually, I would like to talk to you and Angela again if you have time.'

'Go ahead,' said Wang easing his chair back and crossing his legs while propping himself with his right arm over the back of the chair.

'Thanks,' said Drake. 'This is not the time or place. I have something I would like to show you. Perhaps I could come into the gallery one day?'

'Of course. We both there most days.'

'Thank you. Maybe I could come and see you both tomorrow with my sergeant.'

As he spoke, Drake began the lengthy process of clambering to an upright stance. He slowly rose to all his six and a half feet. 'I see the police car has just arrived for me. I must go back to work.' Wang stood up before Drake had finished the climb from his chair.

'I help you, Inspector.' Wang walked alongside Drake to the Range Rover and opened the front passenger door. Drake mumbled and pointed to the rear door. Wang sprang forward laughing.

'You like back,' he said.

'I need the legroom and headroom,' grunted Drake as he clambered into the car.


Drake had promised Grace a walk through the city centre accompanied by his commentary on the architectural riches of Chester. As they set off the following morning, Drake complained of a problem with his right knee and had been hobbling from early on. Grace knew where the police had marked out reserved parking places that they used for special events and Saturday evenings. She drove the Range Rover to the station's front door and collected the limping Drake. Throughout the journey, Drake complained about his knee and back. He railed against the discomforts of ageing that seemed to delight in attacking his large frame. Grace thought he cut a rather sorry figure and was glad she had suggested driving.

'It's all a conspiracy,' he said to Grace as he eased himself across the seat. The height of the Range Rover was, however, just right for him as he could place his feet on the ground before leaving. Grace cringed as she watched him. She knew better than to offer assistance, which would inevitably serve only to bring more complaints.

'That's saved my knee,' grunted Drake as he turned to see The Orient. 'I would far rather have walked from the car park.' Grace was too busy taking in The Orient to notice Drake's latest groan. The shop was a real treasure trove. She marvelled at the furniture on display in one window. She walked along the extensive frontage, looking in each window in turn. It all looked exquisite and expensive. Drake had remained by the car as he took a phone call from his son Tom. Drake knew full well that Tom was checking up on him, though neither of them mentioned Cynthia's death.

Wang had seen them through the window, so he came to meet them. He ostentatiously shut the rear door of the Range Rover behind Drake just as he was putting his phone away in a jacket pocket. Wang rushed to be in front of Drake and Grace and opened the door. The scent of China wafted across Grace's face, completing the seductive effect. The whole place was weaving its spell on her, just as it had Drake on his first visit. Immediately opposite them was a woman on a stepladder dusting the frames of hanging paintings. She turned cautiously as the ladder groaned. She looked down to assure herself that the ladder feet were secure and then up at her visitors.

'Hello, Chief Inspector,' said Angela, coming down to floor level. Wang laughed and pointed to Angela's brush.

'You be astonished. Much dust collect here.' He beckoned Drake and Grace. 'Come into office where we talk.'

'This is Detective Sergeant Grace Hepple,' Drake said. 'Perhaps Grace could look around the gallery first.?'

'Of course, of course. I show you.' Wang scuttled off with Grace in tow. The limping Drake stumbled along some way behind. 'We start at the far end,' said Wang as Grace caught up with him. 'This is where we make space for big things.' He waved his left arm across the carved wooden frame before Grace. 'This a daybed for Chinese diplomat made in Ming period. Might be five hundred years old.' Wang laughed. 'Is unique. Is very expensive.' Before Grace had taken in something she had never seen, Wang waved her back around the first dividing wall. 'These all old paintings. We not sure of artist's name. Probably four hundred years old.' Grace would have liked less of a whirlwind tour. But she dutifully followed Wang to the next bay. She looked for Drake and saw him at the other end of the shop, or was it a gallery?' He was in conversation with the distinctly western-looking woman who had been dusting. Eventually, Wang's guided walk reached them, and Angela Marchment introduced herself to Grace. Wang headed towards the stairs leading to the office, followed by Angela and Drake.

'I've left the portfolio in the car,' said Grace, excusing herself and dashing back through the gallery towards the Range Rover sitting arrogantly in its privileged parking space. When she returned carrying the portfolio of the work of Imogen Glass, the little tea ceremony was already in progress. Prompted by looks and gestures from Drake, Grace quickly understood that this should be respected, so she sat silently with the portfolio on the floor propped up against her chair. In due course, and after they had all taken their first sip of tea from the tiny cups, Drake broke the silence.

'We have something we would like to show you,' he said as he nodded to Grace. She lifted the portfolio onto the table.

'We found this in the studio of Imogen Glass,' she said. 'It seems to be a complete illustrated catalogue of her works.'

'Good gracious,' said Angela. She stood to look over Grace's shoulder at the first painting. 'I had no idea she had this.'

'She seems to have been very efficient,' said Grace.

'Oh, she was, she was,' said Angela, 'but I had no idea this existed. We could turn this into an interesting publication.'

'Yes,' interrupted Wang. 'It sell well here and in Hong Kong and Singapore.' He pushed forward and turned a page.

'Many we haven't seen,' said Wang. 'How she sold these?'

'There is an index at the back,' said Grace. 'They are all numbered, and in the index, she has made some notes about how they were sold and who bought them. We would like you to look at the final pages. There are three more paintings in her studio. Look at these.' Grace turned the pages.

'Just sketches only,' said Wang. 'She wouldn't allow them to be sold.'

'I wondered about that,' said Grace. Now, the next three. Please look at them. They have your gallery name at the end.'

'These on our walls,' said Wang immediately.

'OK now,' said Grace. 'There are twenty-four more. They don't have anything against them in the index. Just their numbers.'

'Not seen them,' said Wang as Grace flipped through.

'Stop,' said Angela, suddenly. 'Looks like Danqing. Oh my, she develops here! These are exceptional innovations.'

'What is Danqing?' asked Grace. Wang turned several more pages ignoring Grace's question. Then he stopped, stood up and looked at Angela, expecting a reply from her.

'It's difficult to explain,' she said. 'It can mean many things now, which is a typical Chinese way of using words. This goes back to the Zhou Dynasty.'

'When is that?' asked Drake.

'In our calendar, maybe two hundred BC. It means red cyan in modern words. Vermillion is Dansha. Qingyu is cyan. This refers to early sources of colour pigments. Danqing refers to the most common colours in ancient Chinese ink painting. They were usually done on silk or some special paper. The newer plant-based, mineral, and metal pigments lasted longer. So Danqing started to mean faithful or reliable. But it also means a style of painting. Imogen refers to that style in these later paintings. Her work is very clever, very beautiful, unique.' Wang started to turn the pages himself. Grace thought he pushed her out of the way rather rudely.

Drake accepted it as his normal behaviour. It signified agreement and enthusiasm, even admiration, not rudeness.

'Must find these paintings, they fetch high price,' said Wang. 'Exhibition and auction in Hong Kong best way.'

This confirmed Drake's earlier assessment of the roles of Angela and Wang. Wang's head was full of marketing, contracts, deadlines and balance sheets. Angela lived in a different world of history, culture, philosophy and aesthetics. Together, they made an unlikely couple at first sight, but on further thought, this was a perfect partnership for what they did.

'So, could this mean they were stored in her studio?' asked Grace. 'Her landlady said there were usually many more paintings stacked against the wall.' Nobody answered, but Wang nodded his head enthusiastically.

'Is it possible that there was a robbery?' asked Grace. 'An inside job using knowledge about these paintings. Perhaps Imogen disturbed them, and they killed her, either intentionally or accidentally.' Angela shrugged her shoulders. Wang carried on looking at the portfolio as he spoke.

'Robbery, yes, robbery. I tell her not to leave paintings in studio.' Grace made a note.

'New period, new exhibition.' Wang spat out his words.

'I think what Wang is saying,' said Angela, 'is that she may have held all these together as a new period in her work. Perhaps she had an exhibition in mind. If so, I would have expected her to ask us about it. Perhaps it should have been in London. Maybe she didn't want to offend us.'

'I tell her paintings can be stolen. She couldn't keep secret,' laughed Wang. 'She talk about it to people. She always did.'

'Not to me,' said Angela. 'How about you, Wang?'

'No. She say something about new kind of work once. Can't remember now.' He turned more pages slowly. 'Oh, this very good,' he squealed. 'Very good, yes. Oh, look at these two! They have similar numbers 38S and 38D.'

'What does that mean?' asked Grace.

'No idea,' replied Angela. 'She has always used a rather odd way of numbering her paintings and would never explain. She said it was just for her use, not anybody else's.'

'Oh,' said Wang, 'I want to own these two.'

'That's our problem,' said Angela, laughing. 'We are in business to sell paintings, not to buy them.'

'Well, thank you,' said Drake. 'You have been most helpful. Perhaps we have a new line to our inquiry.'

'Need to find these,' muttered Wang. 'Must get rights.'

'I don't suppose you know what her will says by any chance?' asked Angela. 'I know it sounds a bit pushy, but we would want to buy the rights to publish this portfolio. I'm sure we could do a deal with her lawyers or her executors.'

'Do you know who her solicitors are?' asked Drake. 'We need to speak to them anyway.'

'I can't remember their name. They are just by us in Watergate Street,' answered Angela. 'I will check on them and let you know by phone or email.'


'They're a great couple,' said Grace as she drove Drake back to the station.

'Yes,' grunted Drake, who was deep in thought.

'She has all the knowledge and understanding of art. He has the business brains. She drools over the paintings, and he wants the rights to the portfolio.'

'Yes,' said Drake, laughing with delight at Grace's analysis. He was increasingly aware that Grace had promotion prospects. He ought to give her more personal responsibility. 'Well spotted. They make a good team. Can you chase up the will with her lawyers for us? We need to do that anyway. It would be easiest if they were her executors, but I wouldn't mind betting that her sister, Felicity, is at least one of them. She hasn't mentioned it, though.'

As they entered the case room back at the station, Dave, the technician, came rushing over.

'I have some news,' he said.

'Can I just get a cup of coffee?' groaned Drake. 'I need to sit down for a while.'

'Take a seat in your chair,' said Dave. 'I will make you a cup.' Dave caused the coffee machine to hiss and gurgle at its business. Drake idly picked up his crossword. He was annoyed that he had made so little progress that day, so he scanned the unsolved clues. His eyes set on thirteen across, which he now saw the answer to immediately. He had struggled with this earlier and marvelled at the clever way the human brain would come to something fresh and suddenly see it differently.

Dave brought the coffee over for both Drake and Grace. He was hopping up and down as Drake looked up.

'OK,' said Drake expectantly.

'Our boys have worked on the latest data, and we have a match,' gasped Dave.

'A match for what?' Drake was beginning to share Dave's sense of urgency.

'It's the new set of fingerprints that we got from Imogen's boyfriend, Elliott Chan. They match the prints on one of the poles in Imogen's studio. He must have picked it up.'

# 14

It was a long journey down to Fairlawns, the Xi Dong headquarters that Imogen's sister, Felicity, had described. Grace had brought Constable Dan Ford to do the driving. They had to get around London. During her time at The Met, Grace had developed what was to become a longstanding aversion to the M25. She had some notes to catch up with, but she had completed her task by the time they reached the M25. As they talked, she was astonished to discover something Dan mentioned rather casually. They shared a background in ballet. Dan's mother had been a dancer in the corps de ballet, and Dan was brought up knowing the basic moves and positions.

'As I grew up, I changed to ice skating,' he said somewhat coyly. 'My parents were supportive, and I got to be in demand as a partner for pairs. There's always a shortage of boys to partner with the better girls. It was quite easy to transition from ballet, but there was too much travel and early morning practice for my liking, and it seemed a natural progression into ice hockey. I still play in quite a good amateur team.'

'Well, I never,' said Grace. 'You are quite a discovery.'

'So are you,' said Dan, turning rather red-faced. 'I don't think the lads know you were a professional ballet dancer before you joined the police.' They both laughed.

'Well, perhaps mine is not quite such an obvious progression,' smiled Grace, who returned to her notes while Dan concentrated on navigating the rigours of the M25.

'The satnav is telling us to leave the motorway here,' said Dan. 'I think it's only a mile to the place we're looking for.'

'It's called Fairlawns,' said Grace. When I looked it up on Google Earth, it is set back and not visible from the road.'

'Yes,' said Dan. 'Amazingly, the shot from above shows the house all wrapped up like one of those ridiculous, so-called works of art by... I can't remember his name now.'

'Christo,' said Grace. 'However, did they manage that?'

'From what you've told me,' said Dan, 'I think they are quite a secretive lot. Ah, here we are. At least the satnav thinks this is it.'

'Just looks like a driveway that curves out of sight,' said Grace. 'I guess we go down and see where it leads us.' Dan backed up and turned left down the drive. Into sight came a gatehouse standing next to a gate across the driveway. There was still no house visible. Dan wound down his window and pressed a button on the post next to the car. Grace could not hear the conversation out of the car window. Eventually, the gate opened without any particular sense of urgency. Dan was tapping irritably on the steering wheel. As soon as there was room, he drove through, turned behind the gatehouse and parked as instructed.

'Is this it?' asked Grace.

'No idea,' replied Dan. 'The guy told me to park here and wait for him.' Dan got out of the car and tried the door to the gatehouse. It was locked. As he walked back to the car, a golf buggy careered into sight around a bend and bounced along the drive. It pulled up next to the police car.

'Hello and welcome,' said the driver of the buggy. 'I'm Luke.' He pulled out a ring of keys, unlocked the gatehouse door and beckoned them in.

'Is this it?' demanded Grace after the introductions.

'This is as far as we allow visitors to bring their vehicles, I'm afraid,' said Luke. 'But we will be comfortable here. He opened the door from the hallway into a huge room overlooking gracious and well-kept lawns surrounded by what looked like an orchard.

'Where is the main house?' asked Dan, frowning.

'Further down the drive,' replied Luke. 'We are a closed community, so we cannot have strangers wandering around.' Luke beckoned his visitors to take large armchairs near the windows and walked across the room to an elaborate-looking coffee machine, which he began to operate. It hissed and grunted somewhat reluctantly in response. 'We had two rooms knocked into one here,' said Luke, still trying to coax the coffee maker into action. 'It makes a generous meeting room. I hope you like our lawns. We named the house after them. They are quite a feature.' He carried a large tray with three cups of steaming coffee and put it on the low table between the armchairs.

Grace was carefully observing Luke as he spoke. He was young, perhaps in his thirties, and Chinese. Grace was not surprised since, according to Elliott Chan, the movement had begun in China and Hong Kong. Luke seemed well-educated and wore expensive-looking clothes. Grace made a mental note that his use of English was as immaculate as his dress. He sat down opposite Grace and Dan and spoke again.

'Perhaps you would like me to explain a little about us?' Grace nodded silently as she munched a digestive biscuit.

'We are called Xi Dong,' said Luke. 'In Mandarin, that can mean west-east. The movement began in Hong Kong and spread into mainland China. Then, two of our most active members moved to Texas. That is now our headquarters. In these times, our activities in Hong Kong are not always approved. We changed the name to reflect our new international status.'

'I think we might know who these two illustrious members are,' said Grace. 'What are their names?'

'They are called Mary and Peter,' said Luke.

'What about their surname?' asked Grace.

'We are all members of the Xi Dong family,' replied Luke, 'so we don't use family names as they would all be the same. It would be pointless. I am delighted that Mary and Peter have visited us to celebrate the opening of our British branch. We have only been operating here for about a year.'

'You all seem to have rather biblical names,' said Grace. 'Is that significant?'

'Not at all. We do not like complicated names that allow members to sound more important. We use simple names.'

'So, how long are Peter and Mary expected to stay here?' asked Grace.

'I'm not privy to the detailed movements of important members,' replied Luke with a slight air of irritation. 'We were just told to expect them and be ready for them to stay as long as they see fit.'

'How do you operate the house if you don't allow visitors in?' asked Grace. 'What happens if you need tradespeople.'

'Good question. Deliveries are made to this Lodge and are collected in one of our buggies. We actively try to recruit members with all the skills we need to make a self-sufficient community. In addition, members are encouraged to be active in the arts. We love our members to play musical instruments and encourage them to learn if not.'

'So, are you a religion?' asked Grace.

'Some people might think so, but we don't regard ourselves as a religion; we are a movement. We don't have religious ceremonies or a church, but we have communal spaces, which we call forums.'

'So, what do you discuss in a forum?' asked Grace.

'Ways of living better lives.'

'Gosh,' said Grace. 'That's a big topic.'

'It keeps us busy,' said Luke, smiling beatifically. 'I suppose the big question you haven't asked is whether we believe in God. The answer is that we think there must be some greater supreme force. Of course, we allow discussion of that, but so far, no member has been able to persuade us otherwise. None of the narratives offered by the major religions appeals to us.

We believe any benign, external being would approve of our way of life. We keep an electronic library of all our forum discussions, and the three centres, London, Texas, and Hong Kong share those.'

'How do you pay for all this?' asked Grace. 'Do you discuss that in a forum too?'

'We don't discuss money in a forum, only ideas. We encourage members to continue to practice their occupations where possible. Each member contributes what they feel they can. We are all individuals, and there are no rules.' There was a brief silence before Luke spoke again. 'Now, can I ask some questions? Why have you come today? What is the nature of your interest in the movement?'

'We are investigating an unexplained death,' said Grace. 'This took place in Chester, and we believe the deceased had some connection with your movement.'

'Oh no, surely not,' said Luke indignantly. 'We would know if any of our members had died.'

'The person concerned was not a member of your movement, but we believe her parents were. For this reason, I need you to tell us the family names of your members, Mary and Peter. They must have had a name before they joined, and we must know what it was.'

'Oh dear,' said Luke. 'I do not know this information, and I would not ask. That would be quite wrong. It would not normally be revealed. All I could do would be to ask the Texas centre to discuss this matter. We would have to accept their opinion on it. They would take collective responsibility for answering your request. Normally, any conclusion that a forum comes to remains confidential within the movement.'

'How many members are there?' asked Grace, beginning to get frustrated.

'Xi Dong does not discuss its membership with anyone outside,' replied Luke.

'Does that mean you don't know?'

'I could count how many members we have here in London. I don't keep the number in my head, but it would remain confidential. I have no idea how many members we have in Hong Kong and Texas.'

'I have one more question,' said Grace. 'What happens when a member leaves your community.'

'As far as I know, the situation has not arisen. Members take on the responsibility that they remain in the movement for life. I cannot imagine why any member would want to leave this beautiful location and welcoming community.'

'Surely all your centres must come at a considerable cost?' asked Grace. 'Who else other than members could be paying for it?'

'You ask about matters we do not normally discuss,' replied Luke.

'Perhaps I might remind you that this is a police enquiry. We do not ask for discussion, but we can demand answers to simple questions,' snapped Grace. Dan was slightly shocked by her sudden change of questioning style. He thought that Luke was also surprised.

'I will tell you some simple rules of membership,' said Luke. 'We share these with people enquiring about becoming a member, so I am empowered to tell you this. Firstly, we expect members to sign their savings over to the movement. They do not lose these savings. The movement invests them. They could either in whole or part be returned to a member whom a forum agreed had such a need. Any income made by members is paid directly into the movement bank. Again, members may request some of this money if they have a special need. The economics, however, are simple. The total cost of running a centre is much less than the expenses of running all the members' homes. That is how we can make provision of facilities for members collectively.' Luke stopped speaking quite abruptly. His manner had changed. He seemed unhappy about discussing financial matters.

'Can we see the main house and look around the estate?' asked Grace snappily.

'I can take you on a tour in my buggy. However, we do not allow strangers to interrupt members or to go inside any of the main buildings.' Luke bowed and smiled as Grace said that she would like the tour. Luke led the small group outside to his buggy. It had three rows of seats with a canopy over it. The front had only one seat for the driver. There was a small collection of boxes alongside this seat. Grace and Dan were directed to the back seat. They were amused that Luke was now talking to them over an intercom. Grace tried asking a question, but Luke appeared not to hear her.

'This drive takes us up to the main building, which is of historic interest,' said Luke. 'We cannot go to the house as this might interrupt members.' It was the second time he had used this odd phrase, and Grace made a note even though she had already turned on the recording feature of her phone. 'There is the main house,' said Luke, pulling up just before a large and generous house. It was a confident building. It knew how beautiful it was. It stood proudly surveying the surrounding landscape. Grace thought it was from an earlier time. The buggy now turned across the driveway as if to block it. Luke resumed his commentary. 'It is a listed building. We take great pride in it. There are bedrooms for some people who have joined the earliest. The building also houses our main hall where we can hold general meetings and performances usually given by members. As I said, most of our members can either play a musical instrument or are learning. There is also a series of smaller meeting rooms. Then, to the left, there is a dining hall. Behind that, in a newer building, are our kitchens.'

Grace panned from the grand hall across the manicured lawns to the rolling English countryside. It was an idyllic retreat, and it was difficult to believe the snarling M25 lay just out of sight. Luke had stopped talking as if to let his visitors take in the scenery. After what he presumably thought was sufficient time, Luke drove the buggy away from the house before taking a sharp turn around behind it and stopping again. 'Here in our modern wing, you can find workshops, music practice rooms and other kinds of working rooms where members can practice hobbies of various kinds.' Luke started the buggy again and drove through an archway between the original house and the new wing. There were tennis courts and a swimming pool, which Luke pointed out proudly. 'We provide all the major ways of leading good and productive lives.' The buggy swept away from this complex. It turned through an attractive and well-manicured copse. A series of three-storey buildings appeared that Luke told his visitors were for newer members.

Grace had become entranced by the whole place. She could imagine people settling here. It was almost tempting. She could understand how people were seduced by it all. Her mind then moved on. She wondered how long one could remain detached from the world without beginning to feel the need for something else. She glanced across at Dan, who was already showing signs of impatience. He made it clear that Fairlawns was not for him. She snapped out of her reverie as Luke began talking again.

'As well as residents, we also have three more classes of membership,' said Luke. 'We call them leaders, followers and subscribers. Leaders are longstanding senior resident members. I am a leader, as are both Mary and Peter. The other two groups, followers and subscribers, are not residents but have access to all our online material. In addition, subscribers can also book short stays in this building. Usually, followers begin by taking courses from our online life coaching scheme. Wonderfully, that often results in them joining as subscribers, and they may visit us for short life coaching courses.'

'How many followers and subscribers do you have?' asked Grace.

'Again, I cannot tell you the precise number, but it runs into hundreds,' replied Luke. 'Many of them follow our meetings online.'

They passed another single-storey building with long and deep overhanging roofs. Luke did not comment, so Grace asked what this building was for. She received no reply. Then, she noticed a wire fence that appeared to surround the sides and rear of the building. She caught sight of a figure through one of the windows. She thought that the figure may have waved. The buggy had now accelerated and was rattling busily along. To the front, at one end of the building, there was a short, stocky figure standing to attention like a soldier. Luke waved to him, and he waved back.

'What is that building?' she asked again.

'I don't think he can hear us,' said Dan. Grace hurriedly took a photo with her phone. The buggy had reached the original driveway, and they were soon back at the gatehouse where their car was parked. Luke pulled up next to it. Grace asked about the building for the third time.

'That is for our special guests,' said Luke enigmatically. 'Now, if I can draw this to a conclusion, I need to be at a forum in a few minutes, and I don't want to keep members waiting. I will open the gate for you.' Grace was a little put out by being dismissed this way but decided not to cross Luke. She spoke politely.

'Constable Dan Ford will give you a card giving our contact details. Would you use it to send the information about Mary and Peter that we have requested,' said Grace as she drank the last dregs of the cup of coffee she had carried with her. Dan handed Luke a card, and they left silently.

'Well, well, well,' said Grace as Dan drove them through the open gate that Luke was standing next to. 'Money is a sore point. It's funny how often that is the case with these sorts of outfits. It always amazes me that people are gullible enough to be taken in by it. I did some work on religious movements when I was at The Met. They often have extremely cleverly constructed contracts and astute lawyers. A member leaving would have a devil of a job to disentangle themselves from Xi Dong. One of the clever things you can be sure of is that every member has a contract written in another country. They would need a lot of money to hire lawyers to extract them with any money, and of course, they will be penniless at the time.'

'What about Imogen's parents?' asked Dan as he negotiated their way back to the M25.

'I bet he knows their name, and I think we have found them. From what Luke said, they are normally residents at the Xi Dong Centre in Texas but are visiting Fairlawns. No wonder it was hard for the Glass sisters to make sensible contact with their parents. You can see why the parents are anxious to entice their girls into the Xi Dong web. We may be dealing with an international crime syndicate here. Drake needs to plan our moves carefully.'

# 15

Early the following morning, Grace arrived in the case room to find Dan making the final edits to his report of their visit to Xi Dong at Fairlawns. She wanted to share their notes with Felicity Glass. It might help them learn more about Xi Dong. She had called Felicity's mobile number earlier, and it went straight to answerphone. She called it again now with the same result. Drake rocked slowly in his favourite chair, making that characteristic creaking sound. Grace tried not to get irritated by it.

'I'm getting only an answerphone message from Felicity's mobile,' she said.

'OK,' grunted Drake, 'let's try Elliott's number. He is living with her and should know where she is.' Grace checked her notes for Elliott's phone and called it.

'Hello. Please leave a message.' Grace noted that Elliott was always anxious not to give away his whereabouts, so the answer message was terse and uninformative. She left a message, asking Elliott to call her.

'OK,' said Grace. 'Perhaps we should put out a missing person call. That should track her down if she is moving about.' Grace put down the phone and went over to Drake, still rocking noisily. Grace stood in front of Drake to get his attention.

'Neither Elliott Chan nor Felicity Glass are answering their phones. I'm a bit concerned about Felicity. She told us about her anxiety that she was being followed, and Elliott is almost paranoic about being chased down by agents of the Chinese Communist Party.'

'I wonder,' grunted Drake. 'Perhaps after Elliott let us take his fingerprints, he may have remembered that he had handled an incriminating object at Imogen's house. He might have gone into hiding somewhere. After his experiences in Hong Kong, he is probably quite skilled at dodging officialdom. As for Felicity, that is more worrying. Maybe I should have taken her concerns more seriously and given her some protection. In the meantime, keep trying them both. Let's see how you have got on later.'

Dan emailed his report to Drake, who sat reading it closely while Dan made the coffee. Grace attended to her emails until Drake was ready.

'Xi Dong is a secretive outfit,' he growled eventually.

'Luke was OK,' said Grace. 'That was until we asked about membership or money, and then a cloak of obfuscation came down. He was mostly polite and a good host, but anyone investigating them thoroughly would have a tough time.'

'Couldn't we get a search warrant?' asked Dan.

'Of course, we could try,' replied Drake, 'but I doubt we have sufficient grounds to win one, and I would guess that there would be little to find on the premises.'

'Except perhaps for Imogen and Felicity's parents,' said Grace. 'Luke talked of two illustrious members coming over from Texas.'

'Have a look at this, folks,' said Dan. 'I've downloaded Grace's photos and blown this one up. I had a vague feeling about it. Look, the mysterious building has bars over the windows. Rather oddly, they appear to be on the inside. You can also see the outline of someone in one of those rooms waving.'

'At the time, I thought it was waving a greeting at Luke,' said Grace, 'but now I'm inclined to think it was waving in distress at being locked up.'

'Well spotted, Dan,' said Drake slowly while pouring over the image. 'Well done, both of you. I think there is more to discover here. We need to think out our strategy for that. Do we go in all guns blazing with a search warrant and a platoon of constables? Or do we take a more subtle approach?'

'I think we have found Imogen's parents, and I bet Luke knows who they are,' said Grace. She was unhappy about Drake dismissing the possibility of getting a search warrant for Fairlawns, but an idea was already developing in her mind.

'I wonder if the police in Texas have any information on them?' pondered Drake.

'What about Hong Kong?' said Grace. 'Maybe we could use our contact with Martin over there.'

'It's worth a try,' said Drake. 'Yet again, this investigation points to Hong Kong. Why don't you email Martin and see if he knows anything about Xi Dong.' Drake returned to his chair and rocked noisily. Grace momentarily clenched a fist and got on with her emails. Dan made himself a cup of tea.

'I'm going to have to go down to Birmingham,' said Drake, suddenly. 'My sister's husband is about to die. I need to go and support her. She helped me a great deal when Cynthia died. I hope I won't be away too long, but I can't be certain. Grace will take over, but I will be in contact by email and, if necessary, phone.' Grace and Dan muttered some words of support, and Drake asked Dan to drive him home and to the railway station.

When they had left, Grace went down to the evidence store. She put on a pair of the soft plastic gloves they used to handle evidence and opened a floor-to-ceiling metal cabinet. She looked up and down the shelves and pulled out the portfolio of Imogen's paintings. It was sealed in a plastic bag and wrapped in tissue paper. She did not know why it was stored so carefully. So much had happened to it already. She laid it on the small table in the middle of the room and began to sift slowly through it. She glanced at the paintings as they passed in front of her.

She was no art expert, but she felt she could see some of the development of Imogen Glass. There was no doubt about a sudden change quite early on when the work became more obviously original. As time passed, this work seemed to get more confident and sophisticated. Grace knew she would be missing things, but at least this was the first time she had seen the development so clearly. In particular, the last two dozen pieces of work felt different. She came to the final pages, which contained the catalogue of work. She presumed Imogen would have been at the height of her powers when she died. She remembered how Wang and Angela at The Orient were so impressed by these paintings.

She wished she had seen the originals full size. Perhaps they would eventually be found, but she doubted it.

The final sleeves of the portfolio contained a variety of more mundane items. One suddenly caught her eye. She didn't remember seeing it before. Seven paintings were much more graphical and quite different from Imogen's main paintings. They were smaller and came in different overall outline shapes. They were numbered one to eight but no number four. The last of these, number eight, appeared to be based on the number itself. A background of flowers was interlaced with the digit. It fascinated Grace, and she wished there was some explanation. In the next portfolio sleeve was a copy of "Eight". It was much smaller, closely cropped and wrapped around the upper arm of what looked like a female. It suddenly hit her that these were designs for tattoos. She remembered that Philippa Crehan had mentioned that a local tattoo artist had commissioned Imogen to design some patterns for him. Then, a quick white flash caught her eye as a small card dropped on the floor. It looked blank. As she picked it up, she turned it over. It was a business card, and it belonged to a tattoo artist. It was for an address in Chester. It was a studio called "Red Deer." She sat down and called the telephone number on the card.

'Red Deer,' said a voice.

'Hello,' said Grace, looking at the card. 'Is that David Tong?'

'Speaking.'

'I'm Detective Sergeant Grace Hepple. I've just found your business card and the designs for tattoos that Imogen Glass created for you.'

'Good gracious,' said David Tong. 'I thought that had all got lost, and I never kept a copy.'

'Could you spare me a little time to talk about them?'

'Of course. Yes. I have no appointments early this afternoon. Come over if you want to. Oh, and please bring the designs.'

Grace was familiar with the road to Hoole Way. The address was on a parallel street. She drove slowly down Brook Street. There were several massage and beauty parlours, some hairdressers, and two other tattoo parlours. There were also a few oriental restaurants and takeaway shops. It seemed to be a favoured location, and it bustled with business. There was a distinctly oriental flavour to the place. Then, there it was, Red Deer. She parked up, walked over and pushed the door. It opened to an oriental chime and a smell of the far east.

'Welcome,' said a booming voice. She looked around, and a figure appeared from behind a screen.

'I'm David Tong.' He was an impressive character who commanded attention. He was not fat. He was large. He had a shaved head, and Grace could see tattooed arms where his sleeves were rolled up. The tattoos competed for attention with the substantial muscles that rippled as he moved to hold out his hand. Grace saw hers disappear into his and felt a firm but gentle grip.

'Please come and take a seat,' said David Tong. There was an air of the Orient about him. But he seemed too tall and stocky for a Chinese man. It looked as if he made good use of weights. There was an impressive set lying on the floor beside him. He had an open face that drew Grace in. She somehow felt comfortable in his company. He was a big man. He looked strong but behaved gently, bowing slightly as he spoke. The more Grace studied him, there was a deep-seated gloom about the man. It was as if he didn't expect the world to treat him kindly, and sure enough, it didn't.

'As you can see,' he said, 'business is not exactly fizzing. I was so pleased to get this place. I get passing trade, and it is easy to park. But things have become rather slow recently. If it continues, I shall have to get another form of employment.'

'I'm sorry,' said Grace. 'I hope things improve for you. Did you do a tattoo for someone called Imogen Glass?'

'Good gracious, yes,' replied David Tong. 'Some weeks ago.'

'Do you know when exactly?' asked Grace. David Tong was thumbing through his diary. Suddenly, he stopped and looked up.

'Of course, I remember now. It won't be in the diary because she turned up unannounced, and I did it on the spot. She said a friend had recommended me to her. The tattoo was a simple little thing, rather ugly, but I remember she wanted it. She brought a little business card with her. A sketch of what she wanted was on the back.'

'Was it her business card?' asked Grace. 'Do you still have it by any chance?'

'No, it was someone else's card. I can't remember the name, I'm afraid. Imogen was particularly insistent that I return it. She said it was a business contact.'

'Who was it who recommended you to her?' asked Grace.

'It was Wang from The Orient Gallery. I know him a little. He comes from the same part of Hong Kong that we believe my father was from. I thought I had landed a great job. Of course, I know her paintings. I had this idea of producing tattoos to match Imogen's trademark paintings, and she liked the idea and agreed. I gave her my card, and she emailed me some preliminary ideas. The next thing, she is dead, and that idea doesn't work.' David Tong's countenance changed as he spoke. His face knew how to express sadness. Grace thought it had plenty of practice.

'Yes,' said Grace. 'I'm sorry. So, your father is Chinese?'

'Yes. However, he left the family and returned to China when I was young. Neither I nor my mother have ever heard from him again. I hardly remember him. I only have a few photographs. I would love to have met him. It has become an obsession with me. I sometimes think I have spent half my life trying to trace him without success. I would give everything up and fly over there, but the costs put it all out of my reach, and I don't speak Mandarin. My mother wouldn't have anything to do with it and refused to help me. She was understandably bitter about him just walking out and disappearing. She had changed her surname back to her family name. As I grew up, I started to use my father's name. I think maybe that hurt her a lot.'

'Where do you think he is?' asked Grace, noticing a tear in David Tong's eye. His sadness had plummeted to its lowest point.

'I'm not sure, but I've had reports of him more recently in Hong Kong.'

'Do you know what he does?'

'Well,' laughed David Tong. 'By now, I think he would be retired. Perhaps he is not even still alive.' Grace thought it best to wait while David Tong wiped away the tear. It was incongruous to see this great bear of a man crying.

'Do you mind if we finish?' he said. 'I have a client coming soon, and she wants the tattoo to be a secret. Imogen Glass was the same. I was sworn to secrecy, but I suppose it's OK now she's dead.'

The following day, there were some surprises in store for Grace. Usually, she was in early in the morning, but now Drake was away in Birmingham, and she was effectively in charge of the investigation. She felt some pressure to be first in every morning. She overslept and had to dash out to achieve her target arrival time. She just made it. Dan Ford was only a couple of minutes behind her. She sat down with her coffee and remembered taking a letter from the postman on her way out. She pulled it out of her bag. That was when it all started.

She thought the printed self-adhesive address label was a little odd. Not that the address was in any way wrong. It was correct in every detail. But this little label looked more like a mass-produced thing she might have created for herself, not someone else. Presumably, whoever sent the letter expected to communicate with her on more than one occasion. Grace slit open the envelope and took out the paper inside. It was just a single sheet. It was blank. She turned it over. The reverse side was equally empty. She placed it on her desk and ran her fingers along one of the two folds that had neatly reduced the A4 sheet to fit in the long rectangular envelope.

She picked the envelope out of her bin where she had unconsciously cast it. There was nothing unusual, and it was postmarked as coming from Chester. She teased the corner of the address label away. Sure enough, it seemed as she had thought, self-adhesive. The address looked computer-printed.

Why would someone send her a blank sheet of paper? Perhaps the wrong piece of paper was inadvertently used. But since they were so meticulous about the address, this seemed odd. Constable Dan Ford was soon asking her what he was to do that day, so Grace soon forgot about the puzzling blank sheet of paper. Little did she know that it would come back to haunt her in an even more disturbing way.

# 16

Grace was busy thumbing through an extensive list of contacts on her phone. An idea had been worming its way into her consciousness overnight. She wanted her plan to develop before she involved Drake. She brought up her contacts list on her computer and put in a search filter to show only members of The Met Police Service. The system seemed to be doing its best to frustrate her by claiming no knowledge of any Met Police officers when she knew darned well there were dozens. Eventually, her computer cooperated, and she found the name she was after. It was a colleague that she made friends with while working for The Met before coming to Chester. Grace and Drake had come to the Cheshire Police Service directly from The Met. She had worked there for about five years. Drake had been there for half a lifetime, so it seemed to her that he knew almost everybody. The reverse was nearer the truth. Everybody at The Met knew of Drake. She preferred to find someone who didn't know Drake well enough to call and check what she was doing. So, there was the name she needed. Julie Dobbins was a detective sergeant like her but had never worked with Drake. Grace and Julie often had a post-work drink to gossip about their superiors. Julie would be an ideal contact for her purposes.

'Hi Julie, this is Grace Hepple.'

'Grace! How nice to hear your voice. I miss our little chats and lunches. How are you?'

'I'm fine and enjoying Chester. It's just such a lovely place to live. I don't miss commuting, and I certainly don't miss the M25. Working with Drake here is great. By and large, he gives me much more responsibility.'

'Oh, great. I think I envy you. We've had tube strikes and all sorts here. Why the call?'

'I need a favour, Julie. In the case we are working on, we've visited somewhere that turns out to be just in your area.'

'OK.'

'It's an odd lot who are based at a place called Fairlawns. We've been to see them, and they are hugely secretive.'

'Tell me about it,' replied Julie. 'We know. They have been getting more and more in our sights. They seem well connected to several members of parliament who, it is thought, could cause trouble.'

'Oh, my goodness,' said Grace. 'What are you after them for?'

'Not sure I should talk about it. I'm not directly involved. I heard about it from a colleague, Sheila Richards.'

'Oh yes,' said Grace. 'I vaguely remember her.'

'I could ask her if she feels it appropriate to call you.'

'Great, thanks a lot,' said Grace. She sat wondering if she was doing the right thing. Should she consult Drake? No. She thought it was better to get the idea fully developed first. Her thoughts were interrupted by the arrival of Dan Ford, who looked disappointed.

'I asked Dave if there was anything he could do to enlarge the photo I took of the Fairlawns building. You know, the one that Luke said was for special friends. No good, I'm afraid it just goes all blotchy. We were already at the limit of the phone camera's resolution.'

Later that afternoon, Grace's phone had finally stopped ringing. She had tried to get rid of all her callers quickly in case Sheila Richards was trying to get through. It sounded as if she might help her plan come to fruition. She looked at her watch. It was time to go home. She shut down her laptop, and the phone rang again.

'Hello, is that Detective Sergeant Grace Hepple?'

'Yes, speaking.'

'I'm Detective Sergeant Sheila Richards of The Met. I gather you are interested in Fairlawns.'

'Yes. We've been down to see them, but they put the shutters up, and we suspect things are not what they might seem. I was wondering if you might be able to help.'

'We have a couple of witnesses who give us cause for concern about them, but it isn't clear here that we should go in yet.'

'OK,' said Grace, 'can we keep in touch?'

'Of course,' said Sheila Richards. 'I'm certain they are up to no good, and we suspect they are involved in major crime. However, we also think they are rather professional and will have all their tracks covered. I will check if there is anything I can send you. We sent in an undercover agent recently. I've not heard from him yet. Maybe he has something.'

'OK,' said Grace. 'Can I ask, have you heard of Peter and Mary in connection with Xi Dong?'

'Not as far I am aware,' said Sheila. 'What is the connection?'

'We suspect they are parents of a murder victim here in Chester, and her sister has told us of longstanding efforts by the parents to suck the two daughters into Xi Dong. The murder victim has stood out strongly against this. Her sister has suggested a motive for the murder could be the parents' fanaticism over this sect.'

'Oh, really?' said Sheila. 'Our suspicions are to do with fraud and almost modern slavery in terms of the way they retain their members. They begin by luring people in with online life coaching courses. These seem to attract vulnerable people who then get sucked into becoming residential members. Then they seem to lose all their money. I will consult. We may need to act. We have a couple of witnesses here who are both extremely keen to help. I'm sure if you came down, they would both willingly talk to you.'

'OK, thanks,' said Grace, 'we would be happy to do that.'

A couple of days later, Grace and Dan Ford decided to take the train to London. Grace was beginning to regret this a little as she had brought work to do on the journey, but Dan seemed keen to make small talk. However, they soon arrived at New Scotland Yard to meet with Sheila Richards.

'We are going to keep the identity of our witnesses confidential,' said Sheila. 'They are both nervous about Xi Dong discovering they are helping us. The place seems to have a real hold over them. I'll bring in our first witness, who we will address as Linda.'

Grace nodded, and Dan took out his notebook. Sheila placed four cups of coffee on the table in the middle of the interview room and went to fetch Linda. Introductions were made, and Linda gratefully gulped at her coffee. Grace thought she was nervous as she twisted her hands around in a circle. Sheila began.

'Linda, our two colleagues from Cheshire Police have their reasons for investigating Xi Dong, and I think they would find it helpful if you would repeat what you have told us.'

'Yes. I am happy to help as long as it is all kept confidential. Those people can be terrifying if you get on the wrong side of them. I dread how they would react if they knew I was talking to the police.'

'Of course,' said Grace quietly. 'We understand. This conversation will remain completely confidential.'

'Yes, please,' said Linda. 'I was a chef there for several months. It was a good job. Well paid, and to begin with, it felt like secure employment. Originally, I was hired to do lunch, which was a bit boring. It all started to get a bit odd when I did the first evening for them. I was aware they occasionally had a meeting followed by a communal meal. This meant that I was there until quite late. The first time it happened was when I went out to the bins. Suddenly, a van arrived at the building opposite. Delivery vans are never allowed beyond the gatehouse. I had to go with a porter on the buggy there to collect all our food deliveries. Anyway, this van caught my attention. Someone got out and came round the van. It could be male or female. It was wearing a hood. Well, not a hood, more of a balaclava. You could only see their eyes. They came around my side of the van and unlocked the side door. They then helped another person out. They had to help her. I think it was a woman, but she also had a hood over her head. This was a real hood. You know. I don't think she could see at all. The driver then took her into the building. He walked behind the hooded woman, pushing her in the small of her back. They disappeared inside, and I went back indoors.' Linda looked to see if Grace and Dan were paying attention, took a sip of her coffee and continued.

'Well, of course, I kept thinking about it. Was the person in the hood someone famous trying to conceal their identity? Or perhaps they were there against their will. They had never told me what that building was for, and I had never seen anyone go in or out. It kept going around in my head. Anyway, I was having a break one morning. I always go outside because I smoke. I know I shouldn't, but there it is. I just thought about it again and walked over there. It was all completely locked up, as far as I could see. There was no one around. So, I started taking a walk that way while I smoked. I noticed that a few of the windows had bars inside. First, I thought they must keep valuable stuff in there. Then, my mind started racing. What if it wasn't to keep people out but to keep someone inside? So, one day, I extended my walk a bit. I thought I'd go round the other side. You couldn't get there. It had a high fence stopping you from getting behind.' Linda stopped and started twisting her fingers again. Grace, Dan and Sheila waited quietly, and she continued.

'That was when it happened. I was returning from my walk when I saw Luke standing, blocking my way. He demanded to know what I was doing. I showed him my fag and said I was having a break. He turned quite unpleasant and told me not to go walking around. I was quite upset. I wanted to ask about the building, but I didn't dare. He asked me what I'd seen. I said I'd seen nothing. He told me to get back to work, so I did. Three days later, he came into the kitchen after lunch. He said they had decided to do things differently. They didn't need me anymore. He told me to take any belongings with me and not come back again. He said they'd pay my notice. So that's it. But it kept playing on my mind, and in the end, I rang the police and saw Sheila the same day.'

'Thank you,' said Grace. 'I'm sorry that we've had to trouble you again. Can you tell me, did you ever see anyone inside that building?'

'No, never. Perhaps I'm just being silly.'

'Not at all,' said Sheila. 'We are glad that you came to talk to us.'

After Sheila had seen Linda out, she came back into the interview room.

'I'm sorry, but our second witness phoned to say she's sick today. I'm not sure that's true, as she has been nervous. The gist of what she told us also mostly relates to the same building. At least from her description, we think it does. She was a cleaner. She was shown around the whole site by someone. The person never gave her a name. She thought she was told to clean that building once every couple of weeks. The first time she went in to clean, she found several doors were locked. On a later occasion, Luke found her in there and was nasty to her. He told her never to come into the building again. She left of her own volition. However, she was cleaning a room in the main residential building one day when its occupant came in. They started chatting, and then, he suddenly asked her if she could help him leave. He said he didn't know how to get out and wanted to return to his old home before it got sold. She obviously couldn't help him, but it all rattled her, and after running into Luke, she just got frightened and left without getting her pay that week.'

'So, a pattern is beginning to appear,' said Grace. 'It looks as if several possible crimes are being committed here.'

Drake returned from Birmingham. Grace had left him a message to say that, despite repeated calls, she still had no luck tracing either Felicity Glass or Elliott Chan. He decided on some action. Constable Steve Redvers was working at the main table.

'Steve,' said Drake. 'Get the Range Rover. We are going to Felicity Glass's house. If necessary, we will break in. Bring the big red key and door repair kit.'

Half an hour later, Drake and DC Steve Revers stood outside Felicity's house. It was a narrow affair on a long terrace. Steve rang the doorbell persistently, but there was no response.

'Let's see if we can get round to the rear,' said Drake.

Steve Redvers walked down the road and through a brick arch in the terrace wall. A light came on automatically as he walked down a passage. Sunlight was illuminating a garden beyond the end of the passageway. He reached the open air and found a paved path running across the back of the adjacent terrace houses, which he followed until he calculated that he was at the rear of Felicity's property. There was an unglazed, blue-painted door without a bell. He peered through the adjacent window into a tiny kitchen. He banged on the window and again on the door. There was still no response. By this time, Drake had arrived.

'OK,' said Drake. 'I've decided to go in. Because we are concerned about someone's safety, I'm not waiting for a search warrant. Go, get the key.' Drake peered into the kitchen and knocked on the door of the adjacent house. There was no answer. Steve Redvers returned with the large and heavy ram painted in bright red, earning it the nickname of the big red key. Steve Redvers took only one swing of the instrument to break the door open. He entered ahead of Drake. Drake looked at the rear door. It was bolted and locked. The lock was old and, by current standards, hardly secure.

'You take the upstairs,' said Drake to Steve Redvers, 'and I'll look around down here.' The kitchen which they had entered was small but neat and tidy. Drake opened some cupboard doors to discover everything stored in an orderly fashion. It occurred to him that he had a similar feeling in Imogen's flat. He reflected that Imogen and Felicity could probably live together harmoniously. Leaving the kitchen, he was at the bottom of a narrow and steep staircase. He had heard Steve Redvers climb up there. He passed a small cupboard containing mainly outdoor clothes and shoes, and then he was in a small living room, which was also tidy. The front door opened directly into this room from behind a short sofa. He checked the lock. The bolts were undone. The door lock was of the kind that anyone leaving could pull the door to lock it. Wherever they were, Drake thought, Elliott and Felicity seemed to have left in an orderly manner.

Drake's cursory exploration of the ground floor had just about concluded when he heard Steve Redvers coming down the bare wood staircase.

'Two bedrooms and a tiny bathroom,' he said. One seems occupied by Imogen Glass when she is here. There are art magazines by the bed. The other, slightly larger room at the front is, I assume, shared by Felicity and Elliott. There is a combination of male and female clothing in the drawers and wardrobe. Do you remember the testimony of the man from the riverside pub? In one drawer, I found this.' Steve brought his left hand rather dramatically around from behind his back. In his hand was a man's bright red knitted jumper.

'Oh, I say,' said Drake. 'I wonder.'

# 17

The following morning, Grace was less rushed. All seemed well in the investigation, with people appropriately busy. She allowed herself the luxury of a relaxed breakfast. That was until the post arrived. She picked up the small pile of envelopes that had landed on her doormat. She thumbed through, anxious to see if there might be any further incomprehensible posts. She had not admitted to herself that she was just a little worried. Then there it was. Another envelope with her address neatly printed on a small self-adhesive label. The label was perfectly centred on the envelope. There was exactly as much space below it as above. There were equal amounts of space to the left and right. She noted how the stamp was positioned precisely square to the boundary of the envelope. Whoever sent these messages was a careful and precise person, perhaps obsessional. She ran her paper-knife through the top of the envelope. Just as she had expected, it contained a single sheet of A4 paper neatly folded. She opened it. This time, it was not blank. In the centre, was what looked like the capital letter "I". At least, that is what she thought it was. It was in a large font using a rather florid typeface. Gently curving lines looped around the letter.

Grace sat looking at the sheet of paper. What was going on? Someone was trying to communicate with her in a deliberately cryptic way. It crossed her mind that this might be a rather clever, attention-grabbing way of advertising. She was always getting junk mail. She wished that it was just junk. The alternative was not too attractive. She worried that someone wishing her harm might be playing nasty tricks on her. Somehow, a sense of anxiety had crept up on her. Grace carefully put on a pair of evidence gloves. She folded the piece of paper and returned it to its envelope. She put that into a clear evidence bag. It was time to see if technician Dave and his forensics colleagues could yield any information.

Dave took the material from Grace down to the lab. Grace grabbed a cup of coffee and sat to think. If this was a stalker, who could it be? Her mind traced back to find any characters she had been responsible for putting away who might now be released. As she mentally roamed back over the years, her brain landed on Jason Mercer. He was a financial expert who had repeatedly defrauded vulnerable women. He had a distinctly nasty personality, she thought. Even though there was no record of him stalking, she could imagine him holding a grudge. She checked the files on her computer. First, the date of conviction, then the sentence and finally, the reduction for good behaviour. He would easily have managed to imitate that! Yes, it all added up. She dug out what pictures she had of him, but he was a master of disguise, so they were probably of little help in terms of what he looked like now. She wondered what to do. Should she open a case? Should she involve Drake? It seemed unfair to worry him with such a trivial matter. Right now, he had other things to attend to. Could she put one of the constables on it to chase things up? Perhaps Dan Ford. He seemed a sympathetic person and could be trusted. On the other hand, should she shake the whole thing off and stop worrying?

Later that day, Grace had tired of waiting for the forensic results and was nestling down in her favourite armchair in front of the television. The news seemed full of events and issues she couldn't relate to, given her currently unsettled mind, when her mobile phone rang. She instinctively picked it up and answered the call. There was only silence. Grace hurriedly put the phone down. Its display told her that the caller's information was withheld. Of course, this was just another nuisance call. Some remote call from overseas trying to sell her something or, more likely, some scam. Or was it? Could the sender of the weird letters have now taken to making calls? Her phone issued the familiar ping to announce the arrival of an email. She opened it. The message was terse and clear. "I'm everywhere" were the only words in the email. The first letter was again heavily decorated. The sender was named "GuessWho." She saved it in a folder for future attention. Perhaps Dave would be able to track the sender.

Then her doorbell rang, and Grace went to answer it. She was shaking a little. She suddenly felt rather alone and vulnerable. This was not a feeling she was used to. The hallway was in darkness save for a small pool of light from a streetlight coming through the small window in the door. There on the mat, as if in a theatrical spotlight, was a single envelope with the address side face down. She instinctively picked it up and turned it over. There was the address label and a stamp, but it had not been franked. It suddenly dawned on her that it had been delivered by hand. Her hand went to the door handle, and then she froze. It might be better not to open the door. If her stalker was there, she had no defence or security. She dashed into her living room with a bay window overlooking the front of the house containing her apartment. There was no one there. She hurriedly pulled the curtains and groped over to her chair in the darkness.

Grace slumped into the chair. She was shaking and on the verge of tears. She soon felt ashamed of herself. She should be tough enough to deal with this. We can't have police officers breaking into tears, she thought. She pulled herself together long enough to take the envelope to the kitchen and slit it open. She pulled out the single sheet of paper. There were three words. There could now be no doubt that the previous single letter was the beginning of a message. This latest one read, "I am watching."

Grace was aware of the considerable number of victims of stalking who were eventually murdered by their pursuers. She had tried to put this thought out of her mind, but it stubbornly kept returning. She reminded herself that in most of these cases, the stalker made no secret of his activities. She tried to take comfort in the fact that she did not know who it was. Her phone rang again, and she turned it over hesitatingly. She visibly slumped in relief. The display said the caller was Dave, the technician.

'Oh, hi, Dave.'

'Bad news, I'm afraid,' he said. We have tried every trick in the box. We can only detect your fingerprints. We tried DNA but had no luck again. Whoever is sending these letters knows what to do. They have taken great care to remain anonymous.'

Grace sighed. She feebly thanked Dave. Momentarily, she wondered whether to tell him about the phone calls but then mentioned the email.

'Forward it to me,' said Dave. 'I'll see what I can do.'

'Thanks,' said Grace, her voice lowering into no more than a whisper.

'Are you OK?' asked Dave.

'Yes, thanks,' replied Grace more confidently. 'I'm trying not to let it get to me.'

'Should I ask the desk sergeant to get a constable outside your door?'

'Oh, no,' said Grace. 'Don't worry. I'll be fine.'

Grace sat as still as a statue. She tried to think through the situation. Somehow, she had failed to put the light on, and the room seemed darker than she had ever known. Every sound was amplified as if some mystic being had turned up the volume of the world. A car door slammed in the road outside. A baby cried. A gate shut. Someone shouted to a friend to bring some unknown item. Her stalker would have a real problem not making some giveaway noise. Grace began to calm down outwardly, but inside, she was getting more tense. She was listening to these sounds and trying to place them. It just increased her stress levels. She was like a taught wire just short of its breaking point.

This would not do. Grace got up, put the light on and grabbed the TV remote. She selected the news and fell back into her chair to watch. It was about disasters and wars. She turned it off.

Sometime later, Grace woke up with a jump, frightened by her violence. She looked at her watch. It was already the middle of the night. She had never fallen asleep in her armchair before. She would go to bed, and tomorrow, she would take charge of the situation. She needed to get the actual release date of Jason Mercer. The prison should have his home address. She could check with Dave about the email. Was there some clever piece of software that could help?

The following morning, Grace breathed deeply as she looked at the mail. There was no envelope. She checked her email. Nothing from the mysterious poster. She hadn't missed any calls. Was he backing off? She walked round to the rear of the building where her car was parked and set off for the station. Gradually, the traffic got heavier. Then, she noticed the car behind. It was a grey saloon. He seemed to be driving annoyingly close. She took the next left turn and checked in her mirror. He was still there. Now, she was on a more major road; she moved into the outside lane to filter right at the next junction. He followed her again. Each time she took a turn, he followed her. She wondered about making a sudden turn to shake him off. Then, after negotiating a tricky junction, she looked in her mirror again. He had taken the turning to the left. Grace let out a sigh of relief.

Dave was already waiting for Grace to arrive.

'I'm sorry,' he said, 'that I didn't call you last night, but I got the feeling you would prefer not to have your phone ringing.' Grace nodded. 'I'm afraid I've had no luck with the email. He is probably using an account with a VPN.'

'What's VPN?' asked Grace.

'Oh, sorry. It's a Virtual Private Network. It's a clever piece of software that disguises the data an Internet transaction normally gives about its origins. Usually, we can pin down the rough location of an ordinary email. This is deliberately concealed here. We can't tell where the source is located.'

'How does it do that?' asked Grace.

'It sends all your communications through a remote server. It is this server that communicates with the person you are emailing. It also disguises who you are when surfing on the Internet.'

'Clever stuff.'

'Yes indeed. Again, it suggests this guy knows what he is doing and how to cover his tracks.'

Grace's heart sank. Inwardly, she had suspected something like this. Her stalker was a real professional. She was in for some hard times. Grace nervously checked her email. A message told her that, just as she suspected, Jason Mercer had been released about two weeks ago. The only address they could supply was in Manchester. Would he travel over to Chester to stalk her? Probably, she thought, he seemed determined. This only served to make Grace more anxious. On reflection, she was inclined to believe that he was on a mission. She was the target. If so, what was he going to do next? She checked with the police in Manchester, and they agreed to go to his address and check up on him. Things were moving, but Grace had never felt so helpless.

Drake arrived, and as usual, things started to happen. Grace temporarily forgot her troubles.

'We still don't know what happened to Imogen in her final days,' he groaned. 'We need to do something to remedy that.'

'Why don't I put out a press release with a call for information?' said Grace.

'Good idea,' said Drake. 'Get on with that.'

'I'll call the local paper and get onto regional television,' said Grace. 'I'll ask anyone who saw Imogen in the week before we found her body to contact us. I'll give them an email address and a phone number.'

'Excellent,' said Drake. Getting Drake's approval made Grace start to feel better about things. If only she could generate new information, she might tell Drake about her stalker. She did not know what would happen next.

# 18

Constable Steve Redvers arrived at the police station late.

'My apologies,' he said to Grace, 'but I came via the location on Hoole Road. There was a car parked in the driveway of the house next door to our location. There was no answer when we did the sweep up and down the road. It looks like they might be there now. Would you like me to go out and see if they have anything to tell us?'

'Excellent,' said Grace. 'I must go out that way this morning, so I'll call on them.'

'It's a Mr and Mrs Hale,' said Steve, a little disappointed.


Grace pulled up in front of the house where Imogen Glass had her studio. There was a grand-looking car in the driveway next door. She walked past the car and rang the doorbell. A man of medium height and receding hair soon opened the door. He was carefully but conservatively dressed and carried an air of efficiency. Grace guessed he might make a good witness. She held out her ID.

'Good morning,' she said. 'We are investigating the death of Imogen Glass, who used the studio next door. Could I come in and ask you a few questions?'

'Yes, of course. I'm Frank Hale, and my wife is Meg.' He said, gesturing to a figure arriving along the hallway.

'This is Detective Sergeant Grace Hepple.' Frank read the ID card carefully to Meg. 'She would like to talk to us about the awful affair next door.'

'Would you like a cup of tea?' asked Meg.

'That would be lovely,' replied Grace. Meg showed her into the living room. It overlooked a beautifully kept lawn surrounded by neatly trimmed bushes. All along one wall were glass cases displaying items made from silver. Grace assumed that Frank was a collector, and Meg tolerated his obsession.

'We can go from here into our new kitchen,' said Meg. 'Come and I'll show you.' She left the living room to go into an open-plan dining room and kitchen. 'This is my treasure,' she said. Grace walked around admiring the shiny cabinets with marble worktops.

'Ah,' said Grace. I see the large window looks to the side.'

'Yes,' said Meg. 'So, we get a view of the lovely painter's studio next door.'

'Do you ever see anything of Imogen or Philippa?' asked Grace.

'Yes, especially because Imogen has a little terrace there just outside where her studio is. She often sits there. Sometimes, she has a cup of tea, and sometimes, she sits sketching. We say "hello" quite a lot. We don't see Philippa so much, and usually, then, it was because she was with Imogen. Sometimes that's a bit embarrassing when they kiss and cuddle.' Meg gave a disdainful look and sat silently looking at the floor.'

'We don't understand all that stuff,' said Frank, 'do we, Meg? We're a bit old-fashioned, maybe. They were an odd pair in a way. They often seemed to argue, and then usually Philippa would stomp off in a temper.'

'But it was never as bad as that night,' said Meg. 'Philippa was shouting at the top of her voice, and we thought we heard them scuffling. I didn't want to look. There was a terrible scream, and when I looked again, Philippa had disappeared.'

'Are you sure that the people you heard on this occasion were Imogen Glass and Philippa Crehan?' asked Grace.

'Oh yes, certain, aren't we, Frank?' said Meg. Frank nodded his agreement.

'Yes, we can see anyway,' said Frank. 'That fence is of slatted timber, and you can easily spot someone you know looking through the gaps.'

'We never saw Imogen again,' said Meg, and she let out a little sob. 'She was such a lovely person. She always had time to chat. She even invited me in to see her latest painting. It wasn't finished. At least, I don't think so. I've never seen anything like her paintings. They had an oriental look to them, didn't they, Frank.'

'Yes. She told us about her time in China and how she'd been brought up there.'

'I don't think it was China, Frank,' said Meg. 'I think it was Hong Kong.'

'Well, it's the same thing now,' said Frank. 'Hong Kong is just a part of China now, isn't it.' He paused. Meg just nodded her head in silence and shrugged her shoulders.

'So,' said Grace. 'Can you tell me when this awful argument was?'

'It was just before we went away on holiday,' said Frank. 'We were away for three weeks, and we came back yesterday. We didn't know anything about it, but our other neighbour who looks after our garden told us that the police were here for several days, and they say Imogen was murdered.'

'Yes,' said Meg. 'Philippa was sometimes a little violent in their arguments. So, we wondered if she hit Imogen too hard or something. I can't believe she would have meant to kill her. That would be dreadful. Is that what happened?'

'We don't yet know how Imogen died. I'm afraid,' said Grace. 'Tell me, did you ever see anybody else there?'

'No,' said Frank. 'It was a private space that Imogen valued, I think.'

'Well, there was her sister,' Meg interrupted.

'Yes. Of course, her sister came occasionally,' grunted Frank.

'That is Felicity, isn't it?' said Grace.

'Yes, that's right, Felicity. I think we have only met her a couple of times. Oh, she is so like her sister. Lovely, both of them.'

'Thanks a lot for your help,' said Grace. 'If you remember anything else to help us with our enquiries, just call me here.' Grace handed over a card as she stood up.

Grace returned to the station anxious to tell Drake about her interview with the Hales next door to Imogen and Philippa's house.

'That's all interesting,' said Drake. 'So, Philippa and Imogen had arguments and one serious one only a few days before she was found in the river Dee. I wonder what the disagreement was about.'

'Surely we know that, or we could at least have a good guess,' said Grace. 'They seem to have had a tempestuous relationship.'

'Lovers' tiffs maybe,' grunted Drake.

'Yes, but this one was the mother of them all. We know Imogen was breaking up with Philippa after trying to return to her boyfriend, Elliott Chan. What's more, she was reverting to a heterosexual relationship. From what we have heard about Philippa Crehan, she might find that insulting.'

'Yes, we need to have a chat with Philippa Crehan. This time, she will need to be more helpful. See if you can get her to come in tomorrow morning.'

The following day, Grace told Drake that Philippa Crehan had arrived.

'Well,' he said, 'we'll just leave her to stew for a while. Send a cup of tea or coffee in.'

'Already done,' said Grace, who could see that Drake was busy on his beloved Times crossword. In due course, Drake looked up.

'Right,' he said, struggling to get up from his favourite chair. 'Let's go and see her.'

'Good morning, Mrs Crehan,' said Drake as the two police officers entered the interview room where Philippa Crehan was waiting with a cup of tea.

'It's Miss Crehan, actually, and I've been sitting here wasting my time,' she said.

'I'm sorry,' said Drake, 'as you can imagine, we are rather busy on this case. We need to hear more about your relationship with Imogen Glass.'

'I was her landlady. She was my tenant,' replied Philippa abruptly. Drake gave Grace a knowing look that meant she should take over.

'Is it possible that there was more than that to your relationship?' asked Grace.

'I don't talk about private matters,' snapped Philippa Crehan.

'I understand your principle,' said Grace, 'but this is not a normal conversation. This is an interview in connection with a serious crime. You are required to help the police as appropriate.'

'What do you want to know?'

'How did you first meet?'

'I advertised for a tenant, and she applied. She did some building work to make the place suitable as a studio.'

'I understand,' said Drake, 'but we have heard that you formed a more personal close relationship.'

'Why is this relevant?'

'Obviously, the relationships between a person who is murdered and the people she knew are essential to understanding what may have happened. Getting ideas about motives is an essential part of our work.' Drake sat silently, waiting for a further response from Philippa. None came. She sat staring at the table in front of her.

'Perhaps I can help a little,' said Drake. 'Let me put it bluntly. We understand you became lovers.'

'If so, why would that matter?'

'We have witnesses to a raging argument between you not long before Imogen Glass was found dead in the river Dee.'

'Who's told you that then?' demanded Philippa. 'I suppose it's those interfering nosy busybodies next door?'

'So, you accept you had such an argument?' demanded Drake firmly.

'We might have done. I can't remember.'

'So, perhaps, you had frequent arguments that didn't register in your memory.'

'I didn't say that.'

'Imogen had decided not to continue your relationship, hadn't she?'

'Who said that?'

'We have a witness who would testify to that effect. It is true, is it not?'

'Yes, we broke up. It was a mutual agreement.'

'I put it to you that this is not true. Imogen had decided to try to renovate her relationship with Elliott Chan. She told you this, and you flew into a rage.'

'Maybe.'

'In fact, you lost your temper. Perhaps you hit her with some hard object. Maybe you hadn't decided to kill her. It was an accident. Am I right?'

'No.'

'You mean it wasn't an accident then,' demanded Drake. 'What did happen, Miss Crehan?'

'We argued, that's all.'

'We now know that your fingerprints have been identified in Imogen's van. Specifically on the steering wheel. You killed her, perhaps accidentally and drove her body to dump it in the Dee.'

'No. This is all invention. None of that happened.'

'Why were your fingerprints on the steering wheel?'

'It is widely known that Imogen disliked driving. When we went somewhere together, I would drive. That's all. I don't want to listen to this anymore. I want to go home.'

'Very well,' said Drake. 'You are entirely free to leave. We will terminate this interview.'


'What do you make of that?' asked Drake when Grace returned after seeing Philippa Crehan out.

'She's an angry young woman,' replied Grace, 'but I don't think she did it. I may be wrong.'

'You may be right,' said Drake. 'I want to search her house. If she is guilty, there may be something that gives her away. Get a search warrant for tomorrow if you can.'

# 19

Drake sat in the back of the Range Rover parked outside the house next to Philippa's belonging to the Hales. Grace was in the driving seat with the search warrant at the ready. She expected that Philippa Crehan would be reluctant to have her house taken apart. Behind the Range Rover was a large people carrier containing all the constables ready to perform the search. In truth, nobody was exactly sure what they were looking for. Drake had delivered a talk about this in the police station before they left. It might be anything that somehow linked Philippa to the murder of Imogen Glass. It could be a calendar or diary. It might be a credit card slip for fuel on the day they had seen the white van in the videos.

'Is everyone ready?' demanded Drake.

'I think so,' replied Grace. 'I'll check with the van.' She opened her intercom and spoke to the group leader waiting behind. 'Everyone is ready,' she said.

'Right, let's go,' said Drake. Grace spoke into the intercom. 'Go go.'

Drake watched his party leave their vehicle and march down the drive to the Crehan house. Two constables were dispatched around the side of the house to guard the rear door. Others waited at the front door until Grace arrived. One constable rang the doorbell repeatedly, and another hammered on the door. Drake followed in his usual stumbling walk and stood back, waiting. There was no response.

'She must have gone early this morning,' said Drake.

'I wonder if she has done a runner,' said Grace.

Another session of bell ringing and door banging brought no result.

'Has someone got the big red key?' demanded Drake. A constable stepped forward, carrying the heavy door ram and stood waiting to be instructed to break the door down when suddenly it opened. Constable Redvers appeared in the doorway.

'The back door was unlocked,' he said, 'So, we came through the kitchen and hallway. You can unlock this front door by hand from the inside without the key. I'm afraid we are too late. Philippa Crehan is lying face down on the floor in the hall. I briefly checked. There are no vital signs. She appears to be dead.'

'OK, everybody, we still need to do our search.' said Grace as she dispatched pairs of constables to various parts of the house. 'Let's first check out that no one is here. If they are, then bring them down here.'

Drake entered the open doorway and followed Grace into the hall. He bent down onto the floor next to Philippa Crehan's body. It was lying front down with the head turned awkwardly sideways to the right. The face showed an expression of terror. There were two pools of blood. A smaller one on the left next to the neck and head and a much larger one to the right opposite the upper part of the torso.

'She appears to have been shot,' said Drake grimly as he staggered back to his feet and eventually his full height. 'Given the location of the bullet holes, it's most unlikely to be suicide. This is now a crime scene. Please conduct our search of the house, taking care to disturb things as little as possible.' He walked through the open doorway into the rear room. It was used for dining with a table to seat six in the centre. Three drawers and two doors of the sideboard were all pulled fully open. The bottom drawer was half hanging off its runners. Constables started to arrive with similar stories suggesting the whole house had been ransacked. One had inspected the garage. It had its door open, with everything thrown around. One reported more detail about the downstairs back room.

'There is a desk in the downstairs back room. It is set up for working on a computer. There are loads of devices like printers and screens, but their cables are left unconnected and where you would expect a computer is just open space. It looks like they took it.'

'This looks like a multiple crime,' grunted Drake. 'Someone or people were looking for something in a hurry. The missing computer may have been what they wanted. If so, why open every cupboard and set of drawers? The computer would have been obvious. OK, Grace, tell everyone to continue as planned. We will leave this hallway untouched.'

'Yes,' said Grace. 'Already done, but what's that on the floor by your right foot?'

Drake looked down to see a small piece of paper sticking out from under the right leg of the body. He stepped back so Grace could pick it up. She turned it over and passed it to Drake.

'Looks like a photo of Philippa Crehan,' said Grace. Look, there's something scribbled on the back. I think it might be Chinese writing.'

'Yes, definitely,' said Drake smugly. He took a photo of the Chinese Characters and started to write an email on his much-prized new iPhone. 'I've sent it to that Caruthers chap at The Met. He is a specialist in Chinese culture.' Drake looked around, and Grace thought he was almost expecting applause for his advanced use of technology. Drake tapped away on his phone again.

'Hello, is that Professor Cooper? Good, I'm glad I've caught you. We have another body for you.'

Various constables continued to appear, reporting cupboards open and shelves empty. It seemed the place had been thoroughly searched, leaving things carelessly scattered around. Drake put his phone in his pocket and muttered partly to himself but loud enough for Grace to hear. 'Was someone looking for something and got disturbed by our victim? Or was the assailant sent to murder her guided by the photo? Perhaps they dropped this and then searched the house. If so, what were they looking for?'

'Jewels perhaps,' suggested Grace.

'Possibly, possibly,' said Drake, in his characteristically doubtful manner. 'I wonder if this has anything to do with the murder of Imogen Glass.'

'In what way?' asked Grace.

'I don't know yet,' replied Drake, 'but our theory that Philippa Crehan murdered Imogen is probably less likely now. One possibility is that the same person is responsible for both deaths, but why?' A beeping sound seemed to come from somewhere in Drake's clothing. He started patting himself all over and finally discovered his new iPhone. He tapped away on it for a few seconds. "I'm getting the hang of this thing now,' he said proudly. 'Ah, it's Caruthers of the Met. He says it's a name which he thinks is Philip Crayon.' Drake and Grace laughed. 'It's been handed to someone who is Chinese to be sure of identifying the right person. If this is right, it could be a contract job.'

Professor Cooper stood up from his preliminary examination. 'She has not been dead long. I would guess maybe up to a few days.' He stretched up and groaned. 'My back is not as good as it once was.' The wounds suggest the bullet entry was from the rear, so she was probably trying to escape and was shot in the back. She probably died almost instantly. There is likely to be damage to the brain and heart. I will only be able to confirm that after the post-mortem.

'Thanks, Prof,' said Drake. 'Grace, please arrange a door-to-door check to see if anyone saw or heard anything that might help us.'

Two days later, the team were assembled in the case room when the phone rang. It was the pathologist, Professor Cooper. Grace put the phone on speaker.

'This latest case is comparatively simple and straightforward,' he said. 'I can cover it all in this phone call unless you need to come in and view the body. She was shot three times. One shot entered her back and passed through the heart. The other two shots entered her head from the rear. One smashed the skull, passed through the right cerebral cortex and lodged in the front of the skull; the second passed through the upper neck and the lower brain, which we call the cerebellum. The first shot caused substantial damage to the heart, resulting in considerable blood loss. This is evidenced at the scene of the crime. She would not be able to survive this injury. The shot passing through the cerebellum damaged that lower brain element and the hypothalamus. Again, she would not be able to survive this injury. I am drawn to the suspicion that this shooting was done with the intent to kill. You might consider perhaps that the assailant was an expert. He, or she, could not have selected more lethal locations.' Professor Cooper paused to see if there were any questions. His audience sat in silence, so he continued.

'I have examined the bullet and case found at the crime scene. I was suspicious, so I consulted with your forensic scientist and an expert in firearms I know in The Met. It is not a bullet that we can identify so far. I will consult some more experts who might be able to help. For the time being, we know for certain she was shot. As for the time of death, I would estimate about three days before I examined her. Could easily be a day either way, though.'

'Thank you, Prof,' said Drake. He put the phone down and turned to the meeting. 'Why was she shot so deliberately?'

'Perhaps they wanted to kill her to stop her saying something?' asked Grace.

'Possible,' said Drake, 'but why ransack the whole house? They surely killed her so they could search the property?'

'If so, it seems likely that it was something of considerable value that the intruder wanted,' said Grace.

'Value perhaps because of the possible information it contained,' added Drake. 'Of course, it is also possible that the two murders have no connection. We must keep an open mind. What seems slightly puzzling is the extent of their search. Every kind of cupboard, storage, and every type of room has been searched.'

'Perhaps the intruders didn't know what they were looking for,' said Grace.

'Perhaps they expected what they were looking for to be hidden,' said Drake.

Grace got home late that evening. One of the familiar white envelopes was on the mat inside the door. She had almost forgotten about her annoying stalker. She held the envelope in both hands for a moment. She wondered if she should play his game by opening it. She thought it might be better to throw them away unopened. No, that would destroy possible evidence. She just had to open it and read it. The message was typed in the usual way, centrally spaced and in giant characters using a flowery font. It read, "I know when you're alone. Should I come and visit?"

Grace froze. A sense of chill descended over her. Was he the murderer? Was this a hint that she might be next? For a moment, she admired the wretched man. He was clever enough to make her repeatedly think about what he was saying. She had to deal with this now. She would tell Drake all about it in the morning. She collected all the alarming messages and put them in her bag for tomorrow. She was feeling good about herself. The silly tendency to feel like a vulnerable woman had passed and she was dealing professionally with the whole business. She could talk to Drake on a level basis without feeling like the silly woman archetype that these stalkers hoped to promote. She was glad now that Drake had been away when it started. She had become fascinated by the puzzle being presented. Who could it be, or was it someone she had no contact with?

# 20

Grace sat at the table in the centre of the case room with all three letters from her stalker. Drake admired Grace's calm and professional approach. Perhaps he was guilty of assuming she would be frightened. He made a mental note that she was made of sterner stuff than he had thought. Now, she had been tested. It would not be long before she might become eligible for consideration at the inspector level. For now, he must concentrate on this new puzzle. He was inclined at first to think the murders and this game of stalking might well be the evil work of the same individual. How else could the stalker know about both murders? At the least, maybe someone was watching the investigation.

'Right, Grace,' he said. 'The first thing we must do in a case like this is to separate you from the investigation. We are talking about something that has the appearance of being rather personal. For that reason, you cannot pursue the case. I have been increasingly impressed by Steve Redvers. I will put him on it, and you should not discuss it with him, at least for now. He will work directly with me. I will brief him. We must keep this investigation confidential. The fewer the people involved, the less likely our work will leak to the stalker. We need to keep him isolated. Please produce a complete list of all the people you know, mainly people who are in your life in some way, work colleagues, friends, and relations. Create a computer file and email it to me and Steve. Is there anything more you can tell me that might help with our investigation?'

'You think it might be someone I know?' asked Grace.

'I gather from colleagues who have dealt with cases like this that it is likely and a good place to start. Does anyone you know come to mind as a possibility?'

'Yes, there's Jason Mercer,' said Grace.

'I remember that name,' said Drake. 'Who is he?'

'It was that financial fraud case we did at The Met. He was used to defrauding vulnerable women. He had stolen the life savings of several women. He's a nasty man. I'm not sure if you knew, but he kept trying to bribe me. Of course, I took no notice. But when bribing wasn't working, he tried being nasty. He was quite threatening on several occasions about coming after me in due course. Thankfully, I had completely forgotten about him, but now all those memories keep flooding back.'

'That must be a good many years ago, Grace.'

'Well, exactly. I searched the database and discovered he had recently been released. They have an address in Manchester for him on their release notes.'

'OK, I'll get Steve to check him out as soon as he can,' said Drake. 'As I remember, he had several addresses and as many names and aliases. Perhaps he's carried on where he left off. Add past felons like him to that list I asked for. Is there anything else?'

'Not really,' said Grace. 'Except perhaps that a couple of times early on, I felt someone was following me. I carried out our training on being followed and could not get any confirming evidence. I have since stopped getting that feeling. Of course, it could easily mean he has become a better stalker.'

Drake grunted an acknowledgement and went to his chair with Grace's letters and The Times. For a few minutes, his mind ranged around more or less randomly. He liked that early in a case. It avoided shutting down too many possible lines of enquiry too soon. He turned his newspaper over to the crossword only to discover that he had yet to start it that day. He only got as far as five across when he saw Grace standing before him with two cups of coffee. She put one down on his side table.

'There's another development I need to update you about,' she said. 'I contacted an old friend from The Met, Julie Dobbins, to see if she knew anything about Fairlawns. It lies just inside The Met area. They are indeed investigating Fairlawns. She put me in touch with Detective Sergeant Sheila Richards. A couple of witnesses are reporting behaviour there that suggests they are holding some people against their will. One witness recalls an inmate asking for help to get out, and the other saw what seems to be a person being imprisoned.'

'That's good work, Grace,' said Drake. 'I hadn't appreciated The Met area reaching out that far. We must leave any action to them but make sure they know why we are interested.'

'Yes,' replied Grace. 'I've already done that. I'm waiting to hear if they have taken any action.'

'Excellent,' said Drake. 'We mustn't tread on their territory.'

Grace was working on the new Philippa Crehan murder case. She had gone down to the evidence store when her phone rang.

'Detective Sergeant Grace Hepple.'

'Hi, Grace. It's Sheila Richards from The Met here. I need to update you on things in connection with Fairlawns. We went in early morning yesterday. Everyone was in bed, so it was easy to control the situation. We had a huge presence because we thought there might be around fifty inmates.'

'I'm not surprised by what we saw,' said Grace.

'In fact, we found 48 members and two residential maids. By keeping inmates in their rooms, we could speak briefly to them all. I'm just looking up my notes. Yes, a dozen said they were happy to stay, and most of those twelve were almost obsessed with the place. However, 16 said they wanted to leave, and the other 20 refused to speak to us. Two had tried to leave by walking out at night. They were intercepted at the gate and returned to their rooms. As they openly said, they had no idea what they would do if they got out. They would have lost everything. Those who spoke to us admitted they had handed over all their money and credit cards. They had even handed over their phones as part of some so-called corporate regulations. A couple had requested their money back. They had been told it would take a while, as all the money was in accounts in China. They heard no more.'

'It's astonishing how gullible some people can be,' said Grace.

'Yes, it's amazing how easy it can be to keep people captive,' said Sheila. 'There were two maids who looked after the residential buildings. They lived in. Otherwise, we think we have missed something. Many inmates spoke about three short and stocky Chinese males who never spoke English. They seem to be enforcers of one kind or another. A couple of much more critical inmates had, on several occasions, tried to explore more of the estate. They were curious about the separate building. They were apprehended by one or more of these guys. They made it clear by grunting and shoving them that they should return to their rooms. Several inmates reported bad experiences with them and were intimidated. There are reports from several of our officers of a couple of people disappearing down the road to the entrance gate. Whether they were inmates or employees, we don't know. I've got the local police to comb the area for suspicious characters.'

'Sounds as if you did pretty well then,' said Grace.

'Yep. We were quite pleased with the operation. Of course, I haven't mentioned the main character yet. We have arrested Luke. We still don't know his actual name, but we have a safe in his office to break open, and we hope to find credit cards and other forms of ID. He said he was expecting us. I think that may be a result of your earlier visit. I'm not sure he appreciates who you are and has confused us all in his mind. Whether it's because of that, I don't know. But there is virtually no documentation around, and the only computer is password-locked, so we have handed it over to our technical people to see if they can do anything. Luke isn't cooperating but has come out with that old line about having friends in high places. He may be right. The local member of parliament has already been on to me. He told me how wonderful the place is and how it needs protecting, not invading.'

'Oh dear, not helpful. Have you found a couple known in Xi Dong as Peter and Mary? We believe they are called William and Dorothy Glass. They are the parents of our murder victim.'

'I don't recall any of those names. I am thumbing through the list to check. No, I am correct. We found no people using either set of names.'

'Bother,' said Grace. 'We were hopeful we might find them at Fairlawns. We want to question them about the murder of their daughter, Imogen Glass.'

'Sorry to disappoint you,' said Sheila. 'Now, next, we come to the inmates of that locked building. There is one male and one female. The male seemed to be extremely unwell. He has been taken to the hospital. We think he is probably an inmate. The female is probably in her late thirties or forties. She refuses to give her identity, and she has nothing on her. She seems extremely nervous. I'm not sure what they might have done or said to her. She said she had been incarcerated and was also not too well. We have also taken her to hospital. Our impression is that neither of them had been fed for some time. I will email you a photograph just in case you might be able to help us with their identity. The only thing we found on Luke was a small scrap of paper with an undecipherable note scribbled on it. The writing is hard to read, and Luke refuses to explain it. He was surprised to hear it was discovered in a trouser pocket. I will email a picture of it. Now I need to get back to helping to interview him.'

'OK, thanks for all this and for taking the time to call me,' said Grace.

Drake was busy with some administration, causing him to groan and moan, telling everyone who would listen that he didn't join the police to do all this. Grace dashed into the case room. She rushed over to her computer and began tapping away excitedly. Suddenly, she cried out to the whole room to come over and look at her computer screen.

'Look,' she said as Drake hobbled across the room, grateful to find an excuse to leave his administration behind.

'It looks like a picture of Imogen's sister Felicity that we have been concerned about,' said Drake.

'I'm sure it's Felicity Glass,' said Grace.

'Yes, but she looks unhappy,' said Drake. She looks like she wasn't very keen on the photograph being taken.'

'That's because she was being held captive at Fairlawns,' said Grace.

'Well, I never,' said Drake.

'It's come from Sheila Richards at The Met,' said Grace. 'They've raided Fairlawns. They sent me this picture because she won't talk to them, and they don't know who she is.'

'I guess she is paranoic about the Chinese,' said Drake. 'Her now boyfriend Elliott Chan has probably made that worse. So, some strangers locked her up. Then, other strangers let her out and questioned her. You wouldn't be surprised if she clammed up. You'd better let Sheila Richards know and tell her that, as far as we know, Felicity is an innocent victim. I can only assume some of the Xi Dong people have kidnapped her. If necessary, we can arrange to collect her. She may not want to return to her home, so tell her we will find her a safe place to stay for the time being.'

'OK,' said Grace. 'One more thing first. Look, this scrap of paper was found in Luke's pocket. He won't tell them what it means. It's hard to read, but I think it says "PM Grosvenor," whatever that means.'

'Surely not,' grunted Drake. 'The only Grosvenor I know is our favourite local hotel.'

'Oh yes,' said Grace. 'So, Luke had a meeting in the afternoon one day at the hotel.'

'Possibly, possibly,' said Drake in that drawl he uses to indicate that he doesn't think so. 'What if PM stands for Peter and Mary?'

'Wow,' said Grace, 'do you think so?' The room went quiet as they all took this in and wondered, each forming their own opinion.

'Why don't we get Dan to call the hotel and see if they have had a couple of residents called Glass or Peter and Mary?' Dan got busy while the others sat looking at Grace's computer screen. It wasn't long before Dan came back across the room.

'You were right, Sir,' he said. 'They were called Peter and Mary with family names Xi Dong. The hotel remembered them because they seemed to have Chinese names but did not look Chinese.'

'Are they still there?' asked Drake.

'No, they had booked in to stay longer but left yesterday saying something had come up that they needed their attention back home. They had a taxi booked to take them to Manchester Airport Terminal 2. They left early in the morning without having breakfast.'

'When did they arrive?' demanded Drake.

'Oh, look said Dan, checking his notes, 'they arrived a week before Imogen was found dead.'

'Check with airlines to see if you can find flights to and from airports in Texas, USA that had those particular passengers,' said Drake. 'So, this mysterious couple have been dogging us all the through this enquiry. Now we discover that they were in Chester when Imogen was murdered.'

'Not only that,' said Grace, but they were staying at the Grosvenor Hotel when we took a room there as a safe place to interview Felicity.'

'Oops,' said Dan.

'How ironic,' groaned Drake.


Several hours later, everyone was getting ready to go home when Dan suddenly let out a whoop followed by a curse.

'What have you got, Dan?' asked Grace.

'OK, I searched for flights from the States to Manchester. After all, if they were coming to Chester, that would be their best point of arrival rather than Heath Row.'

'So?' demanded Drake.

'Bingo,' said Dan. 'Singapore Airlines flies from Houston to Manchester most days of the week. I've checked with them in

Manchester. At first, they were a little uncooperative until I explained the situation. Sure enough, Peter and Mary flew from Houston to Manchester in business class on the day in question.'

'What about return flights yesterday?'

'There was a Houston Flight early in the morning. It comes in from Singapore, but they were not booked on it. Nor were they on the ongoing flight to Singapore. The airline couldn't help us anymore. I looked up the flights from Terminal 2 around mid-morning. There is an obvious candidate, which is Cathay Pacific at 11:25 to Hong Kong. The airline refused to discuss the passenger list.'

Drake walked silently across to his case boards and started shuffling around. Eventually, he spoke.

'Felicity told us how the family lived in Hong Kong, and the parents left there to go to Texas. Hong Kong is a good possibility. Leave that with me,' said Drake somewhat enigmatically. 'It's been a long day, everyone. Let's all go home.'


The following morning, the team was assembled, getting on with their various tasks, when the door was rattled quite aggressively.

'That will be Drake,' said Grace, dashing across to open it.

'I think I must have left my keys at home,' said Drake. Various people exchanged knowing smiles. Mostly, they guessed the recalcitrant keys could be found in one of the many pockets in his overcoat, but no one dared to suggest such a ridiculous idea. Drake hung his coat up and went to make a coffee. After the machine had done its hissing, he slumped in his chair.

'We're in luck,' he said. 'I contacted our old colleague Inspector Martin Henshaw, who is now with the Hong Kong Police. He has promised to do a small favour for me.'

No sooner had Drake consumed his coffee and completed the across clues in The Times Crossword when his phone rang. Drake's colleagues could not overhear his conversation, which went on for several minutes. He put his phone back in his pocket, collected the small notebook he had been scribbling in and addressed the impatient team.

'That was Martin from Hong Kong. He has come up trumps after getting a senior Chinese colleague to call Cathay Pacific. Sure enough, Peter and Mary were on flight CX216. If they are who we suspect they are, Imogen and Felicity's parents are somewhere in Hong Kong.'

# 21

All the others had gone home for the evening, with just Drake and Grace left behind.

'That confirms it,' said Drake, suddenly.

'Sorry, confirms what?' asked a puzzled Grace.

'So many lines of enquiry now point to Hong Kong,' said Drake. 'The Glass parents are probably there, and it's where Xi Dong has a key base. Imogen frequently went to Hong Kong and, according to Angela Marchment at The Orient Gallery, a good proportion of her paintings were sold there to an enthusiastic following. The mysterious Irene Lee is based there. She seems to have her finger in the pie somehow. As you know, our Detective Inspector Martin Henshaw is on secondment to the Hong Kong Police. I have contacted him, and he says sorry for not responding to the email you sent a little while back, as he has been busy, but he is more than happy to assist us. One of us needs to go over there. Normally, of course, that would be me. But I have been thinking about it. I know you and Martin had quite a relationship before he left. Perhaps you would both appreciate some time together. If you went, it would get you away from the stalker situation. It would be excellent on your CV. Would you like to make the trip?'

An electric shock travelled through Grace's body, or so it felt. She was still conflicted about Martin. On the one hand, it would be good to sort out their relationship. On the other, this could seriously endanger the investigation if it all went wrong. She knew Martin had expressed a wish to pick up their relationship. But she was so uncertain about it that she didn't want to get into a situation from which she couldn't escape. However, an opportunity to go to Hong Kong does not come often. She would have the chance to make a real difference in the development of the case, maybe even solve it altogether. It certainly wouldn't do her chances of promotion any harm.

'Can I think about it?' she asked hesitantly. 'I'm not sure.'

'Of course,' said Drake. 'Let me know tomorrow. We need to get on with it.' Grace got on collating all the reports from constables going house to house along Hoole Road. Drake went back to walking around his boards, adding little pieces of information that he had missed earlier.

That evening, Grace found another of her stalker's messages waiting for her. This one was even more threatening than the others. "First Imogen Glass, then Philippa Crehan. Who is next?" As Grace read these words over again, she caught her breath. Was he threatening her with murder? A trip to Hong Kong suddenly seemed more attractive. It would indeed be good to get away from this stalking situation. However, the stalker would still have her email, and she might feel more concerned about being disconnected and not knowing how the case was developing. Just how did her stalker get his information? Of course, how silly; he only had to read the local newspaper. Grace idly flipped through her email. There was one from the police in Manchester. They had checked up on Jason Mercer and were sure he was not responsible for all the stalker's messages. He had good, validated alibis, showing that he had not been away from home. Grace felt a sudden pang of disappointment. That would have sorted it all out. Her pursuer was still unknown and free to cause her misery. She went to bed, still unsure what to decide about Hong Kong.

The following morning, Drake greeted Grace as he came through the door. Somehow, his daily hunt for his keys had proved successful.

'Have you decided about Hong Kong?' he demanded.

'I have. With regret, I prefer not to go,' said Grace. She heard herself answer without having consciously decided. Somehow, overnight, her brain must have mulled it over. She felt a huge weight fade away from her shoulders. She was suddenly comfortable with the decision.

'That's a pity,' grunted Drake. 'It could have been good for your career.' Grace gulped and shook her head.

'I'm sorry, but there it is,' she said. She turned abruptly towards the coffee machine and made two cups, taking one over to Drake, now sitting in his rocking chair. He was silent and absorbed with his crossword. Grace suddenly thought that this was almost certainly the first time Drake had shown any disappointment about her performance. She took her coffee to her desk and turned her computer on. There was a message from Sheila Richards saying that Felicity Glass was in a car on her way up to Chester and asking where it was to deliver her. Grace replied that they wanted to question her at the station.

The interview room was windowless but with a small overhead roof light. When Drake and Grace entered, Felicity was seated at one of the longer sides of an oval table. Grace sat at the sharper end to her right and opposite Drake. The remaining chair was left empty.

'Why have I been brought here? I want to go home.' Felicity sounded both weary and angry. Drake nodded to Grace to answer her.

'Felicity, we are sorry, but given your concern about being followed and now having been kidnapped, we think you should stay at a safe location rather than go home. We have arranged a pleasant place, and you will be guarded and looked after.' Grace sat back to let Drake take over.

'Felicity, do you know why you were imprisoned in Fairlawns?'

'So, it was Fairlawns! I sat trying to work it out and wondered if I was there. I half expected my parents to come in any minute, but they didn't. The last thing I wanted was to meet them again, so I was apprehensive. My memory is rather fuzzy about it all. It seems unreal now.'

'So, can you tell us what you recall?' asked Grace.

'I remember opening my front door. I think there might have been two or three men. The one at the front was Chinese. I'm sure of that. Then, my memory goes blank. I have confused memories of waking up and trying to work out where I was and what happened to me.'

'Where was Elliott when you opened the door to these men?' asked Drake.

'I think he was out. I've lost my phone. I haven't had any contact with him. Do you know where he is?'

'He's not at your home,' said Grace. 'We have been there.'

'Can I ring Elliott now?' asked Felicity.

'Please do. We are anxious to speak to him as well. Use my phone.' There was silence while Felicity called Elliott.

'It is just going straight to answerphone,' said Felicity. 'I'm worried about him. I've left him a message to contact me.'

'Please rest assured we are doing our best to find him,' said Drake. Felicity nodded and smiled. 'In the meantime,' continued Drake, 'perhaps you could fill in a few details that might help us. Do you think your parents were at Fairlawns?'

'Possibly, yes, but I had no contact with anyone.'

'Could they have returned to Hong Kong, do you think?' asked Drake.

'Again,' said Felicity. 'It is possible, but I have no idea where they are.'

'What about your family home?' asked Drake. 'Where was it?'

'Oh, we were so lucky to grow up in it. We had a luxurious house in Happy Valley. When Immy and I went to The Chinese University, we left and went somewhere in Shatin. The university is near Shatin, and the journey from Happy Valley was just too much every day.'

'Perhaps you would let Grace have the address in Happy Valley, please. She will take you to your temporary safe house. Thank you for all your help. Just one more thing before you go. Did you know that Imogen had a tattoo?'

'Yes, horrid thing. I have no idea what she was thinking about.'

'We think someone suggested it to her. Have you any idea who it was?' asked Drake.

'Yes. I think it was a Chinese woman that Imogen saw occasionally. She told her it would be a lucky charm. I think there was something Chinese about it.'

'Was it by any chance Irene someone, Grace, I forget the name, what is she called again?'

'Do you mean Irene Mei Lien Li?' asked Grace.

'Yes, that's her,' said Drake. Felicity screwed her face up and thought for a moment.

'It sounds like it?' said Felicity, 'but I can't be sure.'

'Thanks for all your help, Felicity. Detective Sergeant Hepple will arrange for you to be taken to a safe house we have arranged. I suggest you stay there for a few days at least and don't leave without informing us. Ring Grace if you want to move.'

Grace called Constable Steve Redvers over to drive Felicity to her temporary home.

'Do you know what, Grace?' said Drake. 'I will send the tattoo in an email to my Chinese expert at The Met. Perhaps he can tell us something about it.' Drake fumbled around on his new iPhone, and suddenly, it rang.

'That's a shame,' said Drake. 'He can't immediately see any significance in the tattoo but says he'll have a bit more of a think about it and call me back if anything occurs to him. It doesn't sound too promising.'

'Hi Grace, come in,' said DS Sheila Richards as her door opened.

'Sorry to keep you waiting,' said Grace. 'I got down here again as soon as I could.'

'No problem,' replied Sheila. 'The delay caused by waiting for you to join us has worked in our favour. My Inspector suggested we let Luke stew before questioning him.'

'Glad to be of assistance,' laughed Grace. 'We assume you will do all the questioning unless you want to hand it over to me. We need to know why Xi Dong captured and imprisoned Felicity Glass. She is Imogen's younger sister. She is now in a relationship with someone called Elliott Chan. He was Imogen's lover. It's all a bit complex.' Grace and Sheila laughed.

'OK,' said Sheila. 'Let's go.'


'Luke,' said Sheila as they sat across a small table from Luke. 'Can you confirm that is your name?'

'Correct,' said Luke.

'And your surname is?'

'I don't have one. We don't use them in Xi Dong.' Luke stared at his interrogator defiantly.

'But you must have had one before you joined Xi Dong,'

'That is the past and not relevant now.'

'How about your bank account? Surely you can't just have an account in the single name of Luke?'

'I don't have a bank account. In Xi Dong, whatever we need is provided. We use a series of accounts as a movement.'

'What is the name on your birth certificate?' persisted Sheila.

'I don't have it. I've never seen it.'

'What about your passport?'

'I use Xi Dong as my family name on that. We are all part of the Xi Dong family.'

'Very well. We are not making any progress. Let us move on. What you call your movement has imprisoned two people at Fairlawns. The first is a male and, we think, middle-aged. Why was he imprisoned?'

'He's not imprisoned. He is a member of our movement but sadly has lost his mind. He turned violent, and we thought it best immediately to separate him temporarily from our other members.'

'What about the female, Felicity Glass? Why was she imprisoned?'

'I have no idea.' Luke spat out the words.

'You didn't know she was imprisoned?'

'No. Who is she?'

'We have some testimony that she was brought there by your men. We understand they might be Chinese.' Luke remained silent.

'Surely,' said Sheila. 'If you think the male has lost his mind, he needs treatment. You have isolated him in a locked room?'

'He is having treatment. One of our members is a psychiatrist who is helping him. Where is he now?' demanded Luke.

'We have transferred him to a hospital where his condition is being assessed and he is being cared for.'

'I think you should return him to us.'

'What is your precise role at Fairlawns?' Sheila demanded, changing tack.

'I am known as The Convenor. I arrange events and manage the property.'

'You were visited by Detective Sergeant Grace Hepple and her assistant. We have a record of the conversation. Do you have anything more to say about Xi Dong?' Luke shook his head silently, maintaining his defiant stare. Sheila Richards turned to Grace. 'Is there anything else you want to ask at this stage?' Grace shook her head. The two detective sergeants left the room. As they walked back to her office, Sheila spoke to Grace.

'OK, thanks for coming. I will keep you informed of anything we learn further. I gather you now have Felicity Glass back in Chester. Perhaps she can help us.'

'Not so far,' said Grace. 'She remembers being assaulted by at least one and maybe a couple of Chinese men when she opened the door of her house. Her memory then goes blank. We suspect she was drugged. She woke up in her prison at Fairlawns.'

# 22

Grace's phone rang. It was Sheila Richards from The Met.

'Hi, Grace. We need your help again over this Fairlawns business.'

'I'll do my best,' replied Grace.

'Last night after dark, two of our constables guarding Fairlawns were on duty near the gate. This shady character came creeping along carrying a crowbar. He climbed over the gate and set off in the shadows of the trees on one side of the road. It was a moonlit night here. One of our guys followed him to see what he was up to. He went up to the main building and was intercepted by another of our constables. We searched him and found a set of lock-picking instruments in his pocket. He had a mobile phone that was switched off. It is locked, and he won't unlock it. A little strangely, he has no ID on him. He has quite a fair bit of cash in his pocket. The only other item on him was a map of the area folded open to the Fairlawns location. We still don't know who he is. We arrested him for trespassing with the intent to commit a burglary. He was reported to have been both uncooperative and nervous. He has since been brought here, and I have tried to interview him. He gives the no comment response at every stage. Just before coming on the phone, I emailed you a mugshot. Can you look and tell me if you know who he is.'

'OK,' said Grace. 'I can't imagine that I will be able to help, but if you hang on, I'll have a look.' Grace tapped on her laptop and opened the email. She was surprised and not a little pleased by what she saw.

'Sheila, are you still there?'

'Yes, just waiting. Any luck?'

'Absolutely. It's someone we've been looking for called Elliott Chan. We want to ask him a few questions about the murder of Imogen Glass. It's her ex-lover, now in a relationship with Felicity Glass, who you found imprisoned there.'

'OK. Perhaps he knew she was here and was trying to rescue her. If so, we can let him go. If we give him the all-clear, would you like us to arrange for him to be brought up to Chester?'

'You bet!'

'So, we meet again,' said Drake as he and Grace entered the interview room where Elliott Chan was waiting. He smiled weakly and shuffled his feet. He picked up the glass next to him and sipped some water.

'So, what were you doing last night at Fairlawns?'

'I have been in hiding,' said Elliot. 'I got information suggesting that people I don't want to meet were getting close to me. I had created a hideaway in our house, and as the doorbell went, I climbed in there. When I came down later, Felicity had gone. I was in no doubt that she had been abducted. Perhaps they intended to use her as collateral. I had other information that her parents had flown into the country. I guessed they would be at Fairlawns and might have had her taken there. I was hoping to break her out.'

'Why on earth didn't you go to the police?' demanded Drake.

'I didn't believe they would take the situation seriously and that no good would come if they went stumbling in.' Elliott sighed. 'Do you know where Felicity is?'

'Yes, we do,' said Grace. 'She is in a safe place. You were right that she was held against her will at Fairlawns. The Met Police are dealing with that situation.'

'We would like to turn our attention to the death of your ex-lover, Imogen Glass,' said Drake sternly. Elliott Chan looked startled.

'There is nothing more I can tell you about that,' he said.

'On the contrary,' said Drake. 'We think you can.' He paused and looked at Elliott, who shuffled his feet and stared at the floor. 'You told us that you had not seen Imogen for several months. Would you like to rethink that, or must I jog your memory?' Elliott Chan shook his head and remained silent.

'I believe you own a red sweater,' said Drake.

'I don't think so,' said Elliott Chan. Grace opened the bag she was carrying. She pulled out the red sweater.

'Is this yours?' demanded Drake. 'It was found in your drawer at Felicity's house.'

'Oh, yes,' said Elliott, his voice cracking slightly. He cleared his throat. 'I forgot about that. I haven't worn it for ages.'

'We have a testimony that you were seen wearing this jumper on the riverbank along the Dee arguing violently with a female all dressed in black. Imogen always wore entirely black clothes, didn't she?'

'Yes, she did.'

'This incident was only a few days before Imogen's body was recovered from the river,' said Drake. Do you deny the arguing couple was you and Imogen?'

'Yes, it was us,' said Elliott with a sigh. 'She was trying to persuade me to go back to her. It had got very heated. I suggested we take a walk to calm down. She just got angrier. I didn't push her into the river. In the end, I just walked away and left her. She was shaking with rage. I have wondered ever since if she lost her footing and fell into the river. If so, then I suppose it was partly my fault.'

'So, why did you deny this in your earlier testament?'

'I should have thought that was obvious. You would have charged me with her murder.'

'Let us assume for now you are telling the truth at last,' said Drake. 'There is one more thing we need to talk about. Do you remember being in Imogen's studio?'

'Yes, of course.'

'Do you remember that on one side of the room was a double bed covered in pillows?'

'Yes,' Elliott looked genuinely puzzled.

'Do you remember, on the other side of the room was a pile of heavy wooden poles?  We believe she intended to use them in a sculpture?'

'I'm not sure. There were lots of things in her studio.'

'Perhaps you might remember picking up one of these poles?'

'Not really.'

'That's strange, Mr Chan. Perhaps I might be able to jog your memory again,' said Drake. 'Your fingerprints have been found on one of the poles.'

'Perhaps I picked one up to look at it.'

'So that would be three months ago. That is when you say you last saw her. Is that right?'

'I suppose so.'

'Well, that is even stranger, Mr Chan. The poles were only delivered to the studio two weeks before Imogen died. How do you explain that?'

'I've no idea.'

'I put it to you, Mr Chan. You did see Imogen Glass again. You went to her studio not more than two weeks before she died.'

'No.'

'Mr Chan, I think you did visit her studio. There is no other explanation for the presence of your fingerprints. We have excellent evidence about them. This leads us to think you are hiding this meeting at her studio for some reason. Perhaps it was not only Imogen who was enraged. Perhaps you were angry about her relationship with Philippa Crehan. You went to her studio. You argued. You picked up a pole and threatened her with it. Maybe you had a struggle, and you hit her. Perhaps you didn't mean to kill her. Perhaps that was an accident.' Elliott Chan sat silently, looking at the table. Drake and Grace waited for his response. It did not come, so Drake spoke again.

'This gives me enough information to arrest you for the murder of Imogen Glass.'

'No. I didn't do it. You are right. I did go there once more. I wanted to be on good terms with her. It was causing a rift with her younger sister, and I didn't want to be the source of an argument between them. I wanted to explain to her.'

'So, when was this?'

'Probably only a week before her body was found. It was a difficult meeting, but I thought I had calmed her down.'

'So why did you pick up one of the poles?'

'I don't remember, except we talked a bit about her current work. She might have mentioned she was trying to work in three dimensions.'

'Why then did you deny having this meeting?'

'Because once you took my fingerprints, I started to worry that I might be accused of murdering her.'

'Let me tell you one more thing,' said Drake. 'Our pathologist has suggested that Imogen was not drowned but was already dead when she entered the water. It could be that the blow you delivered with the pole was fatal.'

'No.'

'You then discovered she was dead and panicked. You drove her body in her van to the river. You pushed her lifeless body into the water. You hoped it would look like an accident or perhaps suicide. Unfortunately, the science was against you. It has revealed what happened to her.'

'No. That's not true. Perhaps it was an accident. She was in a deranged state. I imagined she might have committed suicide.'

'Our pathologist is almost certain that it is not suicide. She died before she entered the water. Science tells us that unequivocally.' Elliott Chan shrugged his shoulders. He pulled out a handkerchief and dabbed his eyes.

'I did not kill her with one of her poles.'

'I agree,' said Drake tersely. Elliott Chan suddenly wore a startled expression.

'She did not die from the blow to the head you delivered.'

'I never hit her with a pole.'

'Then why did you pick it up?'

'Probably, I was just looking at it.'

'You mean to tell me that in the middle of this huge argument about your relationship and her relationship with Philippa Crehan, you stopped to discuss art?'

'I don't know. Perhaps I did pick it up to quieten her down, but I didn't hit her. I might have just waved it in the air.'

'Perhaps you didn't mean to hit her, but you lost control,' suggested Drake. Elliott shook his head silently and gulped. 'Perhaps, Mr Chan, in a rage, you got a pillow from the bed and suffocated her.'

'No. None of this is true. We parted amicably. Well, not exactly as friends, but we came to terms with the situation.'

'What do you make of all that?' asked Drake when he and Grace reached the case room.

'I think we might have found our murderer. He is making it up on the hoof.' said Grace.

'Possibly, possibly,' grunted Drake. These Chinese thugs might be significant. We need to interrogate Luke more about them. I guess our friends in The Met are doing that already. We need to know why Xi Dong wanted Felicity and what they intended to do with her. Maybe we should hang on to Felicity in her safe house for now. We need to hold Elliott Chan, for now, to see if you are right and he comes clean. In the meantime, get onto your contact at The Met. Make sure they are interrogating Luke along these lines. We also need to find these Chinese thugs.'

Drake collapsed into a comfy chair in his living room. Tom was already sat opposite, having arrived earlier from his trip to London.

'Success?' asked Drake.

'Yes, I think so,' replied Tom. 'I've been offered a position with good remuneration. I asked for a little time to think it over, and if I decided to take it, I needed to work my notice and move, which would be quite a business after so long in Singapore. How is the investigation going?'

'It's progressing, but we can't see a clear path forward. I have a new problem which is beginning to bug me. I think you know Detective Sergeant Grace Hepple.' Tom nodded. 'Well, she is being stalked in quite an unpleasant way. It's not something I've ever tackled before. I put Steve Redvers onto it, but he hasn't made progress. It's making life hell for Grace and consequently taking her mind off the case. I vaguely remember you mentioning having this problem once.'

'It can be a nasty business,' said Tom. 'Yes, I had experience of it in Singapore. Luckily, one of the world experts on the psychology of it is at NUS, National University Singapore, and we went to see him. He helped us a lot, and we gave the police information that eventually resulted in an arrest. The person who was doing it surprised us. I will contact the chap we consulted. Perhaps he can help.'

# 23

Drake stood looking up at the Eastgate. He had opted to be dropped just outside the pedestrian zone. It was a sunny morning, and his intended walk was on flat ground. He had emerged from a side street in Foregate Street just outside the gate in the ancient city walls. It never failed to fascinate him with its giant filigree ironwork supporting the clock over the heavy red stone arch. If his increasingly dicky right hip would allow, he would climb the stairs to the level of the gallery walkway known as The Rows. The view down onto Eastgate Street was of a bustling city, with people going about their business. Tourists jostled with business folk as some small children ran around them playing tag. He paused and leant over the handrail. He wondered why we could not design cities like this today.

Then he imagined Cynthia's voice reminding him that this had never been designed in the contemporary sense of the word. Historians debated how exactly this arrangement of first-floor covered walkways came about. The most popular explanation was that the upper level had been built over the ruins of earlier Roman buildings, which were later removed, and a new ground floor was inserted under the galleries. Reluctantly, Drake moved on along the Rows. He took the next staircase down to ground level, hobbling slightly as his grumbling hip reminded him of its complaint about this kind of activity.

In truth, this walk had now become almost a ritual. It was the third time he had made it. He was on his way to visit The Orient art gallery. He had some more questions growing in his mind that he hoped Wang could answer. The bell emitted its gentle chime as he opened the entrance door, and he was met with the calming perfume of China. Immediately, he saw a woman standing with her back to him. He knew instantly who it was. The slim and elegantly dressed figure of Angela Marchment turned to speak to him.

'Hello, Inspector,' said Angela. 'Nice to see you. Come and join me in a cup of tea.' She set off upstairs and waved him into the office and to the small round table that Drake had sat at previously. Drake observed a custom he had instinctively picked up in the Far East. Business conversation must wait until at least the first sip of the refreshing brew.

'As always,' said Drake. 'You satisfy all the senses here. I wish I could make tea like you.'

'You can, you can,' replied Angela. 'If I have learned from Wang, you can learn from me. I will give you a piece of Wang's best Pu-Erh.' She picked up a substantial dark brown lump that hid its delightful taste behind a rather unappealing appearance. Angela cut off a piece, gently rolled it in a paper napkin and put it next to Drake's cup. 'This has been nicely aged. Before you leave, I will give you a sheet of instructions for making wonderful tea. Now, Inspector, you have not come to drink tea. What do you want of me? How can I help?'

'Well,' said Drake. 'I would like to know more about how you sell Imogen's paintings in the Far East.'

'Oh dear,' said Angela. 'I will tell you what I know. You should ask Wang, but he is not here.'

'When will he be back?' asked Drake. Angela laughed and looked at her watch.

'Any minute now, he takes off for Hong Kong,' she said. 'I'm afraid I've no idea when he will return. It all depends.'

'Depends on what?' asked Drake, sipping his tea.

'He has gone to talk to agents over there. Things must change.'

'Why so?' asked Drake.

'Imogen is no more. Sad though it is, this is also a big blow to our business. Wang decided it was time for new ideas, new artists, maybe new agents, new contracts.' Somehow, Drake's brain dragged up the conversation with Bristow about the interest that MI5 had, and it suggested a new question. He decided to try it out.

'Angela, have you ever heard of Li Mei Lien, also known here in the UK as Irene Lee?'

'Let me think. The name is familiar. Ah, yes, she came to see Wang a couple of times. I had forgotten about her. She said she was in Chester and just popped in for a chat with Wang. He never mentioned it again. I don't think there was any real business. Perhaps she was only checking up.'

'Checking up about what?'

'I do not know. I'm sorry.'

'When was it she came?'

'Not long ago. Maybe a month or two. I can't recall precisely.'

'Is she perhaps one of these art agents?' suggested Drake.

'I think maybe she has links with our Hong Kong agents. Sorry, I don't know for sure.' Angela shrugged her shoulders.

'Surely Wang would have told you about their discussion,' retorted Drake.

'No. He meets with many people about our business. He would have told me if he thought there was anything I needed to know. Why do you ask this?'

'I'm afraid I can't tell you that,' said Drake sharply. 'Do you know where Wang is staying in Hong Kong?'

'No. He still uses email and text.' Angela wrote Wang's email address and mobile phone number on a scrap of paper and handed it to Drake.

'So,' said Drake. 'I get the impression you do most business with Hong Kong.'

'Yes, it represents a substantial part of our business. Wang comes from Hong Kong.'

'How do you do that business?' asked Drake.

'Most of it we do with Far East Trading.'

'Who are they?' asked Drake, jotting the name in his notebook.

'They do all the actual importing and exporting. I'm afraid that I don't understand it. Unless you know how, it is difficult. I don't think even Wang understands all the detail, but it's his side of our business, so I don't interfere. Far East Trading do a lot of work moving things between here and Hong Kong. They have a couple of British agents working for them here. Usually, one of them will come and collect paintings. He crates them up and takes them to the airport. Far East Trading is insured. They take full responsibility, so everything is covered while in transit. You might find talking to them would give you more information than I have. I know the name of the guy we usually deal with here is Geoffrey Bragg. I might have an email from him. That would give you his contact details.' Angela fiddled around on her computer for a few minutes. 'Yes, here it is. I could send it all over to Grace. I have her email address.'

'Thank you, Angela,' said Drake. 'That's helpful. So, this Far East Trading, are they an art dealer?'

'No, they're not art dealers. They only do all the commercial and legal side of importing and exporting. I think they have many art dealers with whom they do business. They also buy things from them. Some sell art, furniture, ceramics, and all sorts. Far East Traders bring them here. We sell them. It is a well-oiled machine. Imogen's paintings are always collected from our gallery here. We have limited storage space here. Far East Trading may take some larger items to our secure lockup on the Sealand Road Industrial Estate. I hardly ever go there. Wang deals with things there.'

'Do you know the names of any of these art dealers in Hong Kong?' probed Drake.

'I think the main one is the Cheung Brothers. There are three of them. Each brother is interested in different kinds of art. We buy paintings, ceramics and antique furniture from them. Wang could explain it all to you much better than I can. Why do you want to know all this, Inspector?'

'We are naturally interested in what happens to Imogen's work. Where it goes and what it is worth may help us.'

'I see,' said Angela. 'When we send Imogen's work to Hong Kong, where she is incredibly popular, we do it through Far East Trading who then deliver her paintings to Cheung Brothers, who exhibit and sell. Wang believes that Cheung Brothers have the best opportunity of any dealer to sell in what is a special market. I understand that most of Imogen's work goes to serious collectors, and Cheung Brothers knows the market inside out. It's all a cunning arrangement that Wang put together some time ago. Wang is an extremely clever man. His English is a little abrupt and halting. He may seem slow or even stupid at times. But he plays a role that suits him. He is constantly thinking about how to do things. He is a remarkable negotiator. I could not begin to work out all the things he does. He may not be a highly educated scholar, but he is brilliant. He arrives at arrangements that, at first sight, might not seem obvious, but he sees all the possibilities. I'm lucky to be his partner in life and business, and I leave many things to him. That's all I know. I'm sorry I can't help you more.'

'One final question, Angela,' said Drake. 'Do either of you know Philippa Crehan?'

'No, the name means nothing to me, I'm afraid.'

A disappointed Drake stumbled back into the case room and stood looking at his case boards. He made minor alterations to The Orient business, linking them to Far East Trading and Cheung Brothers. He also inserted a possible but previously unknown link from Irene Lee to Far East Trading. He wondered about the significance of what he had learned when Steve Redvers came dashing over.

'You look desperate to impart some news, Steve,' said Drake. 'What can you tell us?'

'Yes,' said Steve Redvers. 'As it happens, it seems we have struck some gold. We've seen a few security cameras around the street where Philippa's house is. None are near the house and pointing outwards. Dave has found a security system in the house, but it is not working. We checked that out when investigating the Imogen Glass murder. However, the real gem is from a chap eight doors down. He is a complete nut about dog training. He goes to shows and competitions with his two dogs. I get the impression that he often wins prizes and is well-known on the circuit. He is not married and lives alone. On the night we believe Philippa was attacked, he had been working late and was out walking his dogs. As he passed Philippa Crehan's house, he noticed a car in the drive, near the entrance and pointing outwards. He remembers it being a white Ford. He has no idea what model, but he said it was of medium to large size. Since he was a regular walker along the road, he was familiar with normal behaviour in the neighbourhood. He said Phillipa never parked her car like that. As he reached the house, he saw a man rushing to the driver's door. He thinks he heard three car doors being slammed. We know that one was the driver's door, and he thinks perhaps one or two people got in on the nearside, but he didn't see them as his view was obstructed by the car, which drove off in what he described as something of a hurry. However, the real gem is that he thought the driver looked Chinese.'

'Do we have the car registration?' asked Drake.

'No, but we are searching for more cameras that might have caught it,' replied Constable Redvers.

'If the unseen rear nearside passenger or passengers were also Chinese.' Drake was pondering aloud, but Grace, for once, knew where he was going. 'We've run across three stocky Chinese characters at Fairlawns. Grace, your mates at The Met are trying to find them.'

'Yes,' said Grace. 'I've heard from Sheila Richards that they were apprehended trying to leave the country at Heath Row. The Met people haven't got anything out of them. Whether they are pretending not to understand English or just being tight-lipped, I don't know. I think The Met made the mistake of calling in a Mandarin interpreter, which didn't help. The original Xi Dong Centre was in Hong Kong, so I suggested they would probably speak Cantonese. I haven't heard from her since. I'll call her now and tell her we might want to speak with them before she lets them go if they are not charging them.' Grace dashed off to pick up her phone. Drake hobbled over to his case boards. He cursed himself for climbing all the stairs on the city Rows earlier as his right hip was aching. He linked the two sightings of the Chinese men and the two locations of Fairlawns and Philippa's house. It was a dashed line until they proved these were the same people.

'OK,' said Grace. 'Not much progress, I'm afraid, but some promise. The Chinese men are still not talking, but the good news is that they have opened the safe in Luke's office at Fairlawns. There are dozens of credit cards and passports in there. Amongst the latter are the men in question. They are from Hong Kong and came here on a short-stay visitor's visa. They have been here for many months and have no work permit. So far, they haven't found any employment contracts, but they have at least outstayed their permit. Sheila says they will charge them with immigration offences to give themselves more time. They are sure they are up to no good and are delighted to get our news. They could be brought up here if we want to do an identity parade.'

'I guess we could try,' said Drake. 'But our witness only saw one briefly in the dark from a distance, so the chance of a successful identification must be slim. Our passports don't show the holder's address, but maybe the Hong Kong passport does. If so, maybe we can track them down over there. Not sure if that would help.' Grace was furiously hammering away on her laptop, and Drake sat silently, waiting for her to say what she was doing. Suddenly, she spoke.

'The Hong Kong passport does not have an address as far as I can see, but it does have the holder's Permanent Identity Number.'

'I bet Martin could get the address from that. I wonder if he could help us. Angela Marchment has emailed you the contact details of the UK representative of this company, Far East Trading, which handles all the exporting of Imogen's work to Hong Kong. He's called Geoffrey Bragg. See if you can get him to come and chat with us.'

# 24

Drake flopped back into his seat on flight CX216 from Manchester to Hong Kong. He let out a "thank goodness for that" kind of sigh. He hated this travelling business. No, correction, that wasn't entirely true now. Thanks to him getting an allowance to travel business class for long haul flights with his ridiculous height of six feet and six inches, he no longer had to press his knees against the seat in front. It wasn't the flying he had hated so much as the airports. This time, he got through more quickly than he had feared would be the case. His ticket allowed him to check in at a less crowded desk and then use the fast channel to emigration and security. The usual nonsense of having to get half undressed and fire up his iPad was carried out by a woman who seemed to take delight in keeping him away from the sanctuary of the lounge.

Now they had taken off, he was able to think again. The two engines were not only doing their day job, but they also issued a reassuring thrum. Drake felt it quite comforting and reflected for a moment as to why such a noise should add to the peace of the cabin that he was in. He fought for several minutes with the in-flight entertainment system. It seemed to be trying to prevent him from having any fun. Eventually, he won the battle and found a recording of the Four Last Songs by Richard Strauss. He looked everywhere for the socket to plug in his sound-deadening headphones, only to discover it was behind him on the seat headrest. He had meant to take out his iPad and do some work, but the gloriously melancholic music of Strauss took over completely. It occurred to him that he had never done this before. Sit and do nothing but listen. A flute soared, and he thought he would willingly give up his whole career to sit in the middle of an eighty-piece orchestra for one evening and play such a part in such a sound. Which of the songs was his favourite? Each time a new one came on, he changed his mind except for the fourth. By then, he was fast asleep.

According to the live map on the screen, he woke up somewhere south of Russia. All the countries that he could see ended in "stan." He shamefully admitted that he could not locate any of these countries accurately. It was a part of the world in which he had no experience.

Refreshed and happy to start the recording again, he felt rather smug. He took out his iPad and opened the pictures app to display his first achievement on the new iPhone that Tom and Lucy had given him. Before leaving Chester, he had photographed all his case boards. As if by magic, here were the photographs on his iPad. Tom had assured him they would be, but he had no idea how this happened. He just knew he had nothing to do with it. Something to do with the cloud, so Tom said. He didn't care. He knew too well that he was now too old to become a computer buff, but he was secretly proud of his modest achievements with the latest technology.

He turned the iPad into a portrait orientation and began scrolling through all his images for the case. That was when his smugness evaporated. He wanted to move something from one board to another, but of course, they were stubbornly static images. He wondered if Tom could find some clever way or secret app to do this for him. Could some bright spark be encouraged to write an app for it? Even so, this dedicated time looking at the boards was beginning to clarify where he was with this case. Many arrows were pointing to Hong Kong, but so far, he had not thought out how to progress all these separate lines of investigation. Perhaps it was just as well that Grace hadn't made this trip. It didn't look as if it was going to be straightforward.


As promised, the hotel sent a car to collect him from the airport. He had often heard remarkable stories about how tricky it was to land at the old airport in Victoria Harbour, but this new one seemed to have a complete island to itself. He checked the useful map he had found in his guidebook. Sure enough, Chek Lap Kok Island was devoted to the airport where he had arrived. The Mercedes car soon glided over towering suspension bridges and through collections of massive high-rise housing blocks to reach the mainland. He opened his guidebook again at the map page to follow their progress. The car pulled up outside a rather unremarkable-looking hotel.

Once Drake had discovered that Hong Kong sported not one but two hotels in his favourite Far East chain, he had asked Martin's advice on which one to choose. The one on the island was more expensive and luxurious looking. However, Martin had promised him that the Kowloon Shangri-La was in an excellent location for getting about, and he would not be disappointed with the view from his room. As soon as he opened the door, he understood what Martin had meant. His room had a wall-to-wall, floor-to-ceiling window offering a dramatic view of Hong Kong Island with the harbour in the foreground. Over to the right, he could see the famous Hong Kong peak. A massive ocean-going liner was gliding past like some gigantic, elegant swan. Large birds were swooping about in the foreground. This would do nicely. The hotel had thoughtfully provided a pair of binoculars. He delayed unpacking, made a cup of coffee and settled down to study the view with them.

The gentle tap on the door interrupted his study of Hong Kong's Victoria Harbour. It was Inspector Martin Henshaw. The two men had worked together for several years before Martin took his leave of absence to accept the invitation to join the Hong Kong Police. They instinctively hugged and slapped each other on the back. Drake sat Martin on one of the easy chairs in the window and made two cups of coffee.

'It is great to see you again, Martin,' said Drake. 'Thanks for recommending this excellent hotel.'

'Ah yes,' said Martin. 'Let me explain. Many visitors are a little confused by the layout of Hong Kong. It comes in at least four distinct parts. First, there is the famous island that you see out of this window. That is the most expensive part of Hong Kong. Next are a couple of areas, leant to the British rather later. They are connected directly to mainland China proper. This hotel is in Kowloon, a business and tourism centre like the island. Beyond is a less dense but much larger area known as The New Territories, and beyond that is China. Then there comes a whole raft of small islands, including Chek Lap Kok where you land at the airport. You can get trains to the mainland areas from the nearby terminus. You can take a short walk along the harbour front to the Tsim Sha Tsui ferry terminal and get one of the many vintage ferries over to the island.'

'Martin,' said Drake. 'That's just marvellous. I understand it now and see why you recommended this hotel. Thank you.' Martin smiled, bowed his head slightly and continued.

'I think before we go any further, I had better explain my situation to you and why I was so late in replying to Grace's earlier email. As I am sure you know, the Chinese Government, or more accurately, the Chinese Communist Party, is taking a much stronger position than has been the case before over Hong Kong. They have tested the water with the UK and discovered they had much more freedom to change things here. The UK can protest but, in effect, has absolutely no power to influence the course of events in Hong Kong. Slowly but inexorably, Hong Kong is becoming closer to being a province of China. Party members are taking over senior positions in major government bodies. The idea of asking a member of a UK police force to come and advise is no longer a realistic possibility. To begin with, I was welcomed and involved in major management meetings. That has all gradually changed. Now, I am tolerated. One or two people have even suggested it would be better if I left.'

'Martin, I had no idea,' said Drake. 'Obviously, we have heard things on the news and in the press, but I didn't know things had gone so far.'

'In the last month,' said Martin. 'I have begun to think it would indeed, and very sadly, be better if I came home. Then came your request. I have researched the case a little from this end and think I might be able to cut some tedious corners for you. I am happy even to annoy my superiors a little. Probably once you have finished here, I will resign and return to Chester.'

'I see,' said Drake. 'I will consider you on the case.' The two men laughed.

'Well, I've researched your Imogen Glass,' said Martin. 'She has quite a following over here. There are at least three Facebook groups, where they all chat about what she has done, when she might come to Hong Kong again, what her work means and so on. I don't profess to understand it all, I'm afraid. The main news for you though is that they have heard about her being murdered and some of them talk about that, but the big news is that they have just opened an exhibition of her work. I think one guy came up with the idea, and a small group persuaded collectors to lend their paintings for the exhibition. A couple of chaps were hesitant, saying their paintings were too valuable and that unless they had a secure location, they wouldn't cooperate. Anyway, one fellow found that the art gallery in the Heritage Museum was free for several weeks between other exhibitions. That is very secure. They even held a Picasso exhibition there with paintings worth millions of dollars.'

'So where is the Heritage Museum?' asked Drake.

'It's out in Shatin,' replied Martin. It's where they also have a racecourse. They held the equestrian events there when China hosted the Olympics. Incidentally, there's another important lesson about the Chinese here. They are unbelievably superstitious. They were desperate to get the 2008 Olympics. Eight is a lucky number here. Perhaps you didn't notice that the Beijing Olympics started on the eighth of August 2008, or 8/8/2008.' Drake laughed.

'Funnily enough, I did recall the business about eight and the opposite, four being unlucky. Do you remember that cropped up on our Singapore case?'

'Oh yes, so it did. I'd quite forgotten about that,' said Martin. 'If you like we could go to the exhibition one day. I suggest you have an early night and a late pickup tomorrow to shake off some of the jet lag. Do you have anything that you particularly want to do first?'

'Yes,' said Drake. 'I would like to see this exhibition you mention. I had not heard about it. It seems as if my visit is well-timed. However, I have one important issue on my mind. I want to visit this location.' Drake handed a scrap of paper on which he had written an address. 'I have no idea where it is.'

'No problem,' said Martin. 'This is Happy Valley, which is over on Hong Kong Island. It's a rather odd combination. In the centre of this large area is a horse racecourse. In the centre of that is a series of sports facilities. Then, around the whole thing is a circular road with rather up-market housing. Some of it is high rise and some mid and low rise. We could plan a special route to get there. We can walk along the waterfront to the ferry. We can then take the ferry to the island, take another much cooler walk to the main road and get one of the lovely old trams right to the end of the line at Happy Valley.'

'That sounds excellent,' said Drake. 'We can combine business and pleasure and catch up with each other's news.'

'What is at this address?' asked Martin.

'It is the home that our murder victim, Imogen Glass, was brought up in. Her parents became somewhat obsessed with a quasi-religious cult called Xi Dong and left the home. Then, they went to a cult centre in Texas. However, some information suggests the parents have travelled to Hong Kong recently. I am anxious to interview them if possible. I suppose that, technically, I will have to leave the interrogation to you as I am beyond my jurisdiction.'

'OK,' said Martin. 'That sounds interesting. On the way, we can talk, and you can bring me up to speed with the case. Now, I suggest you have an early night to sleep off your jet lag. I will call for you mid-morning to give you a chance of a late rise and a leisurely breakfast.'

# 25

Drake woke in a blacked-out room. He tried to decide what time it was. More importantly, he had no idea where in the world he was. His brain decided to play silly games with this investigation. As his eyes gradually dark-adapted, he found the bedside light. Of course, it was Hong Kong, and his watch told him it was already ten in the morning. Now, his brain was more cooperative, and he knew Martin would call for him around eleven. He rose, showered, dressed and found his way via the lift to the rather pleasant restaurant. Refreshed and ready to go, he was soon back staring out of his bedroom window. Several birds with long wingspans were circling over the edge of the waterfront. Then, they were joined by a couple more, and as one came closer to his window, he wondered if they might be eagles. It seemed odd that there were so many close together. He was interrupted by the doorbell. It was Martin.

'Good morning,' said Martin as he entered. 'Did you sleep well?'

'Too well,' said Drake in mock grumpiness. 'I would have liked longer to watch these amazing birds. Are they eagles?'

'There are some eagles around,' said Martin, 'but these are black kites. They are famous residents of the harbour. You see them everywhere, often in quite large groups. Are you ready for our walk to the ferry?'

'Of course,' said Drake, 'but I am surrounded by sights I want to take in.' He heard Cynthia's voice in a jumble of architectural criticism. 'Cynthia worked on some buildings here, but I can't remember what they were. What a place to be an architect!'

'Yes, many Hong Kong students chose to study in the UK and return to fantastic opportunities. Not long after I arrived, I met quite a few at a social event.'

'Let's go,' said Drake. Martin didn't remember ever hearing him so enthusiastic. His memory of Drake was of a rather gloomy man. In the last few years before Martin left Chester for Hong Kong, Drake had been trying to deal with the loss of his wife. He was pleased to see Drake so cheerful. The two men set off. Martin led the way out of the front of the hotel and round to the other side on the waterfront.

'This walkway is full of representations of cinema stars,' he said. 'Some from Hollywood but others from here in Hong Kong.'

As they walked, Drake told Martin more about the Imogen Glass case. Martin was already delighted to get back into a proper murder. His work here in Hong Kong had not been hands-on, and he now knew how much he missed it.

'Here we are,' said Martin as they cut inshore and entered a cluttered building. 'This is the Kowloon Pier. They call this Tsim Sha Tsui. Ferries leave here for several destinations but mostly on the island. I recommend you buy a sort of season ticket. It's incredibly cheap, and you can use it on the ferries and the trams. They will even give you your leftover money back when you leave. It puts cities like London to shame. We'll take the Star Ferry to Central.'

They purchased their tickets, went through the barrier and clambered onto the already-moored ferry.

'These wonderful old vessels remind me a little of the ferries in Sydney Harbour,' said Drake. He watched people getting onto the upper deck where they had arrived. They automatically flipped the back of the bench seats across to face their destination. It was only once they set sail that Drake could see these boats had bows at both ends and, unlike the Sydney boats, did not have to turn around when they left the pier. Drake remembered his feeling of sheer pleasure in Sydney and felt the same here. They were soon out in the middle of the harbour with vertiginous high-rise buildings on both shores. There was a sensation of both being in the most exciting modern city and yet on a quaint old vessel with many years of tradition.

'How old are these ferries?' asked Drake.

'I'm no expert,' said Martin, 'but the Star Ferry began at the end of the nineteenth century. These boats are called fourth generation and date back to the 1950s.'

'Charming,' said Drake.

'Much nicer than the overpopulated underground trains,' said Martin. 'After another short walk, we will transfer to another delightful Hong Kong fixture, the trams. The tramway is over a hundred years old, and the trams have a similar history to the ferries.'

They emerged from a delightfully cool shopping centre onto a bustling city street. The tram they needed came to a halt with its rear door and staircase right next to Drake, who clambered up the steps but had still to reach the top when it lurched into action. He was buffeted from side to side and had to duck his head at several places before they got to their seats.

'The trams are not designed for super tall westerners,' laughed Martin. Drake sat entranced by the old and the new Hong Kong passing by his window. The ancient tram also seemed happy as it rattled cheerfully along past some of the most hi-tech modern buildings. He heard Cynthia's voice telling him he would love Hong Kong. After all these years, he finally knew what she meant. He also recalled Angela Marchment and Wang talking about how the Chinese culture seemed comfortable mixing tradition with modernity. He began to understand Imogen Glass more. She had delightfully expressed what he felt about this place. It was a mixture of east and west, old and new.

'We go right to the end of the route,' said Martin. 'Happy Valley is where the trams circle around and then return to Central, where we came from.'

As the tram stopped and Martin stood up, Drake was reluctant to leave what had proved to be a privileged view of the centre of Hong Kong Island. Martin looked at the address again and briefly consulted his map. They were soon at the right level, and then there was the door of the Glass home. Drake drew a long breath. What, if anything, were they to discover? Martin pressed the doorbell. A muffled sound emanated from deep inside the residence. There was no reaction. Drake always anticipated disappointment. Even so, this was a long way to go without a result. Then suddenly, the door opened. A tall, balding man of Western appearance stood in the open doorway. He looked over a pair of rimless half glasses.

'Yes.'

Martin held out his Hong Kong Police ID.

'I'm Inspector Martin Henshaw of Hong Kong Police, and this is Chief Inspector Drake.'

Drake noticed that he cleverly didn't admit to Drake's police service.

'Are you William Glass?'

'Oh no,' the man was laughing. 'He and his wife left here several years ago.'

'We understand that William and Dorothy Glass are here in Hong Kong. Have you any idea where they are staying?'

'You'd better ask our visitors in,' said a slightly squeaky voice, and a diminutive woman appeared from behind the man who had opened the door.

'Thank you,' said Martin as their host stood aside. They entered a generous hall and were shown into a classically designed living room. This was not the residence of people from an Eastern culture. Martin and Drake took seats as they indicated.

'We are Ruth and Michael Atkins,' said the squeaky voice. 'We are close, long-standing friends of William and Dorothy. Would you gentlemen take a cup of tea?' Drake smiled and nodded his head. Martin uttered some thanks. Both their hosts left the room. Drake looked around. The sofas and chairs were upholstered sumptuously, and the fabrics generously draped either side of the large window. There was a highly polished mahogany table behind. Between the chairs and sofas was a glass coffee table. Ruth and Michael Atkins appeared with a tray full of teacups, a teapot, and a cake. Soon, everyone was munching and sipping.

'I'm sure if William and Dorothy were in Hong Kong, we would know about it,' said Michael. 'We believe they are in Texas.'

'Perhaps I had better explain,' said Drake. 'Our people have tracked a couple from Texas to London. They then left for Hong Kong. They are known as Peter and Mary, but we believe these are just the names they have taken in a sect known as Xi Dong.'

Michael and Ruth looked at each other with quizzical expressions. They briefly stared at each other, and then Michael spoke.

'I'm afraid Peter and Mary are most definitely not the Glasses. We have recently encountered them, and you can be assured of that.'

'Perhaps you could go back to the beginning of this story,' said Drake, 'and explain to us why you are here and how you know where the Glasses are.'

'These are matters we are sworn to secrecy about,' said William, 'but since you are policemen, you may be able to help us too. William Glass and I used to work together at the stock exchange. We both did well, and we are comfortably off. William, however, was nothing short of a genius. Everything he touched seemed to turn to gold, almost literally. Our two families got to know each other with the children at the same English school. So, we also know Imogen and Felicity. William and I got too old for the hectic life demanded by the international finance world. For some time, we talked about retiring. In short, work had been our lives, and we both felt we had neglected our families.' Ruth was nodding her head in agreement and smiling. Michael continued.

'We both retired at the same time. I previously had a hobby of playing music, and I now found time to join a small orchestra, though I had to practice a great deal. I found retirement a joy, but William was lost. He had no pastimes or interests. Somehow, he got involved in a new sect that had started here in Hong Kong. It all began innocuously as William took some online life coaching courses, then they had some short residential courses, and eventually, it escalated to them becoming residential members. That sect is called Xi Dong. I felt that William and Dorothy got too involved and lost their perspective. The sect started to rule their lives. Their two daughters went to university, and they took up an invitation to help open a new branch of Xi Dong in Texas. William was absorbed and excited by it. I think Dorothy was just a little more cautious. One of the sect's rules was that members gave up their income and savings and, in return, were provided for by the sect. They were assured they could always have their money back if they left the sect. This worried Dorothy more than William, but in the end, he agreed with her to transfer the deeds of this place to us on the unwritten understanding that we would look after it and hand it back if they came out of the sect again. Perhaps you might appreciate that this property is worth millions of Hong Kong dollars. Even in the UK, it would provide a handsome pension fund. Some other investments went undeclared, which we monitor but remain in the name of Glass even though we have custody of them and get all the correspondence.' William paused and took a drink of his tea before continuing.

'Thank goodness that Dorothy had the foresight to arrange all this. As far as we can see, Xi Dong has become progressively more extreme. We now know that William and Dorothy want to leave Xi Dong. William was an enthusiastic convert. But he is no fool, especially about money. He originally expected to play a major managerial role in Texas. But that was not how it turned out. Xi Dong is clever. They moved William and Dorothy halfway around the world, separated from all their contacts and resources. Now, they are effectively trapped. It's not easy to walk out of the centre they are in. It is in a remote part of the country and well-guarded. However, even if they could walk out, they would lose millions. It's a clever trap that Xi Dong springs on its members. They effectively become helpless.' Michael stopped and took a breath. He looked at his wife, and she nodded her approval.

Drake said, 'I assume from some of the things you have told us that you are in communication with William and Dorothy.'

'We have ways of communicating. Their use of the internet is monitored. It is not unknown for recalcitrant members to be kept isolated as punishment for communicating about matters such as membership and finance. This is all dressed up as needing a period of meditation.'

'What are these methods of communication?' asked Martin.

'In the early days, we used Imogen as a go-between. However, that avenue has been closed, and we did not want to cause trouble for Imogen. We now use a supplier in Texas who frequently delivers to the Xi Dong campus. We prefer to say no more for now.'

'Felicity has spoken to us several times,' said Drake. 'She seems to be under the impression that her parents have become progressively more extreme in the sect and are constantly trying to persuade the two daughters to go and join them.'

'That was true early on,' replied Michael. 'However, we are sure Peter and Mary have taken over William's email and computer. The Xi Dong hierarchy is extremely professional in what they do. They are either aware of or suspect there are resources belonging to William and Dorothy that they want to get their grubby hands on.' Michael turned to his wife and asked her what, Drake thought, was a delicate question.

'Shall we tell them about Peter and Mary?' he asked.

'Yes,' said Ruth. 'I will tell them.' She turned to Drake and lowered her voice to almost a whisper. 'We had a visit only a few days ago from these two people known as Peter and Mary. They were outwardly polite but ultimately quite threatening. They told us that William and Dorothy were now old and unwell. They needed money for medical treatment. They said they had been sent over here to collect that money. If we wanted William and Dorothy not to come to harm, we needed to help them financially. They said they knew that this place belonged to William and Dorothy. They said we needed to sell it and give them the money to help William and Dorothy. They said William was seriously unwell. Then they said that if selling the property was too much for us, they could arrange for the deeds to be transferred to Xi Dong, and they would look after the sale for us.' Ruth stopped talking and started to sob. Michael patted her on the shoulder.

'We are both upset about all this,' he said. 'We have gone over it time and time again. We know it is all a lie because we have communicated with William through our courier. We have a friend here in Hong Kong who has warned us that Xi Dong here has friends in high places. We would struggle to take any action against them. Nowadays, things have changed in Hong Kong. We Brits are no longer respected. It's all a terrible mess.'

'As a Brit in the police force here,' said Martin. 'I understand your problem.' William took up the story.

'We do have some hope for William and Dorothy. I cannot say why, except that a route out of Xi Dong is being planned. We don't know if it will happen, and if so, whether it will work. We are also worried about Imogen. We haven't seen her for ages, nor have we heard from her. We are worried that she might have fallen foul of Xi Dong.'

'I'm afraid I have some news for you,' said Drake. 'I am a member of the Cheshire police in the UK. Imogen has very sadly died.' Drake paused and sat still while Ruth sobbed uncontrollably but shaking silently. Michael went over to sit by her on a sofa and hugged her.

'I knew, I knew it,' sobbed Ruth. 'I knew something was wrong.'

'There are suspicious circumstances surrounding Imogen's death,' said Drake quietly. 'We strongly suspect that she was murdered. I am here informally with Martin to see what we might be able to discover in Hong Kong, where Imogen has spent so much time.'

'Oh Michael,' sobbed Ruth. 'I knew it could end like this when they got involved with this wretched Xi Dong outfit. Now, everything has gone wrong. What do we do?' Drake looked at Martin, who spoke again.

'I should be careful about involving the police,' he said. 'Most are straight and honest, but some have suspicious contacts. If you have solicitors, I suggest you get them to play for time.'

'Yes,' said Drake. 'Things are coming to a head. The Metropolitan Police in London have raided the Xi Dong place there. Their investigations are proceeding. I would be confident that they will eventually involve the police in Texas. I believe that

Xi Dong has a limited future. For my part, I will do my best to keep you informed of progress.'

'Do you think Xi Dong is responsible for Imogen's death?' asked Michael.

'That is a possibility. If so, we don't know why they should go to the extreme of murder. Do you know if Imogen has tried to contact her parents recently?'

'I believe she has recently steered clear of them,' said Michael. 'She came to see us a couple of months ago and told us she was here to research. At the time, we assumed she meant investigating more about Chinese art for her work. However, now I wonder if she was in some way investigating the people behind her parent's detention. If only we could have helped, but we didn't know what danger she was in.'

'I'm sorry to bring you such awful news,' said Drake. 'Thank you for telling us so much. We now need to progress our investigations further. I need to understand a whole new web of skullduggery that complicates the situation. I am sorry that we cannot, at this stage, bring it to a conclusion.'

'Thank you so much for coming,' said Michael. 'I hope you will be extremely careful. These people are dangerous. If they know about your investigation, you are in considerable danger. Please be careful here in Hong Kong.'

# 26

'Good morning,' said Martin as Drake opened the door for him. 'Did you sleep well?'

'To begin with, yes. But then I woke up and started to turn all the information from yesterday over in my mind. I'm a bit cross about it because I'm sure my old brain works on things better in the background, and I've never let work interfere with sleep before.'

'I know the problem,' said Martin, 'The jet lag doesn't help, and it worsens as you age. So, did you work anything out?'

'Not so much worked out, but we have a major new line of investigation. The Xi Dong people are ruthless in their pursuit of money. They are quite obviously now an internationally coordinated outfit. They have been able to fool many members into parting with their money. They are obviously after the Glass fortune. What is new to us is the different state of play regarding William and Dorothy Glass, who are no longer taken in and want to get out without losing too much money. It seems likely that Xi Dong has discovered the substantial previously hidden wealth, including the property in Happy Valley. If they are worried that Imogen's parents want out, there may be some urgency to persuade the current residents of Happy Valley to part with the property. However, could they be responsible for Imogen's death? If so, why would they want to take such a drastic and dangerous step? There is a lot to think about.'

'Yes,' said Martin. 'You are possibly up against some dangerous people. Now, how about we visit this exhibition of Imogen's work?'

'Excellent,' replied Drake. 'I'm looking forward to that.'

'I've left my car in a car park. I think it is easier if we go by train. It will give you a better view of Hong Kong, and my car doesn't have a satnav, so I would probably get lost and be unable to find parking places. The station is only a short walk from here.'

The train departed from a central station in the great metropolis that is that part of Hong Kong. It ran along the main line in the area Martin said was called Kowloon. As they watched, they could see the landscape gradually change to a less dense and more rural kind of urbanism. Shatin itself appeared to be a new town. Martin explained that it was part of a much larger planned townscape. This would be the last development before reaching the border with China itself. Then, you would be in a rapidly developing new town called Shenzhen. Martin explained that it had a population of nearly twenty million. Drake struggled to imagine such a size. It was hard to believe. This town had a population of a third the size of the United Kingdom.

The walk from Shatin station to the museum was relatively quick. Martin deliberately took them through a shopping mall to give Drake a feel of the place. Soon after, and down by the river, they found the museum. Drake was having a mental conversation with Cynthia about the building itself. It was a great lump of concrete and certainly not suggestive of the glorious Hong Kong heritage that Drake's guidebook said it housed. Once inside, it was a different matter. Drake couldn't resist looking at the section on Chinese opera first. It first fascinated him when he briefly encountered it in Singapore. He knew about Commedia dell'arte, and he could see some similarities. There seemed to be a mainly fixed cast and a series of ritual scenes and displays. Drake was entranced by the idea of such a well-developed art form appreciated by a colossal audience but about which the West hardly knew anything. Martin could see that he was not just looking but also thinking. Suddenly, Drake turned to him.

'This is fascinating,' he said. 'I need to think about it more.'

Eventually, Martin managed to drag him away, and they went into the Imogen Glass exhibition. It was a surprise. This was not some amateur show. It was a large and highly professional display. Drake made a quick estimate of the number of paintings on display. He thought it was certainly more than thirty and possibly quite a few more. He collected the catalogue, which was dual language and tucked it under his arm to read later. He began to photograph every painting he could. The images on his iPhone also showed a short text explanation against each one. Martin was sure they shouldn't be taking photographs, but no one was bothering about it. Drake was taking great delight in his ability to use the phone's camera. He soon found he could zoom in on each picture. He made a mental note to send some to his son Tom and daughter Lucy to prove he had mastered at least this simple function on the phone they had given him.

'I wish I understood all this more than I do,' he said to Martin. 'She is known for combining elements of Western and Oriental traditional art. I can see the latter. It is clear as daylight that these works are influenced by Chinese culture. It's the combination with English technique that I am not sufficiently clever to see.'

'Well, it's certainly popular,' said Martin. He pointed out several little clusters of people chatting earnestly about what they could see.

'It's also rather expensive, I gather,' said Drake. 'The market here drives up the prices.'

'Yes,' said Martin. 'I read that two Imogen Glass paintings have already been stolen. Art theft and the associated crime of forgery are common here. This is such a widespread habit that you must assume everything offered for sale is a forgery. That doesn't necessarily reduce its value.'

'I can't understand that,' grunted Drake. 'The world has gone mad.'

'I imagine,' said Martin, 'that this exhibition has paintings worth in total many millions of pounds.'

When it is all put together like this, you see how prolific she was,' said Drake, scanning around. 'Presumably, most of this has not been imported just for this exhibition but belongs here in Hong Kong.'

'I should think all of it,' replied Martin. 'They wouldn't have had to curate and import paintings. I understand that is both technically difficult and an administrative nightmare.'

Another viewer came to look at the same painting as Drake and Martin.

'Her work is wonderful, isn't it?' he said.

'It's quite charming,' said Drake, 'but can you explain what is so special about it?'

The stranger spoke enthusiastically for several minutes before moving to the next painting.

'Did you understand that?' asked Martin.

'I understood quite a few of the words,' replied Drake, 'but not many of the sentences.'

'Have you seen enough?' asked Martin, laughing.

'Yes,' said Drake. 'Just let me speak to the man at the desk.' Drake walked back to the entrance to the exhibition, where a small group were setting off inside with tickets in their hands.

'Is this exhibition going well?' Drake asked the newly free receptionist.

'Yes, sir,' he replied. 'It is extraordinary. It has been arranged so quickly that we haven't had time to advertise it. There have been reports in the newspaper and on our website, but otherwise, it must just be word of mouth.'

Drake thanked him and turned to Martin.

'I want to take one final look at the Chinese Opera display,' he said, setting off with Martin in tow. The display was only just round the corner from the reception desk. Drake stopped and turned to Martin again.

This parallel with Commedia dell'arte has made me think. I have just "heard" Cynthia "retelling" me about a group of her architecture students who became fascinated by it. Just like this Chinese opera, it used traditional characters and settings to tell contemporary stories. They started using ideas and elements from classical architecture in modern buildings. I never really understood her, but today, I have begun to. I am beginning to appreciate Imogen's obsession. It is not about the trivialities of style but rather about much more deep ideas. I am stumbling to some understanding. How I wish I had been better educated. OK, let's go.'


Drake opened the door to his room in the Kowloon Shangri-La Hotel. Martin followed him in.

'Wow,' said Drake. 'That view just hits you. It is unbelievable to feel you are in the middle of the harbour. Thank you for recommending it.'

'I thought you'd like it,' said Martin. 'Why don't you just take it in while I brew some tea?'

Drake sat in one of the two easy chairs placed appropriately in the window. Lying on the coffee table between them were several magazines. He picked up a copy of a magazine called The Peak. He flipped through it, one page at a time.

'You need an awful lot of money to buy anything you can see in there,' laughed Martin, bringing over a teapot and two cups. 'It's mainly expensive houses and apartments and equally pricey fashion, especially handmade stylish watches.'

'I've seen this before, said Drake, pointing to an article about a house. Look, I'm sure this picture of the gateway was in one of Imogen's paintings.' He pulled out his phone and started to scroll through his images from the exhibition. Martin looked through the article. There was no address of the property or name of its owner. The caption below the picture on Drake's phone read, "loaned by kind permission of the owner."

'I am looking this up in the portfolio of all her paintings we found in Imogen's studio. I have an idea that I know where this painting is.' Drake started to thumb through the images from the portfolio on his phone. He began at the back. 'Thank goodness Tom and Lucy gave me this phone. Yes, I thought so. Imogen had left behind a folio of all her paintings and often a note about where they went or who had bought them. This is one of the paintings that have gone missing. As far as we were aware, they have never been sold. They appear in her portfolio at the end, so we assume they represent her most recent work. The people who sell her paintings at The Orient Gallery in Chester had not seen them before. This picture has found its way over here remarkably quickly.'

'There's only one place where this house could be,' said Martin. 'It must be on The Peak somewhere.'

'Now I'm going to say something dangerous,' said Drake, 'because I don't know what I'm talking about. You can see how this scene fits into some of Imogen's obsessions. She is in love with those Chinese paintings of vertiginous mountains and waterfalls. It would be interesting to find it.'

'Yes, of course,' said Martin. 'I can go and get my car, and we can explore. You'll enjoy the views from up there.'


About an hour later, Drake was woken from a nap by his phone ringing.

'Hi,' said the voice. 'Martin here. I'm outside the front of the hotel in a car.'

'Right. I'll come straight down,' said Drake. He left the room, called a lift and was soon in the lobby. As he reached the main door, he saw Martin waving from behind a car. Drake settled into the front passenger seat and took out his map of the city he had picked up in the lobby. Martin pointed to the map.

'We're here,' he said. 'Look, this is where we are going. I doubt you'll be able to follow it. The route is not particularly logical.' By the time they entered the tunnel under the harbour on their way to the Island, Drake was already confused.

'Complicated one-way systems,' laughed Martin. They emerged from the tunnel and made several sharp turns before climbing.

'We are on the lower levels of The Peak now,' said Martin. The route started to be surrounded by trees, and from time to time,

Drake glanced at a briefly stolen view of the harbour below. His new surroundings were quite enchanting.

'Beautiful, isn't it,' said Martin. 'You probably need at least five hundred million pounds to buy a house here.'

Martin drove up and down a series of roads that seemed to Drake to each follow a contour around The Peak.

'Those are all the roads where I thought this house might be,' said Martin with a puzzled air.

'I have seen anything like it yet,' said Drake, with the magazine and his phone open at the relevant pages.

'I've one more idea,' said Martin. 'There are a couple of gated developments where all the houses are beyond a single entrance gate. Luckily, with my police pass, we can get inside that gate.' He drove up another couple of roads, both curving around The Peak until they pulled up at a gate with a small gatehouse alongside. He showed his ID to the man coming out, who promptly opened the gate. After they turned along a long curved road, Drake suddenly shouted.

'That looks like it,' he said, and Martin stopped. In front of them was a high-trimmed hedge interrupted by a strongly built gate. Next to it, there was a generous parking space. Drake guessed it was for delivery lorries. There was no number or name on the gate. Drake took several photographs. 'It's no good us trying to get in here,' said Martin. 'You will almost certainly have to call a number and talk to someone who can open the gate. We don't have a convincing reason just now. I could get a search warrant, but I don't want to try that as I doubt my superiors would issue it. I have a pretty good idea who lives here, but I would have to check some closely guarded maps back at the office. If I'm right, this would be an interesting outcome. I won't take you to the office, so I'll drive back via the hotel.'

'Look,' said Drake. 'I've been studying this, and there seems to be an inconsistency. If you look at Imogen's painting, the gateway and hedge are to the left, but to the right is a view looking down over the harbour. They are not positioned like that.'

'No,' said Martin, 'and if I know anything about these houses, the grand view of the harbour will be visible from the main rooms in the house. That can't be possible in Imogen's painting.'

'Perhaps this is part of her mystery,' grunted Drake. 'Presumably, she must have got the permission of the owner to paint this unless there are other published views of this house.'

'I doubt this is a widely published property,' said Martin. 'There were only interior views in The Peak Magazine that you were looking at. You would not be able to identify the place from the outside. If I am right about who owns this, he is notoriously secretive and, probably, with good cause.'

'I wonder,' said Drake. 'I wonder.'

'I'll come for you again tomorrow morning,' said Martin. 'Be prepared for an interesting day.'

# 27

Grace woke, suspecting that she had overslept. She checked her watch on the bedside table. Sure enough, it was already half past nine. For a moment, she panicked. She would be late! She swung her legs out of the bed and sat frozen. It was then that her brain started to do its job. It was the weekend. She was not due to work today. She relaxed. She was anxious to check the post. It was almost a week since the last message from her unwelcome stalker. She had managed not to think about him for the last couple of days. She hoped that he might have tired of his fruitless pursuit of her. She got up and went down to collect the post. Her hands began to shake slightly as she looked through all the envelopes. They were mostly junk mail and bills. Never had she been so glad to get an electricity bill. She took the post to the kitchen and left it on the table while she made a cup of coffee. She only allowed herself one caffeinated brew a day, and this was it. From now on, it would be decaf only, and she felt better about that. It was so easy to drink coffee at work. She had managed to persuade Steve Redvers to order lots of decaf pods. She picked up her laptop and retired back to bed. She briefly checked the post again and then opened her laptop. She needed to check her email. Perhaps the stalker had sent an unpleasant message.

Her inbox only had one message. It was from Drake. Thank goodness nothing from her stalker. Perhaps he had given up. She looked at it and checked her watch. She had one of the little clocks on the time app set to Hong Kong time. Drake's message had been sent at a late hour. Perhaps he was not sleeping any better than her. She opened Drake's mail. It was full of the things he had discovered so far. He described, in detail, his visit to the Imogen Glass exhibition and his meeting with Ruth and Michael Atkins.

There was his analysis of what they might mean. He also told of how Martin was helping him, and then he broke the news that Martin was resigning and coming back to Chester. To begin with, he would join the team. Her internal conflict about Martin surfaced again, and she lay back, turning it all over in her mind.

Grace was woken again suddenly. She had dropped off with her laptop open beside her on the bed. There it was again. It was her doorbell. She pulled on a dressing gown and rushed to the front door. Just as she arrived, her brain relaunched all her anxieties about the wretched stalking. She opened the door and felt the blood rise across her face as she did so. A parcel that had been leaning against the door fell into the hall. Thank goodness again. Calm down, she said to herself. She turned the package over in her hands. It was a large square but relatively thin box. She had not ordered anything. She leant out and looked up and down the street. She saw only one figure scuttling away back to a van. Why was he rushing? Of course, all these white van drivers are permanently in a hurry to keep up with their demanding schedules. She read the lettering on the top of the box, "handle with care, flowers." Who could they be from? Perhaps Martin was sending a message about his return. She tore open the box. Out fell a tastefully beautiful circular flower arrangement. There was a folded card with a flower on the front. She opened it. "Grace Hepple, RIP," shrieked the message inside. It was a funeral wreath! She instinctively dropped the whole thing on the floor. She put her head in her hands and sobbed.

Drake was idly sifting through his copy of The Peak and was halfway through his breakfast when his phone rang. It was Martin.

'Good morning,' he said. 'I hope we are not too early for you?'

'I'm just in the restaurant having breakfast.' There was some discussion that Drake couldn't quite decipher.'

'That's OK,' said Martin. 'We'll come and join you for a coffee.' Drake ordered two extra places to be laid, and Martin came striding in together with a stranger. They sat at the table.

'This is Chief Inspector Drake from the UK,' said Martin as Drake held out a hand.

'It is best not to use my real name,' said the stranger. 'Please call me George. Inspector Martin has told me of your interest. Formally, I should not be assisting you. However, we are interested in similar things, and your enquiry may yield information we might want to use too. Of course, you accept that you are working outside your jurisdiction, so if any formal procedures are required, you must leave those to me.' Drake nodded his head.

'Yes, of course, totally understood.'

'Perhaps you could explain where you have got to,' said George.

'We are investigating the death of an artist called Imogen Glass,' said Drake. 'This occurred in the city of Chester, where I am responsible. The circumstances of the death strongly suggest murder. Some of her paintings are missing, so we are naturally interested in what happened to them and where they are. We found this painting in the exhibition of her work in The Heritage Museum. It is in the group of paintings that went missing from her studio. As far as we know, these paintings have never been sold, at least legitimately. Yesterday, we found the house where this gate is. It is in one of the gated communities on The Peak. There is an odd feature. The painting shows this gateway and the view over the harbour, but this is physically impossible.'

'Ah yes,' said George. 'That is one of her trademarks. She often juxtaposes different views from the same place. Often, they are all assembled like traditional Chinese landscapes. Martin and I think we know who owns this house. If we are right, it is an important and influential member of Hong Kong society. If it is him, then after many years of being ultra-careful, he may have made a mistake. I suspect his pride got the better of him. He has allowed The Peak to show his house, mostly interiors and inaccessible to ordinary folk. He has also allowed his painting to be used in the exhibition. Martin, it is best that we don't use his real name. What do you suggest we call him?'

'I don't know his name. How about DH for Dragonhead?' said Martin. George laughed. Drake looked puzzled.

'I get the impression you have been after him for some time,' said Drake.

'Yes, we strongly suspect he is the dragonhead of a triad crime syndicate here.'

Drake interrupted, 'What's a dragonhead?'

'It's what triads call the most senior figure in their ranks,' said Martin.

'Yes,' said George. 'The rate at which he has acquired money would be way beyond the means of most of us. He is quite secretive and virtually never gives interviews. I could only talk to him with the backing of the most senior people, and I would need to have far more than just suspicions. This is what he trades on. It probably costs him a whole load of money. He must worry that one day, the whole edifice could collapse. That is why we suspect he is involved in the art trade.'

'I'm afraid that I don't see the logic of that,' said a puzzled Drake.'

'Let's get another pot of coffee, and we can explain,' said George. Drake waved his arms demonstratively, and a freshly steaming pot was brought to the table. As it was being poured, Drake turned to George.

'Do you mind if I say you speak English remarkably well?'

'Ah, my parents' fault,' said George. 'They sent me to expensive schools in England. I learned to speak what I think you call the King's English. This used to be a passport to success here in Hong Kong. Sadly, that is no longer the case. It is good Mandarin that will get you far now. I have always struggled with Mandarin. I speak Cantonese.' Martin and George smiled knowingly at each other. Drake was beginning to appreciate just how well-embedded Martin had become in the place. He was doing well. Drake always knew that he would eventually blossom, and this short-term post here in Hong Kong had created the ideal opportunity.

'Art is a wonderful world for the criminals,' said George, pausing to sip his newly poured coffee. 'There are two main areas of crime. One is forgery, and the other is theft. They are often interlinked. Art theft is most often done at a highly professional and international level. Things once stolen can now be transported extremely rapidly. They may go through several countries in attempts to mask their whereabouts. Unfortunately, this often works, and we lose track of major items. Sadly, there is less international collaboration between police forces than is desirable. In Europe, Italy is a favourite destination for stolen art. Here in the Far East, it is Hong Kong.' George took another sip of his coffee.

'As for forgery, well, that is a national pastime. We are well behind the game when it comes to forgery. Art students are even taught to copy original art as their main form of education. Copying accurately is much admired in our culture. It can be a painting or tapestry. It can be music, watches, or fashion. Anything valuable gets copied. Often, the copies are so good that we cannot tell they are fakes. Go to Hollywood Road, and you will be offered art copies that would defeat the experts. You will even get a forged certificate showing the origin of the work. It is all ridiculous, but many fortunes have been made faking things. It may seem perverse, but often, a painting will be stolen specifically so that it can be copied. Much more money can be made selling countless fakes at attractive "discounts" than from one sale of the original.'

'Good gracious,' said Drake. 'I had no idea that such crime was so international and professional. Hollywood Road needs a visit.'

'Agreed,' said Martin. 'We can go there today.'

'It's a strange world in many ways,' said George. 'Some experts have argued that the more a painting is copied, the more popular it becomes and the more the original is worth. So, a syndicate stealing paintings, copying them, and eventually selling the original has quite a good business model. But it goes further. When valuable paintings are stolen, this is most often from a gallery and, more occasionally, from a collector. That theft will almost certainly be done by what we might call professionals. This is what these people do. They steal to order. They will almost always have some character behind them who will buy the work from them at a fraction of its market value. This will, in turn, be sold on until it comes into the ownership of a crime syndicate. The leader of such a syndicate may hide the work in some unlikely location. A famous one was discovered recently underneath his mother-in-law's kitchen floor. She had no idea that it was there. This Mr Big will certainly be the only person who knows where the painting is hidden. It becomes a sort of insurance policy. If he eventually gets caught, he will offer to trade the painting in for a reduced sentence. If it's a famous work, the police will almost certainly play ball rather than allow it to become public knowledge that they could have recovered this priceless piece of art. This practice originated mainly in Italy, where it is highly successful, but it is also alive and well here in Hong Kong. This practice also works well for jewellery and historic porcelain and pottery.'

'So do you think this is what may have happened to some or all of Imogen's work?' asked Drake.

'We have no way of knowing for sure, though sometimes if we keep our ears to the ground, we get hints about things,' said George. 'If the crooks suspect we are on their track, they might sell the work in the underworld. There, it will eventually represent an insurance policy for a new owner. Imogen's work has become extremely fashionable here. Consequently, it will attract quite a lot of interest. Now that she is dead, the work may rise in value because it suddenly becomes part of a finite sum of work.'

'Thank you for educating me so well,' said Drake. 'I had little knowledge of much of this. So how may we be able to help you?'

'Obviously, you are most interested in tracing this back to the murderer. That is assuming this is who stole the work. We are, however, more interested in the people at the other end of the chain. If, by any chance, this led us to convict one of our high-profile suspects, then we would be particularly grateful. Good luck.' The two men stood and shook hands. George tapped Martin on the shoulder. 'Keep me informed,' he said.

'Did you know all this, Martin?' asked Drake when George had left.

'Most of it, but I wanted you to hear from George's expert account. He remains one of my friends here. His personal history has made him even more sympathetic to the English. After breakfast, I will take you to Hollywood Road. The journey there will be especially fascinating.'

# 28

Drake rose feeling more in step with the local time zone. For the first time on the trip, his brain seemed to accept when night morphed into daytime. It was an altogether quicker process than he was used to. After a leisurely breakfast, he was ready for Martin to collect him. They met in the hotel lobby at the agreed time and set off, taking what was by now a familiar walk along the waterfront to the ferry at Tsim Sha Tsui. Drake pulled out his season ticket, ready to wave it at the machine. Once he saw it, the attendant opened a courtesy gate. It would be a free ride. Martin laughed as they both passed through.

'There is more respect for older people here,' he said. 'Just being in your company saves me money. A pity it's not like that back in the UK.'

They were once more ready for the incoming ferry. Now that he was familiar with the system, Drake took in more of his surroundings. Martin had deliberately chosen a time after the mad morning rush. Their boat ride was both comfortable and quick. Martin had promised Drake one more unique Hong Kong system of transport. He had been rather coy about it, so Drake was anxious to experience this journey. They left the ferry at Central Pier as before, but this time took a right turn into a shopping mall. They passed what Drake thought might be the biggest Apple shop in the world. As far as he could see, it occupied a two-storey bridge that ran right across a multi-lane highway. He took out his iPhone and snapped it. He would send a picture to Tom and Lucy. Taking a left turn, they came out of the mall onto a pedestrian bridge, which he could see crossed over the tram tracks they had travelled along the day before. Martin decided to explain their journey.

'We are going to Hollywood Road,' said Martin. The further inland we go, the more the land rises onto the foothills of the peak. Hollywood Road is on what they call the mid-levels. Here is our transport.' He pointed to an escalator that Drake thought was unremarkable. 'This is claimed to be the longest escalator system in the world,' said Martin. It cannot all be in one span since it crosses so many streets that people must get on and off at intermediate levels. I believe there are at least twenty escalators in the system. So, get ready to get off at the end of this first one and take a few paces to the next. We go up until we reach Hollywood Road.' Now and then, Drake got a glimpse almost to the top of the system and was duly impressed. Of course, there was a covering roof going the whole way, so it looked like the most extraordinary tunnel, crowded with people consulting the iPhones they had presumably bought tax-free down at the bottom.

'We get off here,' said Martin eventually. 'We are probably just less than halfway up the entire system. Normally, they run uphill, and, as you can see, there is a staircase alongside for going down. However, if we had met a little earlier in the rush hour, it would have been switched around to bring the masses of people down from the housing beyond. We would have had to use the stairs. I didn't think you would enjoy that.' Drake laughed and patted Martin on his back in gratitude.

Under Martin's guidance, they began to stroll along Hollywood Road. Almost every other shop seemed to sell art of one kind or another. There were ceramics, pottery, sculptures and, of course, paintings. There were also furniture shops, many antiques, gift shops and cafes. Drake thought you could fuddle around for hours and still not see a repetition.

'Let's have a look in this gallery,' said Martin. 'We can see if they have heard of Imogen Glass and whether they can get any of her paintings.' Martin held the door open for Drake as a chime sounded. There was an air of quiet calm in the place, but this was, to some extent, broken by the riot of colour displayed by the dozens of paintings.

'Imogen Glass, yes, of course,' said the short and slightly stocky man on duty. 'Come this way, please.' He walked towards the rear of the shop, and there, suddenly, there were no less than four paintings, all claiming to be by Imogen Glass. To Drake's still poorly trained eye, they looked like her paintings. He started to flip through his collection of images on his iPhone. Their host backed away, bowing as he did so.

'Only fresh in yesterday. I leave you to enjoy.'

'Look,' said Drake to Martin, 'I've found this one in her portfolio. We think it's quite early.' He continued to flip through his iPhone. 'Here's another, and another. None of these are in the newly apparently unsold paintings, but we saw several in the exhibition in Shatin.'

'Interesting,' said Martin as he waved over the hovering assistant. 'Can we see the proprietor?' he said.

'Owner, yes me,' came the reply.

'Are these originals?' asked Drake. The owner nodded his head silently but enthusiastically and with a broad grin. 'How much is this one?' asked Drake, pointing to the first picture he saw.

'Depends how you pay,' said the owner. 'If cash, then fifty thousand dollars.'

'That's about five thousand sterling,' said Martin helpfully.

'OK,' said Martin. Let us talk about it.' The owner nodded his head and beamed a toothy smile. He backed away again and started shuffling papers on a desk.

'My guess is,' said Drake. 'If this were original, it would be worth many times that price. I'm looking at the note beside this in Imogen's portfolio, and it says it went to The Orient in Chester. We need more information about the destination and price of these paintings. I will email Grace and ask her to get this information pronto. We could then come back better informed and delve further into this murky business.' Drake fell silent and started to tap a message on his phone while Martin had just opened his to read a text.

'That's interesting,' said Martin. 'I've got a message from George. He says he has some new information about Mr DH. He doesn't want to put it into a message that could be intercepted, and he is not far away. I suggest we meet somewhere nearby. It's a place that I'm sure will fascinate you.'

'Excellent and intriguing,' said Drake. Martin beckoned the owner, who scuttled over, smiling and bowing.

'We would like a little time to think about this,' said Martin. 'Can we come back in a couple of days?'

'Certainly, certainly,' said the owner. 'You give me your phone number. I will inform you if anyone else makes an offer for painting.'


After a short walk back along Hollywood Road, the two one-time colleagues made their way down and past a park which Martin said was a kind of city zoo. They entered a garden that Drake thought was beautiful and arrived at a charming colonial-style building. Several men were planting brightly coloured plants into beds. The scene reminded Drake of a passage from Alice in Wonderland, where minions disguised as playing cards were similarly employed. Drake wondered if the Red Queen would appear. Perhaps she would demand that all their heads be chopped off. He speculated for a few seconds why his brain made these curious connections. He was glad it did, as he was sure this often helped him to solve cases. He wished he understood this ability and could call on it at will. Cynthia had told him that the famous American architect Frank Lloyd Wright was instructed by his mother not to inquire into his creativity, or he might lose it. Drake stood smiling at this memory until Martin interrupted his reverie. He pointed to the colonnaded building.

'I'm sorry if that was too long a walk,' he said, 'but we are here. This is the Tea Museum.' Drake was even more sure they were in Alice's Wonderland as he followed Martin inside. Ahead of them was a carefully curated exhibition explaining the history of tea growing and brewing in various parts of the world. They stopped for a few minutes to watch a video showing the best way to brew tea. Drake had become fascinated by the Chinese rituals surrounding tea. Here, it was all explained. Martin had to drag him back into the lobby and past a shop selling everything to do with tea. There were some cunningly designed mugs that you could use to make tea. Drake wanted to buy one. Martin stood patiently while Drake made his purchase and showed him into a café. There, sitting at a table on the far side, was the member of the Hong Kong Police that Drake had been instructed to address as George.

'Hello, again,' said George, standing up to shake Drake's hand and slap Martin on the back. 'I have taken the liberty of calling for teas all round. Strictly the Chinese version rather than Indian, of course.'

'What a wonderful place,' said Drake. 'A piece of colonial history housing the most fascinating exhibits.'

'Absolutely,' said George. 'It is called Flagstaff House and was built in the nineteenth century as a grand residence for important members of Hong Kong society. However, now it offers us somewhere to meet, which is exactly the sort of innocent place we might take a visitor. More importantly, we are as sure as we can be that it is not bugged. We can talk freely.'

They all sat down, and Martin told Drake more about the place while tea was brought to the table. George performed the ritual of serving Chinese tea.

'Now,' said George. 'I have some news for you, but it concerns rather sensitive matters, so I thought it best to communicate directly rather than by insecure emails.'

'I'm all ears,' said Drake.

'Martin took you up on the Peak, and you found a house we believe is owned by a man who is simultaneously a well-known and much-respected figure and is also rather secretive and private. Some of us in the force suspect he also moves in other, less respectable circles. He certainly has more wealth than we think he could have acquired legitimately. Martin sent me some pictures of the house, and I can confirm it is where we believe this person lives. Because of our interest, we have done two things. Firstly, our wonderful IT people have managed to hack into his computer. He is careful never to use it to communicate with people he is connected to, but occasionally, he is a little careless and gives away things. You know that he may have loaned one of his Imogen Glass paintings to the exhibition in Shatin. This looks like carelessness. His desire to demonstrate his good taste and flaunt his wealth may have got the better of him. Of course, he is not referred to by name in the exhibition, but you cleverly spotted a painting that is clearly of his house and its privileged view over the harbour. I have spoken to the secret team we have monitoring him, and they think that he may own several Imogen Glass paintings, and this is almost certainly a recent acquisition. I understand from Martin that you have information that suggests it was painted not long before she died. So far, this is interesting. However, we have connected this with some of his recent computer searches. He belongs to a Facebook group of art collectors who collect paintings as investments. He has taken part in a discussion concerning the effect of an artist's death on the value of their work.' George paused.

'Oh, really,' said Drake. 'That is indeed interesting. Grace will send information about the sum exchanged for this work in the UK. As a start, I believe it was imported to Hong Kong from Chester by Far East Trading. They are a company who do a great of import and export business. Have you learned anything from this Facebook group?'

'Yes,' said George. 'Apparently, there is a variety of opinions about what happens to the value of paintings when an artist dies. Some think it goes up. Others think the biggest rise in value is when an artist is terminally ill or very old, so there is some real prospect of them not lasting too long. They believe the value may rise in these circumstances but may drop again once the artist dies.'

'I see,' said Drake. 'So, if you could predict the imminent prospect of a death and circulate this information, you might cause the value of a painting that you own to rise.'

'Exactly,' said George. 'There are all sorts of ramifications, but that is certainly one of them. Of course, the question that had interested us is why DH would want to know all this.' Drake nodded his head and grunted.

'You said you had done two things in your investigation of DH,' he said.

'Yes indeed,' replied George. 'Our lads have discovered a security camera on the dwelling just down the road, which bends and shows the entrance to DH's property. So, we have been monitoring the comings and goings. Mostly, it is delivery vans. DH is a recluse and seldom goes out, but we have observed him doing so occasionally. More interesting are his visitors. Not long ago, we monitored a top-of-the-range white Mercedes visiting on two occasions just a few days apart. We traced this to a car hire company. From them, we were able to discover who the visitor was. It is a female who uses several names, one of which she uses when acting as an art expert. Her name then is Irene Lei Mien Li. Martin tells me that you have an interest in her. I can say that she crops up now and then in various investigations using her several identities. In one guise, she sometimes travels to Beijing and, we believe, has meetings in government circles. We also suspect she has a high role in the triad that, we think, DH runs.'

Drake sat sipping tea, contemplating all this. He wondered what turns and twists this story would take next.

# 29

The following morning, as had become the pattern, Martin joined Drake for breakfast in the Kowloon Shangri-La Hotel restaurant.

'What is on the agenda today?' he asked as he sat down at Drake's table, where a place had been set for him.

'I would like to visit the art dealers who sell Imogen's paintings here in Hong Kong. I want to understand how a piece of work gets from The Orient Gallery in Chester onto the market here in Hong Kong. The dealers here are called Cheung Brothers. As I understand it, there are three brothers. Bobby, David and Kenneth. Bobby is the one who deals with paintings.' Drake pulled out his notebook and turned to the page recording his meeting with Angela Marchment at The Orient. 'The address is somewhere called K11 Art Mall.'

'No problem,' said Martin. 'That is a remarkable place not far from here in Kowloon. I can drive you there, or we can take a walk. If you like, I can call them to announce our arrival to ensure Bobby is available.' Drake nodded silently as he munched on his toast. 'OK,' said Martin. 'I've found their website and telephone number.'

Breakfast was finished, and calls were made. Drake and Martin left the hotel and walked around to the waterfront esplanade. A substantial ship was making its way steadily through the harbour towards Tsim Sha Tsui.

'Now, Martin,' said Drake as they walked. 'Perhaps you can solve a little mystery for me. I see this ship coming in every morning. It seems to go out in the middle of the evening. I assume it is a sea-going ferry. Last night, I took a walk this way. It seems to dock at the terminal down from the shopping mall. There were hordes of passengers getting on, but I saw no sign of a destination board. I looked at the map back in the hotel to find where it might be going in China, which would warrant a daily trip. You know, Martin, how I love mysteries. I have become a little obsessed with trying to solve this one. Have you any idea where it goes?' Martin laughed.

'It doesn't go anywhere,' he said. Drake looked even more perplexed.

'Surely it's not some sort of pleasure cruise?' he asked.

'In a way, yes,' said Martin. 'It's the gambling ship. The authorities in Hong Kong try to control gambling. Unfortunately, the Chinese here love gambling, but it results in people getting into debt and falling into the hands of crime syndicates. It is a serious problem here. There are a few places where gambling is allowed and controlled. For example, the racecourses at Shatin and Happy Valley, both places you have already seen. However, Chinese culture is one where people don't confront problems. They tend to work around them. So, there is a great deal of illegal gambling. One legal way of getting around the problem is to take the gambling ship, which sails out past territorial waters to a place where the Hong Kong government has no authority. They spend the night gambling, drinking, and dining. They return exhausted in the morning. The ship goes nowhere.'

'How fascinating,' said Drake. 'I have come to understand that the Chinese are a resourceful lot. So, they find ways of forging and faking valuable items, including paintings.'

'Indeed,' said Martin. 'Now we are almost as far as we need to go along the waterfront. We need to take a right turn here up Nathan Road. The K11 Art Mall is just a short distance up there.'

As they entered the mall, Drake took in a deep breath. It was the most extraordinary space. It soared up in a series of dramatic curved sweeping balconies. It was now that he remembered Cynthia describing it. Her excited and enthusiastic voice was in his head once more, and he stumbled as he closed his eyes the better to remember her, but Martin noticed that he was swaying slightly. He took hold of Drake's elbow and steadied him.

'Are you OK?' he asked.

'Yes, just taken aback. I had the geometry of this place described to me by Cynthia. She loved it. She is always with me still.' Drake pulled out a handkerchief, pushed his glasses onto his forehead and dabbed his moist eyes. Martin waited patiently, having seen similar behaviour in the past. He wondered if Drake would ever totally get over the loss of Cynthia. Martin directed Drake up a level on one of the flying escalators, which deposited them almost outside the gallery belonging to the Cheung Brothers. Drake stood, taking in the air of the place. It reminded him of The Orient in Chester, and he was not surprised that Wang had signed an agreement with partners who held similar values about art. The interior itself was of white walls and light-boarded floors. Drake listened to Cynthia's voice, telling him that the job of the architecture here was to make a background rather than demand attention.

There were paintings everywhere, though each one was hung in such a way as to give it space to appear on its own rather than jumbled all together as they were in the Hollywood Road gallery. Some paintings were hanging on the walls, and others were on elegant display screens of white panels held by stainless steel poles. Drake looked around for Martin, who had suddenly disappeared. He turned to see that he was standing by a series of three Imogen Glass paintings. They were the stars of the show. The panels were lettered in a simple, sanserif typeface heralding Imogen's name. An A4 notice was pinned alongside the first painting. It gave a brief account of Imogen's life. Below this was a simple sheet announcing the exhibition of her work that Drake had seen in Shatin.

Martin came round one of the panels, followed by a man dressed entirely in black with a pair of gold-rimmed half glasses perched on the end of his nose. He held out a hand to Drake, who responded.

'Bobby Cheung,' he said, bowing slightly. 'We are honoured to have a visit from you. We are desperately sad to hear about the passing of our favourite artist, Imogen Glass. The world has lost a great talent. She had so much more to give.'

Drake held out a hand. 'Yes, it is an awful business. I am sorry to visit under these circumstances.'

'I see you are looking at some of her work here. It always takes pride of place in our gallery.' Drake was listening, but in his usual manner, taking in his host. He wore a mandarin shirt buttoned up at the slightly loose collar. Although he had short black hair and an oriental face, he spoke in immaculate English, unlike the choppy Chinese version that was characteristic of Wang. 'We have been delighted to work with Wang and Angela. They have been wonderful partners, and we keep in touch with them by email and phone.'

'So, who would set the value and price of one of Imogen's paintings?' asked Drake.

'We would once it arrives here in our gallery. Sometimes, to get a feeling for the level of interest, we might exhibit a painting before we decide on a value. However, we are lucky to have many patrons interested in her work. They might reach an agreement with us before it goes on general sale. We might keep it on view, and if a better offer comes in, we will inform the original bidder. It is a sort of auction, I suppose. Sometimes, we might hold a formal auction.'

'Have you met with Imogen?' asked Drake.

'Oh yes, on several occasions. She visited us maybe a couple of months ago. For the first time in all our meetings, she came across as trying to be a more astute businesswoman. Previously, she had been glad to sell her work and would always be satisfied and sometimes astonished at its value. On her last visit, she questioned whether we could deal directly. She asked many questions about how it all worked, some of which we couldn't answer.'

'Why not?' asked Drake.

'Well, her work doesn't come directly to us. It goes through a company called Far East Trading. One consequence is that we are often unsure when things will arrive. Sometimes, it seems to take ages. We can never work out why. The plus side of this arrangement is that we don't have to deal with all the export and import nonsense. Making paintings secure and free from the jeopardy of damage in transit is quite a problem, and they deal with all that. They take a fee, so Imogen, The Orient, and we lose a little. The idea that Imogen could cut out Wang and Far East Trading is a complete fantasy. You've probably no idea how difficult all that is. There is the physical side of transit and the administrative side. We are glad not to be dealing with that. We do find Far East Trading to be a little unhelpful at times. I believe they wouldn't talk to Imogen, which seems odd. They argue they don't have a contract with her, so there it is.'

'Where is Far East Trading situated?' asked Drake.

'They have quite a large warehouse in the New Territories and a small office on Nathan Road. We've never been to either place. They always come here. They can unload in the basement and bring things up in a large goods lift. That side of things is easy. We've accidentally driven past their warehouse once. We were astonished at how huge it was. It's more like some massive Amazon business. Of course, they deal with many other sectors and take stuff into China easily from where they are. I think that is a large part of their business. They seem to have no interest in art at all.'

'Perhaps we could try to see them,' said Drake, turning to Martin.

'Good luck with that,' laughed Bobby Cheung.

'I've got phone numbers and email addresses,' said Martin, 'and I've tried to contact them several times. I get no reply.'

'You said that you have many almost regular patrons for Imogen's work,' said Drake. 'Could you give us some names? We will try to contact them.'

'Oh no, I'm sorry,' replied Bobby. 'Most of them want to remain anonymous. There is always the danger of art theft. They prefer it not to be known that they own valuable art.'

'We have seen some of Imogen's paintings in a gallery on Hollywood Road,' said Drake. 'Do you deal with them?'

'Ah,' replied Bobby. 'You raise a sore point, I'm afraid. No, we certainly don't.'

'So how do they get hold of their paintings?'

'You will find many of her paintings on sale in more commercial outfits. Imogen Glass did not paint any of these. They are fakes. They are forgeries. They may be good forgeries. The best ones are all painted individually as copies of the originals by local artists. These people make a living doing such work. The art schools use copying art as a way of training their students. People in this part of the world love forgeries. Of course, some places will sell copies that are done digitally. These are easy to spot because everything is pixelated. You can see the dots quite easily under a magnifying glass. These fakes will, of course, be offered at low prices. However, good forgers try to work using the original techniques and materials. They are remarkably good at what they do. These will fetch much higher prices. But they are not even near what we would expect a patron to pay for a genuine piece of art. Although I could usually spot one of these forgeries by examining it closely, most people could not. This is fine for the sort of customers who buy these. They can hang them in their houses and claim to their friends that they have an Imogen Glass. But it is not just contemporary paintings that are copied. Even the old masters get such treatment. Antiques, especially furniture, are copied.'

'That makes me think,' said Drake. 'The Orient Gallery has an antique daybed that looks wonderful. It appears to be genuinely old. Could that be a fake?'

'Almost certainly,' replied Bobby.

'So how would Wang procure that?'

'Of course, I don't know this. I am only guessing, but I would be surprised if I am wrong,' said Bobby, speaking slowly and deliberately. Drake and Martin waited for him to complete his sentence. 'You might find that our friends Far East Trading have something to do with that. We have often wondered if the delay in something arriving here is that it has gone to a forger first. If so, he would make his first copy and return the original. He can make further copies from his first. Given the real value of the original, Far East Trading would probably make him do the first copy at their warehouse or some other safe and secure location. They will probably sell the first copy and allow the artist to sell subsequent ones. It goes on and on.'

'So, when Wang bought the day bed from Far East Trading, would he know it was a fake?' asked Drake.

'Wang is an astute man. He is no idiot, and his partner Angela has a well-educated eye. I say no more.'


As they drove back to the hotel, Drake and Martin exchanged their impressions.

'This business seems full of rather shady characters,' said Drake. 'People who don't want the public to know where they live. People who want to keep their investments secret. It's a secret society.'

'You may be nearer the mark than you think,' replied Martin.

'In what sense?'

'Secret societies abound in this part of the world. There are all the family clans, triads and just plain secretive people. Politicians escape the sort of scrutiny that we are used to. There are people in high places who also lead other lives. These may be legal or not.'

'Is this just tax dodging?'

'Not here in Hong Kong, as there is virtually no tax. It's just a cultural thing. Things are different here.'

# 30

Drake relaxed in the back of the Mercedes, taking him to Hong Kong Airport. It was a comfortable departure time around midday, so he had the luxury of a cooked breakfast followed by packing. He still had time to sit and admire the harbour view from his bedroom window. He was sad to be leaving Hong Kong. It was a place that had grown on him. He found it more oriental than Singapore and full of charming and fascinating places. He wondered if he would ever be able to return. He hoped so. The driver dropped him right outside the departure hall. As he progressed through check-in and security, he remembered Cynthia telling him how much she admired the building. She had told him how clear and logical it was, and she was right. Just as she had promised, there was a clean elegance about it. English architecture at its best, he thought. Cynthia had several exciting opportunities to design in Hong Kong and loved coming here. He could now understand why. It had been good to team up with Martin again. He had matured considerably during his time in Hong Kong, and Drake looked forward to welcoming him back into the team in a week or so.

Singapore Airlines was typically helpful and efficient in processing him. He was now accustomed to the sense of hospitality and service that this part of the world offered. He also appreciated how this culture celebrated older people rather than treating them like idiots. He settled back into his seat on SQ185 to Singapore. He pulled out his notebook and phone. How marvellous it was to flick through all the photographs he had taken. It was a mobile version of his beloved case boards. He soon lost himself in reviewing the situation.

Arriving at Singapore Terminal 3, Drake checked his watch. It was half past four in the afternoon, local time. His next flight left not long after midnight. He had checked his suitcase through to Manchester, so he headed for immigration with his cabin bag. The formalities having been completed and now landside, he looked for instructions on how to find something called The Jewel. Dr Sun had suggested they could meet there. His son, Tom had made the connection for him with this world-renowned psychologist who studies stalkers. As instructed, he mounted the little airport tram, or was it a train? It set off with quite a jerk, and Drake was glad he had found a seat at the front. He looked for the driver. There was not even a cab. Feeling just a little unnerved by this, Drake managed to watch the airport as they glided along. They travelled both indoors and outdoors, offering a constantly changing view. Suddenly, the train emerged into a circular atrium. He left the train, pulling his bag and taking in this extraordinary space. He "listened" for Cynthia's voice explaining it to him. She was unusually silent. Of course, it had been completed while she was ill, and she never saw it. He would have to explore it for himself. Dabbing an eye with his handkerchief, he tried to concentrate on what he could see. He would "tell" Cynthia about it.

It was a massive and complex space. Drake thought he could count five floors, though it seemed to change as he looked around. A dome spanned across the circular volume. In truth, it was more like a circular glazed barrel vault. Dropping down in the middle of this was a dramatic waterfall. He consulted his guidebook, which claimed this was not just any old waterfall but the highest indoor waterfall in the world. He didn't doubt it. The water disappeared into a void in the middle of the atrium. Surrounding this were circular walkways and shops. In the middle was what could only be described as a forest of trees. Drake shook himself out of the moment and pulled out his phone. He had agreed to send Dr Sun a text message when he arrived. He pulled out his phone but felt a tap on his shoulder.

'It's amazing, isn't it?' said Dr Sun, shaking his hand. 'Now, if we just go round here a little and down one of the escalators, we will find an excellent coffee bar.'

'I understand you want to know about stalkers,' said Dr Sun as their coffees arrived. As customary, Drake pushed his to one side to cool down a little.

'I am trying to find one who is causing trouble in my office,' said Drake.

'Of course,' said Dr Sun. 'I will do my best. The first thing I am going to say may discourage you.' He frowned and stared at Drake as if to examine his student. 'The first thing to say is that there is no such thing as a typical stalker. It would be comforting to think we can easily spot a stalker. However, they vary far more than you might think. They are all individuals with unique combinations of problems. However, there are some things we can say about them. They are almost always male. We have known female stalkers, but they are rare. Their victims are also most often female, but not exclusively so. These men invariably have some problems in their lives. Often, these can be complex combinations of things. Normal people don't stalk. These people are all special in some way. Possibly for this reason, they often have a backstory. They may have needed some time for this to develop, and thus, although they are occasionally young, these are more often mature men. However, I have rarely found them to be particularly old. A stalker can be any age but is frequently in his late twenties or thirties.' Dr Sun stopped and drank from his coffee cup before continuing.

'Having said all this, they are unlike the image you may have of them as sleazy individuals in long raincoats. They also do far more different things than we may imagine. True, they may follow their victims, sometimes making themselves known and at other times not. However, they may also indulge in repeated communication. This can be by sending letters or, more commonly, sending emails or texts. They can even send videos or pictures, sometimes of themselves. Some stalkers are secretive, while others make themselves known to their victims. Occasionally, stalkers can even be the partners or ex-partners of their victims.'

Drake held up a hand and interrupted Dr Sun. 'This is all helpful,' he said, but I may have difficulty recalling it all.'

'Not a problem,' replied Dr Sun. 'I have some articles, including one written for police use, that I will email you.' Drake nodded, smiled and relaxed back into his chair to listen again.

'Now a word of caution,' said Dr Sun. 'It is not helpful to think of stalking as a disorder. Rather, it is a behaviour resulting from a variety of higher-level disorders. There is a well-known study of over a hundred stalkers in New York. It found that, in many cases, offenders were substance abusers. They often have a personality disorder. Again, however, many had neither but still stalked. It is probably helpful to think of stalking as an obsession. As with many forms of obsessive behaviour, it can consume the stalker's life. This may leave them almost incapable of thinking about anything else, although many stalkers hold down jobs. Because stalking may consume their lives, they may hold a deep resentment. Consequently, a stalker often has no other interests or pastimes. There is no time for that.'

'Why do stalkers do it?' asked Drake.

'Their motivation can take several forms. Some believe it is possible to develop a romantic relationship with their victim. This may include the desire to replace a previous relationship. Next comes almost the opposite motivation in holding a sadistic desire to torment the victim. Then, there is the wish in some way to replace the victim. Perhaps this might be in a job or occupation where the stalker wants to hold the position instead of the victim and somehow believes this behaviour could bring this about. There is also the delusional belief that the victim is in love with the stalker. This is often the case when the victim is in a high position or even famous.'

'It's complicated, isn't it?' grunted Drake.

'Yes,' laughed Dr Sun. 'Of course, there is also the stalker who has aggressive intent and wants to harm the victim for some reason. This may be associated with other conditions, including a difficult childhood or period at school. In addition to these longstanding issues, stalkers sometimes develop the condition after a major trauma, such as losing a partner or job or rejection by someone, including the victim. Finally, of course, in this group are simple revenge missions. This is where the stalker thinks he has been slighted or harmed by the victim.'

'I need to mull over what you have told me,' said Drake. 'Do you have any advice for someone in the process of investigating a stalking case?'

'Well, I can say one thing about that,' said Dr Sun. 'I have helped in many cases, but perhaps the north of England is too far away for me to be of any direct assistance. I can say that in around eighty per cent of cases, the stalker knows the victim. In most of those cases, the victim and stalker know each other. I understand this is not a hundred per cent, but it's a good place to start. I suggest you try sitting down with the victim and get her to list all the people she knows in her life. For well-known people, this can be quite a task. But for the average victim, this is at least a job that it is possible to perform. Then, take the checklist I have added to one of the papers I will send you and go through all these people, seeing how many boxes they tick. This can be an unpleasant task. You may have to suspect well-known acquaintances and some in close relationships. Start then by focusing on those with many or several boxes ticked and see how, if it was them, you could flush them out. Your offender may work extremely hard to remain anonymous. However, keeping this anonymity can often be difficult. Eventually, a person you may be suspecting might give themselves away.'

Drake thanked Dr Sun and checked his email to see three files had arrived from him. Dr Sun left Drake glancing through his files. Drake finished his coffee and snack. How nice it would have been, he thought, to be able to bring Cynthia here and enjoy hearing what she thought of the Jewel. That was, of course, not to be, and Drake brought himself back to the present. He rejoined the train to terminal three and checked in for his next flight. He would go to the airline lounge, have a meal and then review the material he had in more detail. That would keep him awake until his late flight took off for Manchester. Perhaps he had some material that he could use to help Steve Redvers find Grace's stalker.

# 31

Grace arrived in the case room early. Thank goodness there was no nasty message from her stalker. They seemed to have died down lately. The lack of activity coincided with Drake's absence. She amused herself by wondering if Drake was her stalker. How would he go about such a thing? She laughed inwardly. She opened her computer and turned it on to boot up while she made a cup of coffee. As she walked back to her desk, the computer beeped its good morning welcome, followed by an assertive ping that suggested she had some emails. She began to scan through them to decide what to work on first. There, catching her eye, was an email from Drake that he must have sent overnight from Hong Kong. It was brief, almost terse. It was an instruction to look under the kitchen floor in Philippa's house. There was no explanation. She called the scene-of-crime search team working in Philippa's house.

'Actually, we've nearly finished,' said the lead sergeant. 'We just have to put a few things back in place, and we should be coming back to the station this afternoon.'

'OK, wait there,' said Grace. 'I'm coming over to have a look for myself.' She put down the phone and called Dan Ford to get him to bring the Range Rover keys. 'We're going over to Philippa's house right away.'

A quarter of an hour later, Dan Ford turned the Range Rover into Philippa's driveway. They opened the front door that gave access to a hall. The lead sergeant was waiting for them.

'I've been instructed to look under the kitchen floor,' she said. The sergeant laughed.

'You look,' he said, grinning. He held the kitchen door open. The floor was tiled wall to wall. 'Of course, we can start breaking the tiles up, but there seems little point as there is a concrete floor throughout the ground level.'

'It's a top-level request without explanation from Drake,' said Grace. 'He must think that she has hidden things under a floor. I have no idea why.'

'We could look upstairs first,' said the sergeant. 'That's all done in timber boarding. We've tapped and listened for creaks. We've pulled a few carpets back. We haven't lifted any floorboards; we could try that.' He called a strong-looking constable to follow them, and the little party climbed the stairs. 'This landing is carpeted, as you can see, but it would be easy to lift it at one end and roll it back.' Grace walked into the bedroom while the constable pulled up the landing carpet. 'There's no sign of any boards having been lifted, but there is a board that's just creaking now we've lifted the carpet.'

The constable went to get a wrench and some screwdrivers. Grace kicked the boards just outside the bathroom door and went it. The bathroom was floored out with a vinyl-looking material that she guessed would be expensive. This was all stuck down with no signs of having been moved.

'Aha,' shouted the constable who had levered up the floorboards just outside the bathroom. 'Look, this is simple to lift, and there is what looks like a laptop computer under.'

'Yes,' said Grace. 'This must be the computer missing from the desk in the downstairs back room. It might be best to leave it in situ until Drake arrives. Presumably, this is what he was looking for. I wonder how he knew.' She texted Drake to tell him of their find and ask for instructions. She was surprised that her phone rang immediately.

'Hello, Grace,' said Drake.

'Hi, Sir. I thought you would be asleep by now.'

'No, it's late in the evening here. I'm in Singapore now. I've just had an interesting meeting. I'm waiting for a ridiculously late flight back to Manchester. No, I hadn't expected to find a computer, so keep looking. If you can, lift the computer and get it to Dave for analysis. I'll explain more when I see you.'

'OK,' said Grace to the constable. 'Lift the computer with gloves and put it in an evidence bag. What about other rooms?'

The lead sergeant came out of the master bedroom and spoke to Grace.

'There's a loose carpet in the main bedroom. We had pulled it back to the bed and not seen anything unusual.'

'OK,' said Grace. 'Let's move the bed back and look a little further.' Two constables heaved and shoved the heavy double bed back against the far wall.

'This wasn't meant to be moved,' said one. The other started to roll the carpet back. There was no evidence of loose or creaky boards.

'OK, lads,' laughed Grace. 'Time to move the bed back this way and look under the other side.' There was more heaving and grunting, and the lead sergeant rolled the carpet back.

'Look here,' he said, pointing to the floor. 'There are three floorboards here that move slightly. All the others are firmly nailed.' A constable tried to lift them but could not get any purchase. They remained stubbornly in place. Another constable arrived with what looked like a large palette knife. After a bit of fruitless poking, it slid down the side of one of the boards. Slowly but surely, he managed to get it to come up.

'Look,' he said. This floor is tongued and grooved, but this board has had its tongue shaved off. It's still a tight fit, and it doesn't creak. You did well to spot it.'

Two more boards lifted out easily. Everyone peered down into the space between the floor joists.

'Nothing that I can see,' said a constable. Another got a torch from his tool bag and shone it under the adjacent fixed board.

'There's something there,' he said triumphantly. He pulled on his blue gloves and knelt to reach along between the joists under the board. His hand came back out. He was holding a large cardboard tube about fifteen centimetres in diameter. It came out slowly and carefully until it was free. It just lifted above the board on the other side of the opening. The tube was about 60 centimetres long.

'Aha,' said Grace. 'I'll call Drake again.' She was busy with her phone while one constable began replacing a floorboard.

'Hang on, stop,' she said. 'Let's try the gaps between the other exposed joists.'

'I can't see anything with the torch,' said the constable.

'Let me have a feel. I've got long arms,' said the other. He knelt as before and lay on the floor with his arm under the boards up to his shoulder. 'Can't feel anything, wait a minute. There's a piece of string. He pulled it, and another tube, like the first, began to emerge. He repeated the procedure in the remaining gap between joists, and they recovered a third tube. Grace called Drake again.

'We've recovered three large cardboard tubes from beneath the floorboards under the bed,'

'Brilliant work,' said Drake. 'Better than we could hope for. You had better take the tubes back to a clean location in the station before you open them. I think I know what might be inside. I've just got some hot grub here. My phone battery is showing empty. I'll recharge it on one of the many sockets by the seats, but it will take some time. 'I'll join you tomorrow.' The phone went dead, and Grace put hers down. She addressed the waiting constables.

'OK. These need to go back to the station in evidence bags. Please look under all the floors and furniture to see if we can find anything else.' One of the searching constables arrived holding the laptop found under the landing floor. It was now in an evidence bag.

'This is odd,' he said. 'I just checked the laptop against the leads found on the desk in the back room. These leads are connected to a printer, a screen, an external disk drive, and a keyboard. They have plugs that wouldn't fit into the sockets on this laptop. It looks like another computer was stolen. It might have been a desktop type.'

'That's odd,' said Grace. 'So, we still have a mystery.'

Back in the station, Dan Ford carried the tubes into the case room. Steve Redvers cleared the table in the middle of the room and put a clean sheet down. Grace donned her blue gloves and carefully removed the first tube from its bag, easing the plastic cap off one end. She looked inside. She could feel and see what she thought was paper. It was thick but not as inflexible as cardboard. This was rolled tight inside the tube. She found the end of the paper. It turned inside its enclosure and loosened. Sure enough, the paper now slid out. She put the tube to one side and began unfurling the paper. As it came out into view, Grace was already guessing correctly. It was a painting. A beautiful painting. It was an Imogen Glass painting. The other two rolls gave up similar works of art. Grace consulted the portfolio of Imogen's work. It took some time, but she gradually discovered these three paintings were from the twenty-four missing ones. They were the final three. She tried Drake's phone to tell him, but it was still dead. She looked at her watch and added eight hours for the time zone shift to Singapore. Drake would probably be boarding his flight.

It was lunchtime on the following day when Drake performed his usual door-rattling trick. Grace let him in.

'Jet lag at my age is just dreadful,' he grunted as he collapsed into his chair. 'It's all so confusing. I left Singapore at about two in the morning. I had a fifteen-hour flight and landed in Manchester at only nine today. It's a young man's game this long haul travelling.'

'Was it a good trip?' asked Grace as she poured him a cup of coffee.

'In many ways, yes,' said Drake. 'I'll brief you on it in due course. Now. I want to see the paintings you recovered from Philippa's house.'

'Over here on the table,' said Grace. 'How did you know they would be there and to look under the floor?'

'Well, it was a matter of putting several things together and taking a chance,' replied Drake. He sipped his coffee unusually hot. 'Philippa was always rather defensive, sometimes aggressively so. I have always thought there might be more to discover about her. I met a chap from Hong Kong Police who I referred to as George. There's a lot of secrecy there and not a little corruption. He suspected a more senior person might be blocking some of his investigations. He told me about how major criminals get paintings stolen for them. They keep them as a sort of insurance policy. If they are ever caught, they hope to have their sentence reduced. The missing works of art can be used as a bargaining chip. It's common practice. He told me one was found recently under the floor of the criminal's mother. Philippa had the opportunity and a motive to murder Imogen. Did she do it to steal these paintings? We knew Philippa had been murdered, possibly by up to three men. Most importantly, her house had been ransacked. Was it searched by these men looking for some of Imogen's paintings? Then you got lucky and found them. We need to think through what this tells us about our investigation.'

Grace was studying the three paintings spread out over the table.

'There seems to be a further development in her work here,' she said. 'It's got a bit more animated.

Drake took his time to look at each painting in turn.

'Yes,' he said. 'Maybe more dramatic, and they include more characters. There seems to be a monkey in one and a weird snake-like creature in another.' After a few more minutes of studying, Drake grunted and returned to read his copy of The Times and sip his coffee. He suddenly looked up and started to brief Grace about his trip. She took in every detail until Dave arrived holding the laptop found under the floor of Philippa's landing.

'Sorry,' he said. 'It's locked, and I can't get it to boot up. It is password-protected. I can try extracting the contents of the hard disk and see if I can read them, but that's a tricky thing to do, and I will need some time.'

'Why does she keep her laptop under the floor?' asked Grace. 'It seems she had another desktop computer in her living room.'

'So,' said Drake, 'we can assume she was up to no good and probably communicating with others. The intruders and possible murderers must have found and taken the desktop but missed the underfloor search we have done. Perhaps she used the missing computer for everyday things and then got out the laptop for work that she hid. Whether all this has anything to do with the murder of Imogen Glass is quite another matter. It may be connected, or it may not. Dave, do what you can with that computer, please.' Dave nodded and left, carrying Philippa's laptop under his arm. Drake followed him out of the room and called him back.

'Dave, I want you to do a special job for me. I'd like you to email everyone, asking them to bring their computer in for you to look at. You can say you have found some nasty virus lurking, and you need to get it cleaned off before it does some real harm.'

'Sure, will do,' said Dave. 'Can I ask what you want me to do with the computers when I get them?'

'Let me know each time you receive one, and I'll tell you then,' said Drake somewhat mysteriously.

# 32

There was no sign of Drake early the following day. He eventually arrived just in time for a mid-morning coffee.

'Sorry,' he said as he stumbled in, looking distinctly bleary-eyed. 'I seem not to be dealing with jet lag well.'

'I wonder what Dan's excuse is,' said Grace. 'There's no sign of him this morning. We've tried emailing and calling him, but there is no answer. I'm just a bit worried.'

'I suggest you send a couple of constables round to his flat,' said Drake. 'If there is no answer, I recommend breaking in.'

'I wondered about that,' said Grace, 'but it felt a bit drastic. It's only just down the road. It shouldn't take long.'

'An hour later, two constables arrived in a hurry.

'No answer,' said one. 'Nothing there,' said the other. 'He appears to have done a runner.'

'Why would he do that?' asked a puzzled Grace.

'Because we asked to see his computer,' said Drake.

'Dave asked to see all our computers,' said Steve Redvers.

'He probably didn't feel confident that he could cover everything up,' said Drake firmly. 'He thought the game was up, and he's cut his losses. Put out a call for him to be found.'

'I just don't understand,' said a puzzled Grace.

'I think we've found your stalker,' said Drake.

'What, Dan?' shrieked Grace.

'Yes, Dan,' said Drake.

'How did you know?'

'I didn't. I just suspected. I did what a chap I met the other day in Singapore recommended. He is an expert on the psychology of stalking. He gave me a sort of checklist against which to measure the likelihood of people being stalkers. Dan has an unfortunate record of some major trauma, being trampled on and nearly killed at a football match. It seemed that this changed his personality enough for him to lose his partner, causing another trauma. Yesterday, I talked to Steve about him in a casual way. Steve said that Dan frequently stared at you in a rather peculiar way. If he was the stalker, he found working with you every day was a sort of torture. He was obsessed with you, but, at the same time, you were completely out of bounds. The information your stalker had about events was so accurate that I began to wonder if it was someone here who had access to all our information. So far, we know that your stalker did much of his work on a computer. I tried getting Dave to flush out any potential stalker by calling in everyone's computers. Dan is a bright, albeit rather twisted character. He worked out that he was in some jeopardy. I guess that if we can find his computer, it will yield information Dave can recover for us. I doubt that he has had sufficient time to remain hidden for long. I'm sure we will find him perhaps sooner rather than later.'

'I suppose we can't just let him go?' said Grace.

'I'm astonished, Grace, that you want to be so lenient. No. We cannot condone what he has done. He has committed a serious crime. If he gets away with it, he may do the same thing again. I expect his lawyers will be able to plead psychological factors that may in some way be considered, but the public needs protection from him. If we don't find his computer, it may prove difficult to bring a prosecution to a successful conclusion. Of course, his disappearance is further evidence against him. For now, your problems are over, Grace. We need to concentrate on the Imogen Glass murder.'

'I'm so grateful,' said Grace. Drake pulled out his phone and started to jab at it persistently.

'Ah, there we are,' he exclaimed. He held out his phone for Grace to see. 'I remember this board on the wall in the kitchen of

Philippa's house. It seemed to be where she hung all her keys. Grace, take Steve and go and see if any of the keys fit the cupboard doors that the locksmith opened in Imogen's studio. Now, I'm still struggling with jet lag. You can take me home on the way there.'

'OK, will do,' said Grace. 'By the way, that chap, Geoffrey Bragg, from Far East Traders, is coming to see us tomorrow.'

Grace was soon dropping Drake at the Boathouse pub. He assured her he was going home and had no intention of stopping at the pub. Drake strolled down the riverbank, taking in the wonderful smell of the place. Hong Kong was marvellous, but he had no wish to live there. Chester and The Groves would do him fine. As he walked, he turned over the events surrounding Philippa Crehan. How did she get those pictures stored so carefully under her bedroom floor? Is it possible that Imogen gave them to her for some reason? Perhaps that was possible during their romantic interlude. Alternatively, had Philippa stolen them? Perhaps in revenge when they split up. Or did she take them after murdering Imogen? He had always found Philippa defensive, and her evidence abruptly delivered. Was it all carefully prepared?

The following morning, Grace's phone rang. It was Sergeant Denson.

'I've got a chap called Geoffrey Bragg down 'ere to see you.'

'OK,' said Grace. 'Show him to an interview room, and we'll be there in five minutes.' She turned to Drake. He was sitting in his chair with his first coffee of the day, working on The Times crossword. 'Geoffrey Bragg has arrived,' she said.

'Mr Bragg, thank you for coming to see us,' said Drake as they entered the interview room. Bragg was a shortish but plump fellow with dark hair and a bustling air of efficiency.

'I suppose you have heard about the death of Imogen Glass.' Geoffrey Bragg nodded his head, and Drake continued. 'There were some suspicious circumstances about her death, and we are investigating. It would help us to know more about how her work was dealt with, and we understand you arranged the export of some of it to Hong Kong.'

'That's correct,' said Geoffrey Bragg. 'I think we dealt with quite a high proportion of it. I manage this end of the process. Our headquarters in Hong Kong will take over once it leaves the UK. Most of it went to the Cheung Brothers. They are art dealers with an excellent reputation.' Geoffrey Bragg pulled a notebook out from his briefcase. 'Ah, yes, I thought so. We had a large batch of twenty paintings only a few weeks ago. There had been a long interval since the previous batch. Nevertheless, Imogen Glass must have been working hard to produce so much.'

'Did you collect them from The Orient Gallery as usual?' asked Drake.

'I suppose so, but I couldn't be certain. My two assistants would have done it.'

'Is it possible for you to get them to confirm?'

'No, sorry. They've both gone back to Hong Kong. I always have two members of staff sent from headquarters in Hong Kong. I need at least one person who can speak Cantonese and read Chinese. I need two people who can do the heavy lifting. We often import major antique furniture. Headquarters tend to rotate them from time to time. I could get headquarters to speak to them, but I wouldn't be surprised if they had left. That seems to be the way of it these days.'

'We believe there was a batch of some twenty-four paintings that had recently been available,' said Drake.

'Well, I certainly only took twenty. Of course, we do not see all her work. Some of it is sold here in the UK. The Orient sold her work on the British market. Between them, they have Chester on the map in terms of modern art.'

'How long does it take to get the paintings from here to the Cheung Brothers gallery?' asked Drake.

'I'm afraid I can't answer that precisely. At this end, it depends on the availability of suitable airline capacity. We only use either British Airways or Cathay Pacific carriers. Sometimes, I can get stuff straight on a flight. Sometimes, it can take a week or even more. It depends.'

'Have you ever met Imogen Glass?' asked Drake.

'Strange that you should ask that. I hadn't met her at all until recently. She asked me to go and see her. Naturally, I agreed. I knew she had been asking a few questions. I had some email contact with her, and she suggested she might consider dealing directly with me rather than going through The Orient. To me, that just complicated matters. So, when she asked to see me, I imagined she wanted to talk about that, but she didn't. She said Wang and Angela had helped her to get going commercially, and she owed them a great deal, so she wanted to keep the arrangement with them. That was fine by me?'

'So, what did she want to talk about?' asked Drake.

'More or less the same things as yourself,' replied Geoffrey Bragg. 'She wanted to know how things were done along the journey. She was particularly interested in what happened in Hong Kong. I couldn't help her with that. It's not my end of the business. She wanted to know if we passed everything on to Cheung Brothers, and I couldn't tell her.'

'I'm surprised that you know so little about the Hong Kong end of the business,' exclaimed Drake.

'Actually,' replied Geoffrey Bragg. 'I've never even been to Hong Kong. It just isn't necessary for my job here.'

'How long have you worked for Far East Trading?' asked Drake.

'A couple of years. It's a good job. It's well-paid, and I often get spare time. Every day is different. We deal with a lot of companies here in the UK. Far East Trading is quite a big company over there, I think. It's a steady business.'

When Grace returned to the case room after seeing Geoffrey Bragg out, she found Drake prowling around his boards. She stood patiently, expecting him to say something about the interview they had just conducted, but Drake had already moved on. Eventually, he turned to Grace and pointed to one of his boards.

'When you went to see the tattoo artist, David Tong, he reported that Imogen had handed him a business card with a drawing of the tattoo she wanted on the back. We think it had been drawn and handed to Imogen by Irene Lee.' Grace nodded, and Drake grunted. 'I think you reported that he described some uncertainty about which way up the design ought to be.' Grace nodded again. Drake started to pound away on his iPhone.

'I've just asked my Chinese expert at The Met to turn the design upside down and see if it might mean anything that way up.' Drake's phone pinged as a text arrived. 'Aha,' he said. 'He says it might mean something. It could be a rough and crude version of the symbol standing for the word mountain.'

'Not sure that helps, really,' replied Grace.

'No, probably not, probably not,' grunted Drake. 'I wonder, though. I also wonder if we could check up a little on Irene Lee. Do you remember The Met contact for MI5, Bristow? He said they were tracking her. I asked him if he could provide any information about her movements. He said he would see what he could do and email you information that was not restricted. I assume you haven't had anything yet?'

'Let me check,' said Grace, tapping away on her phone. 'Yes, here it is. Wow, there's lots of information. Oh, look, it is listed by the places they know she was at. Hong Kong features frequently. Let me check my notes on the videos of her at DH's house. Yes, one of her visits to Hong Kong corresponds. That makes useful corroboratory evidence. But more interestingly, she has visited Chester twice. Look.'

'Ah,' said Drake. 'This could be more important than it might appear. She was in Chester a few days before Imogen was found and again just before Philippa's body was discovered. If we look at

Prof Cooper's estimate of time of death, in both cases, she was in Chester around that time.'

'Wow,' said Grace. 'That must make her a clear suspect. But what can we do?'

'I'll talk to Bristow,' said Drake. 'We need to do something.'

# 33

All was quiet in the case room. Grace was busily tapping on her computer. Drake was absorbed with his crossword. Steve Redvers was making all three of them a cup of coffee. Dave arrived carrying a laptop computer that he opened. He was soon absorbed with whatever he had on it. The near silence was disturbed by the sudden ringing of a phone. Everyone looked up. Grace picked up her phone. It was the desk sergeant Tom Denson.

'I've got a couple down 'ere who have just walked in off the street. They claim to 'ave some new information about Imogen Glass. They won't give me their names. They want to speak to Detective Chief Inspector Drake. What would you like me to do?'

'You'd better show them to an interview room,' replied Grace. 'I'll go and see them and find out what they want.'

A few minutes later, Grace returned to the case room. She stood by Drake, waiting for him to look up.

'We have a curiosity, Sir. A couple, quite old, I would say. He speaks with a rather polished English accent. They want to talk to you about Imogen Glass. I've tried to persuade them to tell me what they want, but they refuse to talk to anybody but you.'

Drake grunted, put down his newspaper and struggled out of his chair.

'Good morning,' he said as he entered the interview room.

'Are you Chief Inspector Drake,' said the man rising out of his chair.

'That's me, and who are you? How can I help?' The man sat down after shaking Drake's outstretched hand. He patted his female associate on the hand she was resting on the table. He grasped her hand as he retook his chair.

'We need to talk to you about Imogen Glass,' he said.

'Of course,' said Drake.

'We are her parents,' said the man.

'Really?' asked Drake. 'I have information that you are elsewhere.'

'Yes,' said the man, 'but we have escaped. I am William Glass, and this is my wife, Dorothy.' Drake and Grace pulled up chairs in unison and looked at each other in astonishment.

'Do you mind if I ask if you have any identity?' asked Drake cautiously.

'Of course, I have a hard-won credit card. We currently hold special temporary passports issued by the FBI arranged through MI6 with the Home Office.' William held out his credit card and a paper document that announced itself as an emergency passport.

'Welcome to you both,' said Drake. 'We understood that you were being held largely against your will at the Xi Dong centre in Texas.'

'Correct,' said William. 'It has been a real battle.'

'Perhaps you had better tell us the story from the beginning,' said Drake.

'I've been a complete idiot,' said William.

'No, you haven't, Bill,' said Dorothy, 'we acted as a couple.'

'Yes, but it was me that started it. I retired from the stock market in Hong Kong. We were comfortably off, but I was looking for something meaningful in my life other than money. Xi Dong offered these courses called Life Coaching. It all seemed to make sense, but gradually, we got sucked into an ever-demanding situation. We became members, but I wasn't satisfied being an ordinary member, and we got more involved. Then we went to the States and eventually found we had given up our freedom. For a while, that didn't matter. Soon, however, we suspected the whole thing was a scam to get our money. Luckily, I had the foresight to make arrangements that kept much of our money and our property secure and hidden from sight. Then they began to suspect this and even went to Hong Kong and threatened our friends Michael and Ruth Atkins. I believe they told you the story. When they told us that Immy had been murdered, we suspected the involvement of Xi

Dong.' William began to shake, and tears ran down his cheeks. Dorothy tried to calm him down. He spoke again.

'We will not rest until Immy gets some justice. So, we came here to see you after we heard from Michael and Ruth about what you were doing.'

'How did you escape?' asked Grace softly.

'Luckily, someone else had got out. We don't know the details, but eventually, the FBI took up the case. They managed to infiltrate Xi Dong, and the secret agent gradually discovered our real feelings. The Atkins managed to get a new credit card from the bank and send it over, and the secret FBI agent brought it in. The FBI arranged emergency passports, and one night we escaped. The secret agent was withdrawn, and the FBI will make a raid soon. We are sworn to secrecy, but I am delighted to be talking to an English policeman.'

'So, you believe Xi Dong killed your daughter?' asked Drake.

'We have no evidence, but we believe Immy was trying to uncover more information. They must have decided she was a danger.'

'Why do you think Xi Dong wanted to kill Imogen Glass?' asked Drake.

'I don't know, but behind them is a violent society, and murder is commonplace in their activities. In the early days, Imogen was trying to contact us. They may have thought she was a danger to their secret identities.'

'Do you know who owns Xi Dong?' asked Drake.

'No, but as far as we know, it started in Hong Kong. Whoever is driving it all is probably there. We want to go back there and sort out our affairs, but we are too frightened to go until the FBI have pulled off their raid and put everyone away in the States.'

'You understand that the Xi Dong movement has a place in the UK near London,' said Drake.

'No!' said Dorothy. 'So, are we in danger here too?'

'We can arrange for somewhere safe for you to stay for the immediate future,' said Grace. 'You may not know, but your other daughter, Felicity, is in one of our safe houses. She seems to live in constant fear. Xi Dong kidnapped her. Thankfully, she was released by The Met police.'

'Oh no,' said Dorothy. 'We thought at least she had not been sucked into this awful business.'

'Would you be happy to share the safe house with her?' asked Grace.

'Of course,' said Dorothy. 'It would be wonderful to see her again. We have so much to explain to her.'

'Right,' said Grace. 'If you both wait here where you are entirely safe, I will arrange transport for you.'

'Oh, thank goodness,' said William. 'It is so good to be back here.'

As Drake and Grace left the interview room, they swapped their reactions to this latest revelation.

'You look after them both,' said Drake. 'I think we need Martin's help. I will see if I can hold a Facetime conference call with him. He should be at his home because it is the evening there.'

'Martin,' said Drake. 'Do you have time to help me with the Imogen Glass case? Are you OK to talk?'

'Yes, of course,' said Martin. 'I'm in my flat. I consider myself already part of your team.'

'Martin, we now have Imogen's parents here. The FBI is probing Xi Dong in Texas and has liberated Imogen's parents. William and Dorothy are convinced that Xi Dong is responsible for Imogen's death. They believe Xi Dong is part of a wider crime syndicate. Would either you or your friend George have any knowledge of that?'

'I don't personally, but it would not surprise me. There is so much serious crime here in what we Brits call the Triads. Over here, they are referred to as Black Societies. I've tried to keep out of all that because it is too dangerous to get involved without knowing what you are doing. I will see if George can help. Why don't I call him and create a conference call?'

'That would be excellent, Martin. Thank you.'

'Perhaps it is easier for me to call him, and then, if he can help, I can join you in the call.'

'OK,' said Drake. 'That might prove one step too far for my technical knowledge anyway. I'll stand down. I'm desperate for a coffee, so I'll wait for your call.'

Drake decided it would be better to remain entirely secure and not involve other team members. He made a cup of coffee and took it down to the interview room, which was now empty. As he sat down, his phone beeped. It was Martin.

'Hi,' said Martin. 'I'm joining you on a conference call with George.' Two windows appeared on Drake's screen. One showed Martin, and George was in the other. Drake thought this was nothing short of a miracle. Martin took control. 'Go ahead, Sir, and put your questions to George.'

'Hi George,' said Drake, still marvelling at the technology.

'Hello again,' replied George.

'I think you know from Martin that we are investigating a movement called Xi Dong. It started in Hong Kong but has spread to the States and the UK. We want to know if it is possibly part of some wider crime syndicate, perhaps a triad.'

'Yes, indeed, we believe it is, though the relationship seems arm's length as far as we can tell. We think that it is likely that Xi Dong needs to keep its business model clean as far as the public and its victims are concerned?'

'Is this the same syndicate you believe the secretive DH is the overall boss of?'

'No, quite the opposite. Xi Dong seems to have a loose relationship with a dangerous outfit called 46Q. DH is thought to be deeply involved with Red Peak. They are sworn enemies. Occasionally, we get outbreaks of violence between them.'

'I see,' said Drake. 'Would that violence extend to murder?'

'Absolutely,' said George.

'Thanks a lot,' said Drake. 'I appreciate your help.'

'Four things,' said George. 'Firstly, I have not helped you in any way, and we have not held this conference call. Secondly, I know nothing about either 46Q or Red Peak. It is not my area of responsibility. Thirdly, please do not reveal anything about the video clips to anyone, as this might screw up our investigations. Fourthly, be extremely careful. You may be in danger if you get involved with these people.'

'Understood,' said Drake.

'OK,' said Martin. 'I am closing this down now. It remains entirely confidential.'

'All safe and secure with Imogen's parents now?' asked Drake as Grace returned to the case room.

'Yes,' I've left Steve Redvers to ferry them to the house where Felicity is staying.'

'OK,' said Drake. 'I need to take you into my confidence about my conference call. Xi Dong is a remote arm of a triad called 46Q. We must prevent that knowledge from going further than the two of us. Even Steve should not know. It's dangerous knowledge, and it must not leak out that we are in some way interested in them. I have a hunch, and I have just sent a text to my friend Caruthers, the guy at The Met who is the Chinese expert there. I'm waiting for his response before I explain a bit more.' At that point, Drake's phone pinged somewhat urgently. Drake opened it and read a text. 'I asked him about the symbol that is in Imogen's tattoo. Remember that he said if you turned it upside down, it looked like the Chinese for "mountain." I've now asked him if it could also mean "peak". He says, "Yes, absolutely. Many Chinese symbols have a range of meanings in English," which I think is interesting.'

'Is it?' asked Grace.

'Yes,' replied Drake with a smile. 'The triad DH is thought to be involved in is called Red Peak. Imogen's ignorance and her tattooist's carelessness mean she has her tattoo upside down. Given that there is a red bar in her tattoo, it might read Red Peak. Does this mean that Imogen was a member of the Chinese triad? Remember that we have been told by Felicity Glass that she thought Irene Li recommended she should have this tattoo and drew it on the back of her business card. Given that Imogen didn't know which way up it should be, we might think that she has unwittingly become a member of a triad. Presumably, being able to display the tattoo would offer her some protection in certain circumstances. Unfortunately for Imogen, this has not worked in her case.'

'Wow,' said Grace. 'I need to take all this in.'

'Drake's phone pinged even more impatiently than before. He had learned that this sound heralded the arrival of an email. It was from an unknown sender, so he hesitated, wondering if it was something suspicious. It turned out to be from George. He read it aloud to Grace.

'Following the videos showing Irene Li arriving at DH's house, we have been going back through the huge collection of such clips. We have found two pairs separated by a month but showing the same female dressed all in black. The first shows her arriving in a taxi and going in on foot. She leaves again approximately three hours later. In the second pair, the same thing happens again. This time, however, she arrives carrying a large tube but leaves without it. Your earlier conference call reminded me of these, and I wondered if they might interest you. I attach all four clips.'

'Do you think it is Imogen?' asked Grace.

'Let's look at the clips,' said Drake, clicking on them. 'They are just too small to be sure, but it certainly could be her. We know he has one of her paintings, which includes his house. I saw it at the exhibition, and it is in the catalogue I brought back.'

'Forward the email to me,' said Grace. I'll put it up on my big screen. Drake duly obliged, struggled out of his chair and hobbled across to Grace's desktop computer.

'My old back is playing up today,' he grunted as the clips started to play on Grace's large screen. She magnified the view.

'Do you know,' she said. 'Of course, we can't be certain, but it certainly could be her. Look, her hair is the same, and she is wearing her uniform of all black.'

'So, the first time she is going to discuss it with DH,' said Drake. 'A month later, she has done the painting and brings it to him in one of those tubes we found under Philippa's bedroom floor.'

'Yes,' said Grace. 'Together with the twenty Far East Trading sent over and the three from Philippa's house, we have now accounted for the twenty-four listed in Imogen's portfolio.'

Drake nodded his head and grunted. 'We also know that Imogen spent several hours talking to the suspected big boss of the Red Peak triad.'

# 34

Grace and Drake were sitting with their first coffees of the day, mulling over the latest state of the investigation.

'So where are we?' asked Drake. 'Who do we suspect? Do you still favour Elliott Chan?'

'Well, he has a clear motive,' answered Grace.

'An affair of passion,' added Drake.

'Yes, and he lied about meeting Imogen on the riverside until we challenged him with his red jumper. We have heard he has a bad temper, and his fingerprints are on one of the rods we think could have been used to hit her on the head.'

'But why would he murder Philippa?' demanded Drake.

'Because he saw her as the generator of all his problems by taking Imogen away from him.'

'Ok,' said Drake. 'So far so good, but we have no hard evidence. Unless he admits it, which seems unlikely, there is no chance of charging him.'

'What about Irene Lee?' asked Grace.

'Well, we have circumstantial evidence only that she was in Chester at the right time. That could be a coincidence. In any case, what is her motive? According to Bristow and MI5, Imogen was her method of making contacts in high places.'

'Perhaps Imogen had seen through her disguise, and she saw her as a danger.'

'It's certainly possible, but again, we have no evidence,' growled Drake. 'Our problem with all suspects is a lack of evidence. We somehow need to remedy that one way or another.'

'Yes, but how?' asked Grace.

'Well,' said Drake, 'William and Dorothy, as well as Felicity Glass, seem convinced that Xi Dong is responsible for Imogen's murder.'

'They have a case,' said Grace. 'Now that we know Xi Dong is an offshoot of the 46Q triad and almost by accident, Imogen was connected to the Red Peak triad. George has told us that these two are sworn enemies. Has Imogen somehow got caught in the crossfire?'

'Possibly, possibly,' said Drake. Grace knew from hard-won experience that this answer suggested Drake was unconvinced, so she kept quiet. Suddenly, Drake spoke again.

'Actually, I'd like to have another chat with Elliott Chan. See if you can contact him and get him to come and see us.' Grace scribbled a note and made a phone call. While she was on the phone, Drake prowled around the case boards, grunting as he went.

'Elliott Chan happens to be near here on his way home,' said Grace. 'He said he'll call in.'

'That's great,' said Drake. 'We seem to have some common characters now. There are three Chinese males at Fairlawns who are built like British bulldogs. Do you remember the male boot prints in the corridor between Imogen's studio and the back door to the carport? Our expert identified three different boots or shoes. Then, at least one and maybe two or three people were seen leaving Philippa's house on the night of her murder. At least one looked Chinese, and our witness thinks he heard a car door slam two or possibly three times before the car drove off. We also now know that the staff of Far East Trading here in the UK is three people, two of whom are Chinese. These four things may be a coincidence, but that feels unlikely. Are they the same people in each case?'

'So,' said Drake slowly. 'The theory is that the Fairlawns thugs killed Imogen because she was in a rival Hong Kong Chinese triad. If so, presumably, they also stole the paintings. Somehow, these paintings have found their way to Hong Kong. However, our contact from Far East Trading reports collecting twenty paintings, possibly from The Orient.'

'It's certainly confusing,' said Grace as Drake's phone rang. It was Professor Cooper, the pathologist. Drake, feeling rather smug, put his iPhone on loudspeaker.

'Hello, Drake. I've finally got some information on the bullet used to kill Philippa Crehan. The cartridge is 5.8 by 21 millimetres. No British or even European or American guns use this calibre. However, it is common in China. It is used by the QSZ92 semi-automatic pistol in widespread use by the Chinese army. I hope that helps you. Must go!'

'So,' said Drake. 'Our dog-walking witness thought the man he saw drive away from Philippa's house was Chinese. This all supports your theory about the Chinese thugs from Fairlawns. Perhaps they killed Philippa.'

'It seems she was killed in a search for something,' said Grace. 'The most obvious thing must surely be the paintings we found. Presumably, they should have gone to Far East Trading like the other twenty. Could the UK members of Far East Trading have been looking for the paintings and killed Philippa? If so, maybe theirs are the footprints we found in Imogen's studio. Perhaps they stole the twenty paintings to cut out The Orient's involvement. It would explain the couple at The Orient not knowing anything about them. Could they have generated the footprints? If so, why would they want to kill Imogen?'

Drake fell silent and walked around his case boards again. Grace went over to the coffee machine. She pointed to it and gave Drake a quizzical look. Drake nodded and smiled. This was at least a two-cup problem. They had barely finished their drinks when Elliott Chan arrived.

'Thank you for coming in,' said Drake. 'I have only one question for you. You and Imogen were once lovers. You must have seen her tattoo. Why did you not mention it to us.'

'Ah,' said Elliott, 'At first, there was nothing much to say. I only worked it out the other day. I was looking at some photographs that I took of her. I turned one upside down. I suddenly saw it as a crude Chinese character representing mountains or peaks. I assume now it was a symbol for the triad,

Red Peak. I didn't know they had a badge if that is what it is. I've never been involved in the triads. It's just too dangerous. I can only think the wretched Irene Lee was responsible. Some say she is a bigwig in Red Peak.'

'You didn't think to ask Imogen what it was?' asked Drake.

'Yes, I think I did when I first saw it, but she said it was just something that made her feel safe. Thinking back, I'm not sure she knew what it was.'

'OK, that clears up something that has been nagging me,' said Drake. 'Thank you for popping in.'

'OK,' said Drake to Grace after Elliott Chan left. 'That hasn't got us all that far. I've never really trusted what he says, but in this case, he seemed genuine. We have access to Felicity at the safe house. Let's go and see if she can give us any more information that might help clear things up.'

Drake and Grace met up with Felicity Glass and her parents. They were sitting in the living room of the safe house on the outskirts of Chester.

'Thank you for seeing us again,' said Drake. 'All three of you are looking less stressed than when we met you recently,'

'It has been wonderful,' said Felicity. 'I thought, as did Immy, that I had lost my parents, and now I have found them again. They have been explaining to me what happened. It seems that the emails Immy and I were getting did not come from Mum and Dad but from these awful people pretending to be them. It was all designed to draw us into the clutches of Xi Dong. It's just dreadful that we have lost Immy. I still can't believe she's gone.' With that, Felicity began to weep and shake. She pulled out a tissue. This set Dorothy off, and the two put arms around each other.'

'Unfortunately, we can't do anything to bring Imogen back,' said Drake. 'But we are doing our best to bring her some justice. Can we ask you a few more questions, Felicity?'

'Of course. I wish I could wave a magic wand to bring Immy back, but that is pure fantasy.'

'We remember you saying that you thought Irene Lee had persuaded Imogen to have the Red Peak tattoo done.'

'Red Peak?' queried Felicity.

'Yes,' said Grace. 'We believe the tattoo was accidentally done upside down. It was meant to indicate her allegiance to a Hong Kong triad called Red Peak.'

'How extraordinary!' said Felicity. 'Immy was always against the corruption and crime in Hong Kong. Why would she join a triad?'

'Perhaps she didn't appreciate what she was doing,' suggested Drake. 'The fact that she allowed it to be done upside down makes me think she didn't understand it.'

'Well, I think it was that Irene Lee woman who helped her,' said Felicity. 'Immy was getting in a state about things in Hong Kong. She never explained it all to me, but she had begun to think she was being taken for a ride and that her trust was being abused. She knew Irene quite well, and I think she still trusted her. Elliott warned her against Irene, but it seems she ignored him. I could check with Elliott. We wondered if he could come to stay with us here. There is room.'

'We prefer to keep your safe house just for you,' said Grace. 'We need to control the knowledge of its existence secure.'

'Well, Elliott told me that when he was seeing Immy, he did some investigating. He is well-connected in Hong Kong. He discovered there was a big scam involving fake copies of her paintings. I'm afraid I don't know more than that. Immy became reluctant to talk about it. At the time, it didn't seem important to me. I forgot about it.'

'I can confirm that I have seen these fakes offered for sale in Hong Kong,' said Drake. 'Many people are involved in distributing her work in Hong Kong. It is a complicated process.'

As Grace and Drake arrived back at the case room, Drake suddenly had an idea.

'Dave, have you had any more luck with the laptop we found under Philippa's floorboards?'

'Not really, I'm working on it now. I'm trying to get the disk read onto another computer, but it's not working properly.'

'Try "red peak" as the password,' said Drake.

'OK,' said Dave. 'No. Not with the space. Perhaps it's "redpeak" all one word.' Dave tapped away for a while. 'Aha,' he said suddenly. It's "RedPeak" with capital letters for each word.' Dave tapped at the keyboard again. 'That's odd,' he said eventually. 'I can't find any user files on this at all. It's a basic Apple Mac notebook. It seems to have all the system files, plus basic applications, such as word processor, spreadsheet and email. The email hasn't been used at all. There's no account set up. Perhaps it's been deleted. There are no images, word documents or spreadsheet files. All a bit disappointing.'

'Surely you don't hide an empty computer under the floor,' said Drake. 'Keep looking.'

Grace's phone rang.

'Is that Detective Sergeant Grace Hepple?'

'Speaking.'

'I'm calling you about your request for information about Imogen Glass in the days before she was found murdered. I'm sorry we have taken so long. We are a clinic in Liverpool, and one of our special capabilities is the laser treatment of tattoos that people want to remove. We have a staff member who lives in Chester, but she has been away on holiday until today. She saw your press release. Imogen Glass called us in the week you mentioned to book a treatment, but she never turned up on the day. We tried to contact her but without success. We now know why.'

'Thank you for your help. It is still useful,' said Grace.

'Extraordinary,' said Drake when Grace told him about the phone call. 'Does this mean that Imogen changed her mind about Red Peak? Perhaps she had found out something about it. I wonder what that was?' Drake got up and added this information to his case boards. Then he stood back and surveyed the scene. Grace noticed that he had begun his slow progress around the boards. He repeated this several times. His movements were slow and deliberate, and she knew not to interrupt. She had seen it all before. She only partly understood this trance-like process, but it usually produced results. Gradually, people were leaving at the end of their day. When Grace left, Drake was still absorbed and seemingly unaware that he was now the last person left.

# 35

Grace was in early, but there was no sign of Drake. Gradually, the staff arrived and started their work. It was nearly coffee time when the door rattled, indicating Drake was hunting for his keys. A second rattle and he succeeded in opening the door. He came in humming to himself. That was unusual, thought Grace. He rarely hummed and never whistled. It just wasn't Drake.

'That sounds lovely!' said Grace.

'I'd be surprised if my crude humming does it justice. It is the first movement of Handel's flute sonata in A minor. I finally managed to play it through last night. Of course, it is the slow first movement, and I haven't even tried the faster movements, but I'm quite proud of myself. Handel was a genius. I've bought the books of Bach's sonatas, but of course, they are more complex. How I wish I could play them. I listened to both sets last night. It is wonderful music to take your mind off everything. Somehow, a problem is easier to solve when I return to it after playing. I've found this frequently with crosswords. You seem to get stuck and are just going around in circles. You leave it and do something else and then return to it. Then, somehow, your brain has worked it out, and a few clues that seemed impossible before have become obvious. Playing a musical instrument requires total concentration, but somehow the old brain keeps turning a problem over.'

Drake took off his coat, made a coffee, and carried it to his case boards. He turned to Grace. 'I was up most of the night reading about Chinese mythology, their folk tales and how their calendar was supposed to have been created. It's all rather fascinating.'

'Oh, I see,' said Grace. 'But why this sudden interest?'

'It is far from sudden. It is a train of thought that started when I saw Imogen's work next to the Chinese Opera in the Heritage

Museum in Hong Kong. Cynthia helped me with it; bless her. I am still struggling fully to grasp these ideas, but at least I can see now why Imogen got so obsessed. Of course, she went into it all in far more detail. She was a remarkably clever girl. It's all about using traditional characters and settings to tell contemporary stories. Look at those last three paintings we have found under the floor. Is it possible that they contain coded messages?'

'How would that work?' asked a puzzled Grace.

'Well, of course, I can't prove anything,' said Drake. 'But look at the first one. It has a figure located high up above the clouds on a mountain. The high location surely makes it important. The figure is not just any person or creature. It must have been chosen deliberately. I don't believe Imogen Glass did anything carelessly. Look, the figure has a long tale and is wearing a crown. I'm sure it is meant to be a character called Sun Wukong. He is the famous monkey king in Chinese mythology. He is first seen in a sixteenth-century Chinese novel. He appears with different names in every culture in the Far East. He is a controversial figure and seems to have had two conflicting characteristics. He was, we might say, a monkey. He was ruthless in his pursuit of power, domination, and immortality. But he also travelled to the West with a pilgrim, who he helped, advised and protected along the way. Eventually, he became a Buddha, a revered figure in the story. So, why is he high above the clouds in Imogen's painting? Because he can never be fully understood and seen clearly from below. Is this a reference to a person in our investigation?'

'I think you might mean the person we have been calling DH,' said Grace slowly. 'If we are right, he lives high on The Peak, leads a charmed life in upper circles, but is also thought to run the Red Peak Triad.'

'Well done, exactly,' said Drake. 'Now look at the second painting. It has a similar, though not identical, mountain, but this time, the figure is below the clouds and seems half female human and half reptile. The snake is a character in the Chinese calendar. The story says that all the animals raced to decide the order in which they would appear in the calendar. Several animals, especially the dragon, rooster and sheep, helped others in the race. The snake, who stood no chance of winning a race, hid behind the horse's hoof. He sneakily took a ride but jumped out at the end, frightened the horse and beat it over the line. So, the snake is considered extremely clever but totally without scruples.' Drake paused. 'In Imogen's painting, the snake is shown as female.'

'Oh, I think I see,' said Grace. 'This is Irene Mei Lien Li. She is such a character and visited DH or the Monkey King.'

'You've got it,' said Drake. 'That took me all night to work out.'

'I think you helped me rather a lot,' laughed Grace. 'But what about the third painting? There is no figure, but it looks like the same mountain.'

'I was puzzled too,' said Drake. 'Until I noticed that it is not signed. She signed all her paintings.'

'Why?'

'Because it isn't finished,' said Drake. 'She thinks there is another person, but she still isn't sure.'

Grace grimaced. 'Are we making a lot out of very little here?' she asked hesitantly. Drake shook his head sternly and stared at the paintings intently.

'Right,' he said suddenly. 'We're going for it.'

'Going for what?' asked Grace, half wondering if he thought he had suddenly solved the Imogen Glass case. Drake answered her question cryptically.

'The clue to our murders lies in identifying the third person,' said Drake. 'I need all the station's resources to be brought to the case room for a briefing.'


'Right,' said Drake. I need two teams this morning. One is under the leadership of Steve Redvers, who is about to do his sergeant tests and will pass with flying colours. That team will go to a private house on Watergate Street. You are to search the property for anything interesting. You will have a minimum of 24 hours, and I fully expect to be able to extend this up to 36 hours if necessary. You are to treat the place as a crime scene.'

Steve Redvers noticeably pumped out his chest.

'What are we looking for?' asked Steve.

'Any possible lethal weapon and male footwear,' said Drake. 'See what you can find and keep me informed of progress. Bring anything that could be used in evidence into the station.'

'Grace, you are coming with me. Choose a couple of constables to help if we have any difficulty.'

'Where are we going?' asked Grace.

'To The Orient,' replied Drake. 'No one is to tell anyone else about these raids. They must both be carried out simultaneously without any warning.'

Later that morning, Drake arrived back at the station with Grace. The case room was empty. All available hands were searching a property on Watergate Street. One of the constables with Drake had accompanied Wang, who had been arrested at The Orient. He was taken to an interview room. He was protesting loudly in his halting English. His speech suddenly sounded aggressive rather than faintly amusing. Drake's phone rang. It was Steve Redvers.

'We've not had much luck so far,' he said. 'We've got quite a few pairs of male footwear but no sign of a lethal weapon.'

'OK,' replied Drake. 'Keep searching. Unlike the footwear, it is probably hidden. Look for all the usual hiding places. Send someone back here with the footwear.'

'What are we going to do with Wang?' asked Grace.

'Leave him to stew for a while,' replied Drake. 'Besides, I need to see more progress before we question him.'

# 36

The case room had taken on the appearance of a footwear museum. Shoes, slippers, sandals and boots were arranged in their categories across the floor, each pair in its clear evidence bag. Drake walked up and down the line.

'There are only two pairs of boots,' said Drake with an air of frustration. 'Not as I hoped. I admit I'm taking a bit of a punt today, but maybe it just hasn't worked out for us.'

Even though Grace had a rough idea of what was happening, she waited for Drake's explanation. It wasn't forthcoming. Eventually, he spoke again.

'OK,' let's cut our losses at the house. Grace, leave a couple behind to carry on searching and take everybody else to The Orient's warehouse on Sealand Road. Take the keys we brought back with Wang and meet them there. Have they got a locksmith with them? They may need one.'

'OK on both counts,' said Grace.

Drake settled down with his unfinished crossword until he was interrupted by an excited Dave.

'I've had success with that little laptop we found under Philippa's floor,' he said. 'I found a file hidden amongst all the system files. It is a PDF of a word processing file.'

'Just remind me what PDF means,' groaned Drake.

'It stands for Portable Document Format,' replied Dave. 'It was developed by a company called Adobe. It's created using their software to produce a file from applications such as word processing or spreadsheets. Such files can be printed but not easily edited. They are almost always free of any malicious bugs. They can be combined, so they are useful for exchanging data without any risk that you may also be sending some virus. You also know they probably haven't been edited.'

'OK, OK,' said Drake slowly. I think I understand. I've seen them before but never really knew what PDF meant.'

'This file was also password protected,' said Dave. 'So, whoever has used and hidden this file in the password-protected computer was determined to keep everything secret. I'm sure it was created by Imogen Glass rather than Philippa Crehan. Unfortunately for her, but luckily for us, there are relatively easy ways of removing the password protection on such files. This file is called The Truth, and it is a substantial report. I haven't had time to read it all because as soon as I began, I thought you would want to know. I've brought you a copy.'

Drake picked up the paper document and began reading. It was not long before he began to work out what it was. He grunted several times and whistled. 'Well, well,' he said. 'This is a report by Imogen Glass of everything she has discovered about Red Peak. It looks as if it could be dynamite. It doesn't name Irene Lee but lists her activities. Neither does it name the person we have been calling DH, but it refers to many things that unequivocally point to him. The author, Imogen Glass, may not have initially appreciated who Irene Lee and DH were. The report also claims that Far East Trading and The Orient are associated with Red Peak. As far as I can see, Cheung Brothers, the actual art dealers in Hong Kong, are not mentioned. However, the brother I spoke to there indicated a degree of frustration, but he seemed careful about what he said. I guess he suspects what is going on. I half expected something like this might exist. You remember that Bristow, the Met link to MI5, said that Imogen frequently travelled and left her phone turned off. That may be carelessness or even laziness. It is far more likely that she was anxious not to let anyone tracking her know where she was going. I suspect that Irene Lee was indeed tracking her and has relayed all she knows to the relevant people in Red Peak. Elliott Chan told us that Imogen still trusted Irene Lee, and he was rightly anxious about that.'

Several hours later, Grace returned carrying three large evidence bags.

'It's been slow progress,' she said. 'There is a whole mass of furniture there. Interestingly, there seem to be four more items identical to that wonderful Chinese dignitary's daybed they've got for sale in the gallery.'

'Yes, I'm not surprised,' said Drake. Far East Trading commissions artists and furniture makers to produce fakes of valuable items. They display one in the Gallery, but probably when it's sold, they deliver one of the copies to the customer. The one in the Gallery might even be a fake itself. It may be so good that even an expert will struggle to prove it.'

'The place also has many large crates that are locked up,' said Grace. 'Some are labelled. Some contain ceramics, others, small items of furniture and carvings, as well as paintings. Some don't have a label, and we started with those. The first two we tried to unlock were empty. The third, however, produced what I think you are looking for. Three pairs of boots are dirty, but the soles look almost new. There is also a desktop computer without a keyboard.'

'Help me, Grace,' said Drake. 'I can't bend down today; the old back is playing up. Let's have the boots on the table.' Grace duly obliged and pulled on her rubber gloves. She opened each bag carefully and lifted out the three pairs of boots. 'What size are they?' demanded Drake. Grace fumbled about, examining each set in turn.

'I think I've worked out your line of investigation,' she said. 'There are three pairs, all apparently quite new and size 10. The other two pairs we found in the house are battered and well-worn. They are size 8.'

'Exactly,' said Drake dramatically. 'We have been barking up the wrong tree. I looked it up. The average size of men's feet in China is two centimetres shorter than in the UK. Our average shoe size is at least 9.5 or 10. The average shoe size for Chinese men is size 8. In Imogen's corridor, we found three sets of footprints of shoes or, more likely, boots. Because there were three Chinese thugs at Fairlawns, we got distracted. You would be lucky to find three Chinese men together, all size 10. If we look through the slippers, shoes and sandals you brought back from the house, we will find they are all about size 8.' Grace started slowly moving down the line, nodding each time she examined a pair of size 8.

'So, he bought three new pairs of boots of size 10, but the pair he used are size 8, battered and worn,' said Drake. 'There never were three people. There was always just Wang. He put each pair of boots on, walked in the wet mud outside the carport, and tramped up the corridor. Being a Chinese man living here, he knows about shoe size differences. It's quite artistic. An artistic murder! He carried a picture and name of Philippa Crehan. This suggests that he didn't know her. Angela Marchment told me they had never met or even knew of Philippa Crehan. He was handed instructions to kill her.'

Grace stopped and thought for a moment. 'I suppose you are going to say that he was clever enough to try to disguise his murder as a theft. Of course, he took all the paintings.'

'Yes, and the guy from Far East Trading said they were picked up in the usual way, but he can't confirm it. I'm sure Wang took them to his lock-up on Sealand Road. We might guess that Angela doesn't know what Wang was up to.'

'But why would he murder someone giving him a living?' asked Grace.

'Here, I am taking a bit of a leap into the dark,' said Drake. 'I guess that he was working to orders. I'm pretty sure he is part of Red Peak. He goes to Hong Kong, always without Angela, and does all these wonderful deals for The Orient. There is a strong suspicion that Far East Trading are no more than a commercial arm of Red Peak. Of course, they commission a whole lot of forgery. Faking Imogen's paintings is probably just a tiny fraction of their business. I bet that most, if not all, of the Oriental art and furniture sold by The Orient are fakes. It's a profitable business.'

'I still don't see why Red Peak would order him to dispose of Imogen,' said Grace.

'Well,' said Drake. 'This is where most of my evidence so far is circumstantial. We know that Imogen commissioned a tattoo from David Tong. There is evidence that perhaps Irene Lee recommended that she had it for her safety. There is also some evidence that suggests Irene Lee is part of Red Peak. I suspect that she is a high-ranking official and is probably known as such. She is the communications officer. I understand that syndicates like Red Peak only use word of mouth to communicate, so there is no trail as there might be with email, phone calls or texts. We know that Irene Lee visited our high society member in Hong Kong that we have called DH. This stands for "dragonhead" or the big chief of the whole outfit. She also visited Wang to instruct him to deal with Imogen, then later to deal with Philippa. She gave Wang the picture of Philippa Crehan with her name on the back. All the orders to kill Imogen came initially from DH.'

'I still don't see why,' said a puzzled Grace.

'Oh well, there is some evidence that originally Imogen didn't know that her tattoo was a badge for Red Peak. The fact that she allowed it to be done upside down suggests that. My guess is, and I can't say yet how this happened, that she discovered what she had done. Elliott Chan called her a terrier. She set out to understand what it was all about and became horrified. I'm guessing that she told either Irene Lee, whom she trusted or perhaps even DH that she had done her research and knew all about Red Peak. She might even have naively told them that she was preparing a report. At that stage, she hadn't worked out that they were both at a high level in Red Peak. Therefore, people, especially DH and Irene Lee, would be exposed. In any event, they couldn't take a risk. Imogen had to go, and her file had to be destroyed. Wang had introduced her to art trading, so he was held responsible. Imogen Glass was killed for what she knew. It was dangerous knowledge.' Drake stopped, got up and walked twice around his case boards. Then he returned to the table where Grace was still sitting. He started to talk to her again as if thinking aloud.

'If so, Wang hoped to find something in her studio giving evidence of her research. He didn't. He later thought that it might be hidden in Philippa's house. It is more likely that Irene Lee instructed him to search there. He went in and threatened her, and when she wouldn't cooperate, he shot her with a Chinese pistol and turned over the whole house. He wasn't being artistic by this time. He was frantic. He was seen leaving by our dog walking witness.' Drake paused and took a drink from his nearly empty cup. 'He took the desktop computer that was missing from Philippa's desk. He hoped the file might be on it. Of course, it was on the little laptop under the floor. The extra car door banging that the dog walker heard was him loading the computer into the boot or the near side doors. So, Philippa was also killed for what she knew or was hiding. It was all dangerous knowledge.'

'There is possibly some more evidence to support this theory. Imogen had unwittingly been connected through her parents to the Xi Dong outfit, which George tells us is an arm of the rival triad 46Q. This might have suggested to Red Peak that Imogen was playing a double game or might give things to 46Q that could harm Red Peak.'

'Wow,' said Grace. But most of this is based on suspicion, albeit with good information, rather than hard evidence.'

'That is what today is all about,' said Drake. 'It became obvious to me that I had to force things to make progress. Hopefully, these boots will match the footprints in the corridor. We need to get them to the experts straight away. I'm sure they will have Wang's fingerprints all over them.'

'But who hid the paintings under the floor in Philippa's house?' asked Grace.

'I can't answer that except to say the obvious candidate must be Imogen herself. It seems that she was nervous about her report being found. Perhaps she wanted to keep those paintings for herself. It is hard to understand. We will probably never know if, during their period of intimacy, Imogen told Philippa what she knew about Red Peak.'

Drake's phone rang to interrupt him, and he answered it, listening intently for several minutes.

'Excellent,' he said, putting his phone down.' They have found the pistol. It was well hidden but not well enough to fox our guys. Bingo. Now we have our evidence! Time to talk to Wang and see what he says.'

Later that afternoon, Drake and Grace collapsed into chairs in the case room. Wang had shut up shop. The boots weren't his. He had no idea they were there. Why would he buy boots that didn't fit him? The gun wasn't his. Again, he had no idea it was there. He didn't know how Far East Trading had got hold of twenty of Imogen's final batch of paintings. The fingerprint expert came in with his report on the pistol. It had Wang's fingerprints on it, and the configuration suggested that he had held it in his left hand.

'Exactly,' said Drake. 'I'm sure you have noticed that Wang is extremely left-handed?' Grace mumbled a reply that suggested she hadn't noticed this detail. Drake raised one eyebrow in mock admonishment and continued. 'The injuries to Imogen were on the right shoulder and the left rear of the head. This would occur naturally if the left-handed Wang stood opposite her. She received the first blow while facing him and the second while spinning away from him in terror.'

Drake and Grace were about to go home when Tom Denson called them to say Elliott Chan had arrived. He was shown up and began a tale.

'Imogen's will has just been read. I was there, of course, and she had left me an envelope. Inside was a lengthy set of instructions on how to find her little laptop computer. She also provided a password and instructions on how to find a file on it. She said I was to do with it whatever I thought appropriate. I have put things together, and I think it might be all the stuff she had found out about Red Peak. I need to lift the floor in Philippa's house.' Grace and Drake smiled at each other.

'No need,' said Grace, 'we already have it. I'm not sure we can let you have the file just yet, as it will be used as evidence in a trial.'

'I suppose I shall have to wait,' said Elliott Chan grumpily. 'She has also told me that there are three paintings for me under the floor in Philippa's bedroom. She said they go with the report, whatever that means. I suppose you have found them too?' Drake nodded his head.

'Yes,' he said. 'We have wondered who put them there and why. It now transpires they were both a way of her amplifying the report and part of your inheritance. I guess they will fetch a tidy sum. But there is also more to them than just the art.'

'I shall certainly not be selling them,' said Elliott. 'They will stay with me forever. Felicity and I will display them in our house to remind us of the wonderful Imogen.'

The following morning, everyone was gathered in the case room. Drake announced that Wang would be charged with both murders, and he was confident they would get a prosecution. As he finished talking to a round of spontaneous applause, the door rattled, and everyone looked at it, then at Drake and then just looked puzzled. Steve Redvers went over and opened it. It was Detective Inspector Martin Henshaw.

'I seem to have lost my keys,' he said. Everyone except Drake laughed.

'I'm here to join the team,' said Martin to another round of applause.

'Just too late,' said Drake, 'but welcome home. We have a report blowing the lid off Red Peak. In due course, it will be my privilege to let you send it with our thanks to George in Hong Kong. He can do what he thinks is appropriate.'

# 37 Postscript

One morning, some weeks later, Grace had come to the station via The Orient Gallery. She was relieved Angela was going to Hong Kong and was confident she could establish a new relationship with Cheung Brothers and some of Wang's other contacts. She had already signed up a couple more artists. They had followed Imogen's work and taken it in new directions. It seemed that The Orient had a future. Grace's phone rang as she took off her coat. It was her friend Julie Dobbins at the Met. They had arrested Dan Ford and found incriminating evidence on his laptop computer. Grace put the phone down and stared into space. Thank goodness that was all over, she thought. She wanted to tell Drake and thank him for flushing Dan out, but he said he was taking leave for a few days. This was almost unknown, and Grace had no recollection of him ever going away on holiday. She had no idea where he was until her phone rang again.

'Hello, Grace, it's Drake.'

'Where are you?'

'I'm in Hong Kong. I got a call from George to tell me of progress, and he invited me to come back and visit. He wanted to tell me how things had worked out but didn't want to put anything in an email or trust telephones. Our team are seen as great heroes here. The Hong Kong Police have been able to arrest a whole raft of people on crimes of varying seriousness, thanks to Imogen's report. They are full of admiration for how much she has uncovered. They combined her evidence with their own and then conducted searches and interviews to great effect. Irene Lee is in custody and will be charged with espionage. As we thought, she was playing a double agent and such things are not well regarded in China. They seem to need less evidence than we might. They are sure Imogen had been invited over here by the man we call DH. They still haven't told me his name. They think Imogen has been a brilliant detective. But they are amazed that she naively told DH all about it without knowing who he was. He didn't want any high-profile trouble in Hong Kong, so he briefed Irene Lee to sort it out in the UK. Everything was by word of mouth, so she instructed Wang on what to do. His business depended on Red Peak custom, and they would have dealt severely with him unless he did as he was told.'

'What's happened to DH?' asked Grace.

'I'm not privy to that in detail except that he has disappeared, and his much-prized house on the Peak is up for sale. I think he is almost certainly somewhere rather unpleasant in China. The Xi-Dong outfit in Hong Kong has also disappeared. I don't think we will ever know all the details. Tell Martin all this. I guess he will think nothing much changes there. I imagine Elliott Chan and Felicity Glass will be extremely proud of Imogen. OK, I must go. It's rather late here, and I've got jet lag.'

'So,' said Grace after passing on all the news to the assembled team. 'Drake's not on holiday after all. Nothing changes there either.'

# A DEGREE OF DEATH
# Bryan Lawson

A member of the Singapore Parliament is found murdered on a footbridge in Chester. A DEGREE OF DEATH is a crime novel about the past sneaking up on the present and making a real mess of things. It is September 2005. Murky oriental history is entangled with events at Deva University in Chester, a brand-new institution doing its best to invent tradition. But do these new ivory towers hide more worldly pursuits, and what goes on behind the genteel façades in the historic city of Chester?

DCI Carlton Drake is widely recognised for being as clever as he is tall and clumsy. He resumes duties after a sabbatical, taken for personal reasons, to investigate this diplomatically sensitive case. By contrast, his high-flying young assistant, Grace Hepple is stylish but inexperienced. Together, they uncover an intriguing mystery.

The investigation takes Drake to Singapore, where he discovers that the past is never far from the surface in this modern metropolis. Chinese societies, illegal ivory trading, academic jealousy and raw ambition jostle together to create a confusing and dangerous cocktail.

**Readers say: -**
"Highly recommended"

"The intricacies of the plot keep you absorbed, and the conclusion certainly does not disappoint."

"From an ex-policeman...a good thought-provoking thriller."

"I look forward to the next in the series of this detective duo."

# WITHOUT TRACE
# Bryan Lawson

Lord Richard MacCracken, a minister for the arts in the British Government, disappears during the interval of a performance at Covent Garden. He seems to have vanished without a trace between the two acts of an opera. The nightmare gets darker when the postman delivers a copy of the Royal Opera House programme. It contains death threats and a set of the victim's bloody fingerprints.

DCI Drake and his assistant DS Grace Hepple are called in to recover Lord MacCracken safely and discover who is holding him. The kidnappers have covered their tracks with a web of deception that leads Drake around the world. The sinister and dramatic crimes he uncovers could have come straight from the operatic stage.

**Readers say: -**

"I really enjoyed it and found it extremely absorbing."

"Another great edition with exciting adventures and drama."

"The plot twisted and turned as a good detective novel should, leading to an unforeseen conclusion...

"...attention to detail in terms of background information from experts brought in to assist the case is incredible."

# FATAL PRACTICE
# Bryan Lawson

An internationally famous architect, Sir Julian Porter, fails to turn up to the public launch of a series of new landmark buildings for the UK Government. Detective Chief Inspector Drake and his assistant DS Grace Hepple are called to investigate. They begin their work in the historic city of Chester, where Porter's architectural practice is located. Drake soon discovers that Sir Julian seems to have made many enemies. Some strangely mutilated bodies become the focus of the investigation. One is in Chester, and another on the Malaysian Island of Penang, where the practice has designed a prestigious housing development.

These two murders appear linked, but the question is how? The case leads Drake into dangerous water involving organised crime and a mysterious oriental cult.

**Readers say: -**

"I have just finished it. I enjoyed all the parts in Penang."

"As well as the intriguing mystery, it transports you to a fascinating part of the world."

"Just finished reading Fatal Practice – very entertaining. Makes me want to visit Penang one day."

"International intrigue and fascinating architectural insights enhance this clever and twisty mystery…"

# THE FLAUTIST
# Bryan Lawson

The historic city of Chester has just built a new concert hall thanks to the generosity of an anonymous benefactor. A gala concert is held to celebrate the opening, and an internationally famous flautist, Evinka Whyte, who lives locally, has agreed to play. Unfortunately, the concert is marred by a dramatically sinister event.

DCI Drake and his assistant, DS Grace Hepple, are called in to investigate. They soon discover that Evinka Whyte had a confusing and mysterious private life. This is made more complex by the history of her illustrious but secretive family. The investigation takes Drake to the most historic and musical city of Prague. During his visit, the mystery deepens.

**Readers say: -**

"In Drake and Hepple, we have two detectives who can rival the best."

"The best Drake and Hepple mystery so far."

Printed in Great Britain
by Amazon

31956958R00155